The Dead

ALSO BY HOWARD LINSKEY
FROM CLIPPER LARGE PRINT

The Drop
The Damage

The Dead

Howard Linskey

W F HOWES LTD

This large print edition published in 2013 by
W F Howes Ltd
Unit 4, Rearsby Business Park, Gaddesby Lane,
Rearsby, Leicester LE7 4YH

1 3 5 7 9 10 8 6 4 2

First published in the United Kingdom in 2013
by No Exit Press

A CIP catalogue record for this book is available
from the British Library

ISBN 978 1 47124 698 2

Typeset by Palimpsest Book Production Limited,
Falkirk, Stirlingshire
Printed and bound by
CPI Group (UK) Ltd, Croydon, CR0 4YY

MIX
Paper from
responsible sources
FSC
www.fsc.org   FSC® C013604

For Erin and Alison, of course

'When sorrows come, they come not single spies, but in battalions'

William Shakespeare

CHAPTER 1

The dead are left with nothing, except the power to destroy the lives of those they leave behind. The girl's body lay on dry land, her head lolling over the edge of the river bank. She was face up, her eyes open and her long, dark hair dipped into the water. The steady, regular movement of the current made the strands sway gently like tendrils. Her left arm trailed behind her, the fingertips of one white, slender hand suspended there, as if she were about to dip it into the cool water. Her appearance gave the illusion there might still be life left in her, but DS Fraser knew better.

'Are you gonna call him?' asked DC Thomas, 'I reckon you should . . .' and when Fraser frowned at him, he added an uncertain, 'prob'ly'.

Fraser gave the Detective Constable a withering look that managed to efficiently convey the words 'don't tell me how to do my job' and Thomas retreated without another word, busying himself at the edge of the crime scene.

Fraser watched the SOCOs as they went about their business. They moved slowly and methodically, taping off the area around the girl and the route her body had taken from the main road to her resting place here by the river bank. The river ran through a small copse at the edge of a farm around fifteen miles north of Newcastle, a dip in the land too deep to be cultivated that had been left to its own devices. The bushes were overgrown here and the tall tree branches stretched forwards to meet each other as if in greeting, forming a canopy of leaves that, in parts, blocked out the moonlight.

It seemed she had been dragged from a car on the main road up above them. Whatever her killer's initial intention, he must have panicked and simply thrown her body over the hedge and Fraser understood why. Whoever had done this probably intended to follow the girl down here to bury her or, at the very least, cover her with something, to delay the discovery of the body, but he would have felt exposed out there on the main road in the middle of the night. Any passing motorist could have clocked him and given the police a description of the vehicle, maybe even the registration number.

He must have known every second magnified his chances of being caught, so he had heaved the girl over the hedge and driven away. Judging by the flattened grass and weeds this side of the hedge, the girl's body hit the ground hard, then gathered momentum, rolling down the hill, before finally coming to a halt when the ground levelled off at the edge of the river, where she now lay, staring mournfully up at the stars.

She'd been found by a man out walking his dog. Weren't they always, thought Fraser? At least she hadn't been there too long, before nature could get to work on her, breaking her body down; all those microbes, all that bacteria, the insects and the wild, gnawing animals. That was the thing about Mother Nature. She didn't fuck about. It didn't take long out in the open before you could become unrecognisable, even to your nearest and dearest.

Fraser could tell she'd been a pretty little thing; long dark hair, brown eyes, fresh face, full red lips. Was that why she was killed, he wondered; a jealous boyfriend who'd been dumped and couldn't cope with the crushing realisation that someone else would eventually have her? Sexual jealousy was as strong and likely a motive as any other, in Fraser's experience, particularly when the victim was young.

Fraser wondered if he would soon be interrogating another fucked up ex-boyfriend or if this time they had a random on their hands. Was this poor lass unlucky enough to be out, in her skimpy little skirt, with the oh-so-thin blouse, when a rapist or killer-for-kicks drove by and spotted her? Maybe the intention had been rape but the guy panicked afterwards, knowing she wasn't going to go home and just forget all about it, so he'd made sure she could never talk. Perhaps it was the murder itself that got the killer off and sex had nothing to do with it? Shame they couldn't just ask the victim, so they could find out whose face she'd been staring up into as she gave out her last breath.

One of the SOCOs turned on the light he'd been assembling, then he turned to DS Fraser, 'are you going to call him?'

'Don't you start,' warned Fraser, but he was already reaching for his phone.

Detective Inspector Robert Carlton had already grown weary of the black-tie do, long before his mobile phone began to vibrate silently against his chest from the inside pocket of his dinner jacket. He exhaled wearily, then reached for it. Carlton was feeling the after-effects of a heavy meal; duck and Armagnac terrine, chicken supreme with Jersey Royals and a generous portion of sticky toffee pudding for afters.

'Carlton,' he answered above the din in the room, caused by the chatter of two hundred police officers with copious amounts of beer and wine inside them.

'Boss, it's me,' it was Fraser, that much he could make out but the rest was lost, drowned out by loud, braying laughter from the next table, a reaction to one of Superintendent Connor's borderline racist jokes.

'Hang on,' Carlton commanded, 'I can't hear you.'

He climbed to his feet and left the room, turning sideways as he did so to squeeze between fellow diners who, as always at these functions, were packed in too tightly, so that navigating his way between tables was like tackling an obstacle course. The room was sizeable and full to the brim with ranking police officers, each one looking for a leg up and feeling obliged to shell out on tickets for a charity dinner, which cost far more than the sum of this mediocre meal's parts. Everyone was expected to support the latest cause adopted by the Northumbria Police Force to justify its obscene annual piss up, which would go on well into the early hours. Already there were some familiar faces looking distinctly worse for wear.

Carlton was grateful to be free of the noise and stifling warmth of the dining room. He crossed the Royal Station Hotel's lobby and went out through its main door. Only when he was on the steps outside and the cool air hit him, did he turn his attention back to the mobile phone in his hand.

'I can hear you now,' he told the Detective Sergeant.

'Sorry to bother you, boss. I know you are at that black-tie do but I thought you'd want to know. It's a young girl.'

'What is?'

'The reason I'm calling. We found one; on the bank of a stream, out in the sticks. She was just lying there. No attempt to even hide the body.'

This piqued Carlton's interest. If he was ever going to make DCI he needed as many high-profile cases under his belt as he could get. He listened while Fraser gave him the facts. The girl's approximate age, 'somewhere between fifteen and twenty,' it was always hard to tell with girls, particularly if they had a bit of slap on; what she was wearing, the usual clubbing uniform of short skirt and skimpy top, and the exact location of her body, a smattering of woodland with a stream running through it, a few miles north of the city. The site was about fifteen minutes' drive from Carlton's current location. Finally there was the suspected cause of death, which, from the abrasions on her throat and bulging, blood-shot eyes, looked like strangulation.

'No ID?'

'No purse or handbag, no credit cards, not even a mobile phone, just the clothes she was wearing. I wondered if you would like me to send a car . . . or I could just call it in?' He meant if the DI had been drinking. Nobody could afford to have a pissed up detective at a murder scene, screwing everything up. Carlton had only had one pre-dinner pint and two small glasses of acidic white wine, which hardly counted.

'Send a car,' Carlton told the Detective Sergeant, 'tell him to pick me up outside the railway station.'

Fraser had been right to call him first. While the brass were sipping their Cognacs and singing 'God Save the Queen' before the charity auction, Carlton would get down there and stake a claim on the case. In his experience, pretty young girls being murdered attracted more column inches in the local papers and national tabloids than just about any other case. The middle-aged or elderly could be shot, stabbed, strangled, gassed, electrocuted or run over by trains and their story would be buried in the middle of the paper, but a pretty little thing with potential was a different matter altogether. If she was educated, wanting to become a lawyer or a doctor, or just about to go off and travel the world, then her death would be seen as even more tragic and the public couldn't get enough of it. This could be front page news, only relegated further into the newspaper if the world's economy was about to implode again or David Beckham had a new haircut.

Carlton retrieved his raincoat from the hat-check girl and fished out the packet of cigs for the short walk up to the old Victorian railway station. It was a mild autumn night and he kept his coat draped over his arm as he walked, lit a cigarette and drew on it. Carlton was used to seeing bodies, many of which were in an advanced state of decay; he'd become hardened to it over the years. The bloke walking his dog had probably never seen a body in his life, unless it was a relative in a funeral home all tidied up and made to look peaceful. Murdered folk rarely looked at peace and the poor bastard probably yacked his guts up on the spot, just like Carlton had done when he saw his first floater, almost thirty years ago now. He'd been a beat bobby back then, one of the first on the scene when they fished that murdered hooker out of the

Tyne. She'd been in there a while, smelled like a wound that had gone septic and, just when he thought he'd managed to force his lunch back down into his belly, something dark and slimy slid from her eye socket and he'd barfed up all over the ground in front of everybody.

Carlton didn't have to wait long before the unmarked car pulled over next to him and he took a last drag on the cigarette, dropped it onto the ground, stubbed it out with his foot and climbed in. DI Carlton was a busy man, with little time for reflection, but the short journey north allowed him to be alone with his thoughts for once. The driver, a DC in his forties, was an unambitious fella who would only speak when spoken to and Carlton was thankful he didn't have to engage in small talk. His thoughts drifted back to the dinner that evening and what really stuck in his mind was the amount of moaning from his fellow officers; about the job, money, the whinging wife and ungrateful kids. By comparison he reckoned he was doing alright. Financially, he was through the worst of the early mortgage years. His oldest was out of university and had eased the strain on their finances a little. John might still need the occasional hand-out but that was nothing compared to funding a university education as far afield as Bristol. It was a shame about the girlfriend though. Helen had seemed like the one. At least John thought she was. They'd been together for three years, almost their entire time in college. She'd holidayed with the family and Carlton had started to view her as a future daughter-in-law. They were all shocked when she suddenly finished with him, with little in the way of an explanation. John was devastated and his dad didn't know what to say to him. The poor lad was in bits but he would just have to get through it on his own somehow.

At least Gemma had chosen to stay in Newcastle for her degree. The girls she was sharing with seemed nice enough and there was no heavy boyfriend on the scene to take her mind off her studies. He had hoped she might just stay at home but Gemma wanted her own independence and you had to let them go eventually. There were times, he had to admit, when they quite liked having the house to themselves again.

Little more than a quarter of an hour into their journey, the driver took a left onto a dirt road that led to a couple of farmhouses, but the car came to a halt long before them, by a dip in the land. There was a clear sky and a bright full moon, but Carlton could make out little more than the tops of the trees from here. Fraser was waiting though, to take him down to the crime scene.

'Hope it doesn't ruin your shoes boss,' he said, as Carlton exited the car.

'Don't worry about that,' answered Carlton as he walked over the wet grass to the edge of the dip.

DI Carlton and DS Fraser paused at the top of the hill to survey the scene below them. SOCOs

9

were moving purposefully, illuminated by lamps on tripod frames, which shone brightly down on the body of the young girl.

DS Fraser started to walk down the hill towards the scene but DI Carlton didn't follow. Fraser turned back to see what was causing the delay and found his boss frozen to the spot, staring intently ahead.

'What is it sir?' asked Fraser. Then, when no answer was forthcoming, 'sir?' he asked again. Glancing back, he looked into the inspector's eyes and was startled by what he saw there. Carlton wore a look of shocked incomprehension. The DI slowly opened his mouth then, abruptly, he let out a blood-curdling yell that made everyone at the scene start and immediately turn towards the sound.

'Gemma!' screamed Carlton, 'Gemma! No!' and to Fraser's astonishment his boss charged past him and started running flat out down the hill towards the stricken girl. Fraser remained where he stood, as DI Carlton barrelled past a shell-shocked SOCO, then seemed to launch himself at the corpse, grabbing the body and pulling it towards him to enfold it in his arms. Fraser remained rooted to the spot while he watched panicked SOCOs attempting to pull the clearly insane Detective Inspector away from the murder victim, while he in turn clasped the dead girl to his chest with one beefy arm, fending them off with the other.

It took three of them to drag Carlton away from the girl and they all ended up in the water, tumbling as they lost their balance while trying to deal with Carlton's bulk. Even from this distance Fraser could make out the crazed and desperate look in Carlton's eyes as he climbed to his feet and ran from the shallow water, back to the body, leaving the three other men dripping in his wake. He grabbed the girl once more and clasped her to him. The tiny body lolled like a doll in his arms.

The three other men emerged from the water together.

'Get away from me!' ordered Carlton, all sense and reason gone from him now, as he pulled the girl's flimsy corpse closer to him, 'she's my daughter, that's my Gemma!' and he began to weep, as he held the girl tighter still. The other men seemed to give up then. Perhaps they realised the crime scene was already hopelessly contaminated or maybe, like Fraser, they just couldn't bear the sound of Detective Inspector Carlton sobbing like a child, as he rocked the lifeless body of his daughter in his arms.

CHAPTER 2

There is really only one way out of this world for me. In a pine box. I wish I didn't know that but I do. I'm not stupid. You can't walk away from a life like mine. You don't just retire and hand it all over to someone else or sell the business on as a going concern. There are too many people with a stake in the firm and if any of them ever believed I was looking to get out, they'd make sure I was retired permanently. You see, I can stay alive only as long as the people who work for me, and all the others I pay at the end of each and every month, reckon I am contributing. The minute I cease to add value to their lives they start questioning whether I am really anything more than a drain on their resources. There's no sentiment in this business. As long as I am bringing in a lot more than I'm taking out, they are happy. If anyone starts to suspect I've gone flaky they will forget everything that has gone before and they will kill me. And I wouldn't blame them either.

So I can't walk away, ever, and that's my punishment. The day I pulled the trigger on my boss,

Bobby Mahoney, was the day I was handed my very own life sentence. I just didn't realise at the time that it will only ever be over for me when I'm a dead man. My flight back from Istanbul was delayed and that gave me plenty of time to think about how I ended up here. You don't set out to be a gangster. At least I didn't. I'm no Henry Hill and the road I travelled was long, tortuous and made up of a million little baby steps, each one a decision that eventually, years later, led me here. There wasn't just one turning point, a single chance to turn my back on this life before I fell too deeply into it. I know that now and often wonder what my life could have been, if I'd suddenly decided to just jack it all in, long before I became Bobby Mahoney's indispensable right hand man, a Geordie *Consigliere* to the north-east's most notorious criminal, a man who held the city in the palm of his huge, gnarled hand for more than three decades.

Then, when Bobby was killed, I stepped into his shoes and found they were a perfect fit. I may not have the brute strength, fearlessness and raw fighting ability of Bobby Mahoney, but what I lacked in those departments I more than made up for with my ability to read people and work things out before they did.

I had time to contemplate my situation because I was waiting for my suitcase to make an appearance on the carousel. I'd travelled first class but it was my suitcase that was acting like the diva, insisting on keeping me waiting and I was the last one there, apart from Palmer, my head of security.

The Gallowgate Leisure Group has gone global. These days we are an offshore company that uses lawyers and bankers more than enforcers or hit men and I have to oversee all of it. I try to look the part of David Blake, Chief Operating Officer, but apart from a few expensive suits, I'm pretty much the same guy I've always been.

In my business, you have to keep on growing and expanding, so you can earn the money you need to pay all of the people who will keep you away from prison or out of the grave. Bobby's era of armed robbery and protection, of gaming machines, porno movies and illegal gambling may have been a brutal and bloody place but it has nothing on the world of international drug smuggling and money laundering I've been forced to take us into.

But business is okay, the money is still coming in and we haven't killed anyone in a couple of years now, which is as good a barometer of the health of our firm as any. As Kinane is fond of saying, 'We've got fingers in more pies than Mister Fucking Kipling,' and he knows because he's one of our inner circle, our main enforcer, the man you fuck with if you fuck with me. Since the guy is huge and looks like he's made out of breeze blocks, this acts as a pretty big deterrent.

My bag finally put in an appearance and I was

relieved because I wanted to get going. We left Heathrow airport, then took the underground to Kings Cross for a train north. I got off it at York but Palmer stayed on for a meeting in Edinburgh with Fallon, a Glasgow hard case who shares the city with us, because we are a sleeping partner in his Glasgow operation. I didn't expect to be gunned down on the mean streets of York but you can never be too careful, so I got Joe Kinane to drive down and meet me. He picked me up in his Lexus and drove me to view an old Georgian hotel I had my eye on. I wanted to buy it, reno-vate the place and run it as a going concern, while laundering some of our drug money through its gilded doors. Once I'd viewed the hotel, we were free to drive back north again, which gave him his chance to brief me on everything that had been going on while I was away. Thankfully it wasn't much. Everyone prefers a quiet life and I'm no exception.

'Amrein's been on a couple of times,' he informed me, 'something about a meeting. He wants you to get back to him.'

Amrein; our fixer, the guy who oils the wheels, greases the palms and keeps us all out of trouble, in theory.

'I know about Amrein's meeting,' I admitted. 'I'm trying to avoid it. I'll call him tomorrow.'

I spent the final miles of my journey in a relaxed frame of mind. I was looking forward to seeing Sarah and my gorgeous little girl again. I'd missed them both. We were almost back in the city, just a few miles to go. I was tired and the last thing I wanted was an incident of any kind but that's exactly what I got. As we were speeding up the A1, a car suddenly shot out from the slip road and cut us up big style as it crossed both lanes. Kinane slammed on the brakes with a 'Fooking Hell!' and scowled at the driver in front.

'Simmer down,' I told him once I realised we weren't actually under attack, 'it's just some young tosser,' the car was small and old but it had been souped-up somehow and the boy racer who owned it had spent a lot of time adding spoilers and spray painting it black. I couldn't even tell what make it had been before he started.

Kinane ignored me and pounded the horn with one hand while he gripped the steering wheel tightly with the other and stepped on the accelerator to give chase. I tried to reason with him, even though I knew it would be hopeless. 'I haven't got time for this Joe,' I said, as he swiftly gained on the other car, 'I don't need the grief of bailing you out if you lamp the lad.'

Kinane forced the car level with the boy racer, undertaking, so we were right next to him on the inside lane. The window on their passenger door immediately came down and the guy riding shotgun put his arm out and gave us the finger. I doubted he would have done that if he could have seen inside our car but the darkened windows meant he had no idea who he had just insulted.

I could see the bloke's pig-ignorant face clearly. It was twisted into a violent snarl of hate, as if we were totally out of order, preventing him and his mate from doing exactly what they pleased.

'Little tosser,' muttered Kinane, his voice going as high as I had ever heard it. 'Joe,' I said it quietly, by way of warning, but you don't give Joe Kinane the finger and get away with it. If you did, there wouldn't be much point in employing him.

Kinane moved as if he was about to wind the window down and give this bloke the shock of his young life but, as he took his eye off the road ahead, I noticed the rear end of a lorry coming up at such speed it seemed to be reversing into us.

'Joe!' I shouted and he slammed the anchors on and swerved to the right just in time, 'Jesus!' I watched the back of the lorry veer past me.

Kinane gave it no attention. He was busy steering the Lexus through the rest of the traffic, chasing the little car as it slalomed amongst the other vehicles on the road. One or two of the other drivers looked a bit panicked as we came charging through them but Kinane paid them no heed. This kind of driving was not new to him and his blood was up.

The little black car suddenly cut across two lanes again, this time from right to left and it shot off the A1, taking the slip road into the city. Kinane followed. I had no idea how we missed the car in the slow lane, as we cut between it and the turn off. 'What the fuck are we doing?' I demanded.

'Chasing-these-two-little-cunts,' Kinane emphasised each word through gritted teeth.

I grabbed the door handle and held on to it tightly as our car swerved to the right and shot across the flyover, the driver of the car that was trying to get onto the road from our left must have had several heart attacks as we flew out and cut him up but Kinane just expected the bloke to brake and get out of our way, which thankfully he did. By the time he'd wrestled with his car, realised he was still alive and composed himself enough to sound the horn at us, the noise was already a distant one.

On the straight, comparatively empty stretch of road we soon caught up with the snarling boy racers. Kinane drew alongside them. This time we were on their opposite side, so it was the driver I could see on my left. His window was down and he was shouting and swearing at us. I couldn't really hear the words over the din of our engines but it looked a lot like he was shouting 'Come on! Come on then!'

Kinane needed no further bidding and he slammed our car to the left. They managed to miss us but it was close. The driver must have shit himself, as he simultaneously slammed on the brakes and swerved wildly onto the side of the road. We did the same thing and Kinane stamped on his brakes until we skidded to a halt, kicking up gravel and clouds of dust in the process. As soon as both cars came to a stop, they were out of theirs and starting their angry march towards us, their biggest worry that we might drive swiftly away and rob them of their vengeance.

I wasn't too concerned about their aggression but I was annoyed with Kinane. As far as I was concerned, he could sort this mess out on his own, 'Fucking hell Joe, you could have killed us.' I told him.

'No danger of that,' he said dismissively but he wasn't giving me his undivided attention. Instead he was watching them in his rear view mirror, 'come on, come on,' he was urging them. He didn't want them to realise who they were dealing with until it was too late.

I sighed and put my hand on the door handle and clicked it so that the door was still closed but the mechanism for opening it was half engaged. The guy who was coming for my side was a little quicker than the one heading for Kinane. I watched him in my mirror and, as he bent low to lean into the window and call me out, I clicked the door handle again and pushed against it hard. The side of the window frame caught the snarling little bastard right in the face, and he shot backwards, falling onto the waste ground at the side of the road.

Kinane opened his door and climbed out. I got out just in time to see the look on the young driver's face as he registered Kinane's huge presence and it was an absolute picture. Normally I would have enjoyed that moment but I was too annoyed at Kinane for putting us in this position to gain any real pleasure from it. Before the lad could turn and run, Kinane snaked out an arm and grabbed his fleecy top in one gnarled fist. 'Come here!' he bellowed and I reckoned the guy probably filled his pants for the second time in two minutes.

Kinane must have given the lad a couple of slaps because he started yelping like a little girl and screaming to be let go. I was preoccupied by the young thug's mate, who was crawling to his knees. He shook his head and blinked, then put his hand to his forehead and wiped fresh blood from it. He surveyed his palm, got angry again, snarled at me and tried to get up but I'd had time to pick my spot. I sent a kick Alan Shearer would have been proud of right into his chin. His head shot back then snapped forwards again until gravity inter-vened and he dropped face first onto the hard ground, his chin smacking into the concrete with a sound like teeth breaking. He wouldn't be getting back up again after that.

I turned away then and set off down the road. I knew I could walk over the Redheugh Bridge then get a cab. Behind me, I could hear the sounds of Kinane's violent retribution. Whatever he was doing to that thug, it must have been crea-tive, because there was an awful lot of screaming going on.

I walked on as the screams continued but slowly grew fainter. Eventually, as I knew it would, a police car could be heard heading Joe's way. I doubted his young victim had ever been happier to hear the shrill sound of its sirens.

CHAPTER 3

By the time I got back my little Emma was already asleep. Sarah was at the top of the stairs when I walked in and she greeted me with a big grin but immediately placed her finger to her lips, so I'd know to be quiet. Missing my daughter was another thing I'd blame Joe Kinane for.

We lived in a house on a new development on the edge of the city; one that was built and wholly owned by the firm. The street we live in has twelve properties, a mixture of houses and flats in a horseshoe shape, making a cul-de-sac. It has a gated entrance and tall fences with CCTV cameras everywhere. From the outside it looks like a normal little residential estate with our house at the centre but nobody else lives on our street, except members of the firm, or security men on a retainer, and the gate is manned twenty-four hours a day. The only genuine civilian resident is Sarah's best mate Joanne, who lives in one of the apartments and helps Sarah with Emma. It's probably as secure an arrangement as I could get in Newcastle.

When I reached the top of the stairs, Sarah was leaning against the door frame looking down at our daughter, who was in the kind of deep sleep only little ones can achieve. She was tucked up in her bed, arms wrapped tightly around her favourite teddy, eyes tight shut, breathing regularly into her pillow. Every time I see her like this I think there is nothing I wouldn't do for our little girl, to protect her and walk her safely through this world.

Sarah grinned at me. 'Isn't she gorgeous?' she asked. 'I know I'm her mother but . . .'

'She is,' I replied, 'everybody says so.'

And they did. Everybody, even the hardened gangsters we employed in the firm came over all smiley if they had to come to the house and saw our little girl, with her big blue eyes and the golden-blonde hair she inherited from her mother. 'She gets it from you.'

'From both of us,' Sarah said, 'she's so cute,' she added in wonderment. Like me, Sarah couldn't quite believe our luck. Neither of us ever thought we deserved Emma, not after the stuff we'd seen and done, but she was here with us now and though we'd only had her for two years, sometimes we honestly struggled to remember a time when she had not been in our lives.

Just when I was feeling that all was well with the world, Sarah said, 'You know there's not a day goes by when I don't think about my dad and

Emma. I wish he could have seen her. He'd have loved her so much.'

'He would,' I agreed, but I wasn't thinking about the way that big, bad Bobby Mahoney, Newcastle's former top boy, would have balanced my little girl on his knee and played with her. Instead I was remembering how I blew Bobby's brains out in a derelict factory and it made me feel sick to think that, along with everything else I took from him, I had robbed Bobby Mahoney of time with his granddaughter. I'd had no choice but to kill him but Sarah didn't know it was my finger on the trigger and I was desperate to keep it that way.

My mobile rang then and Sarah winced. I grabbed it quickly but Emma didn't stir. I walked back down the stairs as I took the call. It was Vince, a long-standing member of our crew who kept an eye on some of our pubs and clubs in the city and Privado, our lap-dancing bar. 'Did you know Kinane's been arrested?' he asked me, his tone betraying his surprise, 'for bitch-slapping a couple of knuckle draggers?'

'Yeah,' I said and he hesitated before continuing.

'Oh, right. I was just wondering if you wanted us to try and get him out of there,' he offered tentatively, 'you know, phone the lawyer or summat?'

'No, fuck him,' I said, 'he's been a dick, let him stew.'

'Oh right, fine, I didn't realise. I was only saying like, sorry.'

'It's alright Vince, you weren't to know. Kinane will be out in the morning but he has to learn.'

Sarah followed me down the stairs and when I'd finished talking to Vince she asked me, 'Are you hungry? Do you want a drink?'

'I'm hungry,' I told her as I leaned in and kissed her. It had been two weeks since I'd seen her, 'but unfortunately I've got to go out again.' Her smile faded. 'I'm sorry, but I promised our Danny.'

'Oh yeah,' she said, 'I forgot it was tonight.'

I kissed her once more and told her I'd be back in a couple of hours. When she didn't break free from the embrace I leaned in and kissed her again and the kiss gradually became more serious. She ground herself against me and I slid my hand under her T-shirt and slowly drew it upwards till it cupped her breast. Then I told her in graphic detail what I was going to do to her when I came back later and she sighed. I slid my hand inside the cup of her bra and her nipple stiffened at my touch. She lifted her hand and let one finger trace the outline of my cock through my trousers, teasing me.

'Hold that thought,' she said, as she broke away from me.

I missed the start and hoped he hadn't noticed. He looked like he was well and truly zoned out, oblivious to everything else, including my presence. Danny was out on the edge of the court and, just as I sat down, he was passed the ball by one of his team, catching it cleanly, then immediately dummied his nearest opponent, ghosted past him like he wasn't even there and threw the ball to another team mate, before powering towards the opposing basket once more. His team looked like they were running the opposition ragged already, judging by the evidence of the electronic scoreboard, the frenzied whoops of encouragement from a sizeable home crowd in the stands and the way they casually flicked the basketball around like it was on a string that stretched between them. Their opponents seemed capable only of waving their arms forlornly as the ball flew by. It looked like the league title was going to be Danny's team's for the taking.

Our young'un, as I usually called him, even though he was a fair bit older than me, made his way inside until he was in a shooting position and, even above the noise of the supporters, I could hear him demanding the ball. Sure enough he got it, catching it cleanly and powering forward once more. He went past an opponent who tried to grab his arm and I watched with amusement as the guy was left trailing in Danny's wake. I loved the look of absolute determination on Our young'un's face as he closed in. He was bloody loving this. As soon as he found himself within shooting distance he released the ball, sending it up into the air in a long high arc towards the basket that I was only dimly aware of, because my eyes were still fixed on Danny and the opponent who had chosen that moment to go steaming into him at top speed. If you have ever seen two wheelchairs collide head on at full pelt you will know the impact is stomach churning. It's like watching a miniature car crash. There was a loud, metallic smash that sounded like a gun going off and Our young'un's chair was upended, just as the crowd cheered the basket he had scored. He shot forward and was flung face first onto the court and I winced and turned away. When I looked back he was already dragging himself along the court. Even from my seat I could see the fire in his eyes and knew what he was going to do. He grabbed the bloke who had careered into him by his vest and hauled him out of his chair, so he too ended up lying on the court, then Danny punched him hard on the side of the head.

All hell broke loose then. The referee, coaches and even some fans ran onto the court, meanwhile blokes in wheelchairs from both sides waded in to one another shouting insults and trading punches. Danny was right in the thick of it as usual. Somehow he managed to right his chair and drag himself back into it. Danny may have been paralysed from the waist down, but his upper body strength was amazing. He re-entered the fray just as the referee and others were trying to calm things down. Even from this distance, as the shouts and the arguments grew more heated, I could tell he was laughing.

CHAPTER 4

'Well, that was mature,' I told Danny as he wheeled himself towards me, across the carpet of the leisure centre bar, the big grin still plastered all over his face, 'red-carded or sin-binned or whatever you call it, after how many minutes? My arse had barely touched the seat and you were causing mayhem. You're supposed to play the game, not miss most of it because you've given someone a twatting.'

'I was just messing with him,' he assured me. Only a former Para could describe a solid punch to the side of the head as 'just messing'.

'Oh it was nowt man,' he continued, 'that bloke just took the piss and he knew it, so I gave him a little slap, but it was all handbags. He's fine with me now,' but he could tell by the look on my face I wasn't convinced, 'howay man, I'll buy him a pint.'

'There's no time for that,' I told him, 'I need to speak to you.'

While the other players congregated around the bar we chose a quiet corner away from them to sip our pints.

'So the Turk wants to retire,' he said, 'I was wondering what kept you so long.'

'There was a lot to discuss.'

'Whoever heard of a drug dealer retiring,' he asked me, 'especially one who peddles the quantity of powder he shifts? They always have too much unfinished business to just sail away. You know that.'

'Yeah,' I admitted, and I did know that because I was also a drug dealer. It might not have been the only thing we were involved in but we did a lot of product these days and most of it came from the Turk. Remzi al Karayilan came on board a few years back when our previous suppliers, the Haan brothers, both got life. We had a rocky first year with Remzi and I hated our irregular trips to Istanbul to negotiate consignments but things settled down after that and we started to get along. That didn't make us friends. It just meant we could do business with each other without constantly looking over our shoulders. He had the contacts in Afghanistan where they grow the poppy and wholesale the powder out to the Turk via, of all places, Iran. They'll let Remzi ship his powder through their country, in return for a large consideration, in cash. He then collects it in Turkey and transports it in huge trucks through his country and out the other side, into the Balkan states where we take over, moving it on to Amsterdam, then finally the Eastern ports of the UK. Hull takes the lion's share. Our consignments disappear in among hundreds of tonnes of shipping freight a year in that port alone. If you pay the right people to look the other way it is virtually impossible to get caught.

But now Remzi has had enough. He wants to quit and enjoy his old age. That's why I'm asking my brother for advice. I keep him well out of harm's way these days, since it is my fault he's in that wheelchair. He stopped three bullets and came close to dying. Danny will never walk again because of me, he's a civilian, but I still respect his opinion.

'I'm taking over the whole thing,' I said, 'paying him a lump sum for the consideration, taking it all in-house.'

'What about his contacts?'

'We'll take on some of his people, the ones with the know-how. They'll keep up the contacts and we'll ensure the money keeps on coming but, without Remzi's cut and a few other savings I can think of, we should be considerable amounts of quids-in.'

'Why not?' he asked, 'that Russian connection is the future.'

Danny was right. We've been pushing product into the east, opening up a cast-iron supply chain with contacts in the Russian mafia Remzi intro-duced me to.

'That's what I figured. I've just got to negotiate a little golden handshake and he will duck out; the lucky fucker.'

We talked through the practicalities of taking

Remzi's empire off his hands until we finally ran out of things to say about it. I was pleased Danny was so on the ball. He'd had a very tough time of it these past couple of years. It took him a long while to come to terms with the fact that he would never walk again but I reckoned a lot of his recent improvement was down to the unarmed combat known as wheelchair basketball.

'I've got a day lined up at our hotel for that charity gala dinner we've been talking about.' I said.

'Great,' but then I told him the date and his smile faded.

'What's the matter?' I asked, 'I thought you were mad keen to do this.'

'I am, it's just . . .'

'What?'

'Well, that's my birthday like,' he seemed a bit uncomfortable mentioning it, as if it was unmanly to care that it was your birthday at his age.

'Yeah, well, we can have a beer on the night,' I said, 'at the dinner I mean.'

'S'pose,' he said, but I could tell he was narked because he thought I didn't give a shit about his birthday.

'So how have you been? Lately I mean?' I asked for two reasons; firstly to change the subject away from his birthday but also because I was genuinely concerned about him.

'I still have my bad days,' he admitted, 'but I'm a lot better than I was. You know that.'

He was right. When he first took those bullets in

the spine, I was terrified he was going to die on me. As soon as I realised he would make it, I had a different problem. He kept telling me he'd have preferred to die rather than face life paralysed and I know he blamed me for it. If he hadn't been working for the firm then he would still be walking. It was a visit I organised from two former members of the parachute regiment, who'd had their legs blown off by roadside bombs, that finally started to convince my brother his life wasn't over. That was just the beginning though. The rest has been a daily struggle that I think he's finally starting to win.

'I've settled for where I am and who I am,' he said. 'Don't get me wrong, I'd have the use of my legs back in a second,' and he clicked his fingers to illustrate his point, 'but, I've thought about this a lot and I'm probably a better person these days than I was before . . . you know . . . all this.'

'You are slightly less of a cunt than you were,' I conceded.

'Thanks. Anyway, life is reasonably sweet,' then he added a little self-consciously, 'I've been seeing a bit of that Linda.'

I couldn't place her for a moment, 'Linda that works the bar at the Cauldron?'

'Fuck no,' he laughed, 'she looks like Andy Murray in drag.'

I laughed, 'actually, you're right, she does a bit.'

'Then credit me with some taste. No, I'm talking about Linda who dances for us at Cachet.'

'That Linda? Fuck me Our young'un, how did you manage that?'

'Used me charm bro, used me charm,' he said smugly and I was pleased for him.

'I would have bet against you landing her if you'd used Rohypnol but, well done. What is she though? Nineteen?'

'No,' he scoffed, 'she's twenty-four.'

'I wondered why you kept her on. You usually retire them at twenty. So only half your age then? Reckon it'll last?'

'Don't know, don't care, life's too short to worry about that shite isn't it? How many relationships do you know that last forever. Look at you and that Laura bird.'

'You have a point.' Was there actually a time when I had considered me and my mad ex Laura to be a permanent item? If there was, it was a lifetime ago.

'Anyway, we're just enjoying ourselves and we can still do stuff, you know sexually and that. I don't mind you asking.'

'Asking? I wasn't asking and I won't be. Whatever you and her get up to in the wee small hours has got fuck all to do with me.'

'I'm only saying that I can still *do* stuff. I know some of the lads think I can't but I can and . . .'

I put my fingers in my ears at that point and started chanting, 'La, la, la, la, la, I'm not fucking listening, la, la, la, la.'

Trouble with Our young'un is he is almost impossible to embarrass, so he just rose to the bait, 'she's got a load of toys and she does all sorts of stuff with them. Did I ever tell you how she does this thing with her finger . . .'

'Oh Christ no, I've gone blind, shut up man before I puke. Have another pint for fuck's sake.'

He laughed, 'You're just a prude, that's your trouble. No, I'm heading off after this one.'

'Bloody hell. You're a changed man Danny. It must be that young lass of yours.'

'It isn't just that,' he informed me ruefully, 'hangovers aren't much fun when you're hauling yourself around in one of these things. Were you planning on stopping like? I wouldn't have thought this was your sort of place.'

'No, it's okay. I've got to be off too.'

'Back home to wor lass?'

'Not just yet.'

'She hasn't seen you for a fortnight.'

'I know,' I admitted, 'but I need a word with Sharp. I'll head home after that.'

His face became a grimace, 'oh god.'

'What?'

'You're not still . . .' and he didn't finish but he gave me a look like I was some new species of idiot he'd only just discovered.

'What?' I repeated.

'You *know* what,' he informed me, 'and you know my view an' all, so I don't know why you are bothering to tell me.'

'I know your view but I thought it might have altered since we last spoke.'

35

'No,' he said firmly, 'it hasn't. I can't see what good could come of it.'

'Well, as always, Our young'un, I respect your opinion.'

'Aye and, as always, you'll fuckin' well ignore it,' he told me as I drained the last dregs of my pint.

I was up on the roof of the Cauldron staring out at the night sky and I was here to meet Sharp. Down below me, the city was bustling along, lights gleaming from every window. Detective Inspector Sharp was my main man in Northumbria Constabulary. We had a few on the payroll but Sharp was our best-paid operative and his expertise and information had helped dig me out of more than one hole before now. He liked to meet me here because the building was right on the edge of Chinatown and he could access it through the big Chinese restaurant next door. He would simply flash his warrant card at the waiters then come up the fire escape.

He was looking stressed when he arrived but I didn't have time to ask after his well-being and I was keen to get home to Sarah. Sharp was the best I had at finding people but, surprisingly for him, he'd drawn a blank this time.

'I'm sorry,' he said when he'd concluded his explanations, or were they just excuses?

'I thought finding people was your speciality?'

'It was,' he protested, 'it is,' and he shrugged,

'but you might have more luck with some of the old crew.'

'Why me?'

'Hey, I'm not being lazy. They just don't like talking to coppers, you know how those old villains are, always think they are gonna be fitted up for something they haven't done.'

'Whatever could have given them that idea?'

'Aye well, that was then, this is now. In the seventies if you were banged up for something you didn't do, it probably meant you'd gotten away with a lot of stuff that you did.'

'So you've not found out anything?'

'Only what we know already; your father left town suddenly one day, a couple of years before you were born. There was some sort of job down south, by all accounts, and he never returned home but he kept in touch with your ma for years afterwards. There's people who've corroborated this. She used to go off and see him and always assumed the family would get back together in the end. Then one day, as the story goes, the calls and the letters from your father stopped and he disappeared for good.'

'I was about two years old when that happened.'

'It looks like he left your ma in the lurch to bring up two little boys on her own while he fucked off out of it. He wouldn't be the first or the last to do that, would he? But there are no records of the man anywhere.'

'So it's possible something bad happened to him down south?' I asked.

'It's possible,' he admitted, 'or he could have changed his name and emigrated to Australia. We just don't know.'

I had never cared about what happened to my father before now. I had always taken the view that, since he walked out on ma, Danny and me when I was little and I don't have any memories of the man, I didn't give a fuck what became of him.

Then we had Emma and it changed my view almost overnight. I could never imagine a time when I would be happy to sit down and have a pint with the old git, assuming he was still alive, but I was curious to know what happened to him and to hear from his own mouth why he did what he did, mainly because of Emma. I wanted to be able to tell her something about him, to be capable of answering her questions about her grandfather when she grew older, so I'd asked Sharp to look into it for me. Danny figured we should just leave it as a mystery, because there was nothing the guy could say to either of us that we would actually want to hear.

'So you reckon members of the old crew might know what really went off before he left the city?'

'I dunno, yeah, maybe,' he admitted, 'he used to hang round their old haunts and didn't Bobby's crew always know everything that went on?'

'Yeah,' I admitted, 'but there aren't many of them left,' I reminded him, 'they might all be dead . . .'

I was going through a list of old names in my head; Geordie Cartwright, Jerry Lemon, Mark Miller, Hunter, Finney and the man himself, Bobby Mahoney; all dead, every last one of them and I was responsible for more than one of those deaths.

'There must be somebody,' he said.

'Maybe. Leave it with me. I'll ask around.' We stood there for a while looking out at the skyline until I said, 'out with it then.'

'What?' he asked.

'Whatever it is that's bothering you. You're still here and I thought we were done.'

He exhaled, 'I think I am being investigated.'

'You always think that,' I reminded him.

'Yeah, I do,' he said, 'but what if it's true this time? You still attract a lot of interest. Maybe someone followed you and saw me with you.'

'Then you explain it away. I'm your high-level source, remember, your grass who's selling everyone else down the river.'

'That story might have held when you worked for Bobby Mahoney but who's bigger than you these days? No one,' he told me without waiting for an answer.

'You sure they are watching you?' I asked and he nodded emphatically.

'I've been hearing things,' he said, 'they've been asking questions about me, speaking to colleagues, some I haven't worked with in years. What else could it be but them thinking I'm bent? I reckon they are onto something. It'll be ten years minimum if I'm caught, more maybe,' he said.

'I know,' I replied.

'So I need you to take this seriously,' he urged me, sounding a little panicked.

Detective Inspector Sharp didn't strike me as the kind of man who would go quietly off and do ten years without cutting a deal and the only thing he had to bargain with was me. I figured I'd probably get life for that.

'I am taking this very seriously Sharp,' I told him, 'believe me.'

Basically, if Sharp went down, well, he would have to go.

CHAPTER 5

I was wide awake, my body clock skewed by a doze on the flight home from Istanbul. As soon as I got in I went straight upstairs, because I knew Sarah was waiting for me and I was 'on a promise'. The light was still on in our bedroom and I walked in to find Sarah lying on the bed, but she wasn't alone. Our little girl was fast asleep next to a fully-clothed Sarah, who was passed out like she'd been drugged.

'Hold that thought,' I muttered to myself and trudged off to the spare bed.

I left Kinane to stew in the cells overnight, so he'd know I was pissed off with him. He was bailed late the next morning and we picked him up off the street. He climbed slowly into the passenger seat next to Palmer, who drove away, then he turned back towards me, like he was trying to weigh up my mood. I must have looked pretty narked because Joe did something that he almost never did. He apologised.

'Soz,' he said.

'What?' I was being deliberately awkward. His

form of apology made him sound like a surly teenager, so I was determined to treat him like one.

'I'm sorry,' he told me, 'but those two little cun . . .'

'Deserved it?' I interrupted him, 'of course they did. They were vermin. A small part of me enjoyed kicking that little bastard in the face but I know that it achieved nothing and so should you. There's hundreds like him and his mate in this city Joe, hundreds. Now do you want to become a one-man vigilante group, trawling the streets of Newcastle, looking for wankers like them and administering punishment beatings for the rest of your days or do you want to work for me instead?'

For a moment I thought he was going to argue with me but then he seemed to think better of it. 'I know you are right,' he told me, 'I do, honestly. It's just,' he groaned then, like he was reliving the moment when they cut us up, 'I can't bring myself to take shite from scummy little fuckers like them.'

'No one says you have to Joe but beating them up on the side of the road, in front of three dozen passing cars, is just taking the piss. The police have to do something about that, no matter who you are and we are supposed to be keeping a low profile.'

'I know, I know,' he held his hands up, 'I'm sorry. I am. It won't happen again.'

'It had better not.' I told him.

'Can you fix it?'

'I'll do my best, but you'll have to go to court and you might have to plead guilty to something.'

'What?'

'There are too many witnesses for it to be called self-defence. You put that lad in the hospital and who's ever going to believe *they* attacked *you*. Look at yourself man,' I sighed, 'no, you're guilty and you are going to plead and apologise to the court. We'll get the lawyers to come up with a convincing bit of bullshit about why you snapped that day and how you were provoked by them. That's as good as it gets.'

'But I've been inside,' he reminded me. He was worried that might get him another custodial sentence.

'That was years ago. I've already talked to Susan Fitch. You went inside but you've reformed your life since then. You've been an honest, upstanding member of society, who has worked in the entertainment industry as a night club manager ever since. You put your troubled past behind you.'

Susan Fitch was our solicitor. She had been looking after members of the firm for nearly twenty years now and the police hated her for it.

'What if they don't buy it?' he asked me, 'what if they send me down?'

'Then you'll have nobody to blame but yourself,' I told him, and he looked like he wanted to hit *me* this time, 'I'll do my best. I can't promise anything more than that.'

'You'll be right Joe,' Palmer chipped in, 'no sweat.'

'Pull over here,' I told him because I had just spotted the familiar, balding, paunchy figure of Henry Baxter emerging from his apartment block. He was edging cautiously towards the kerb, like a blind man approaching a pedestrian crossing. Our accountant had been with us for more than two years now but he still treated Newcastle like it was chock full of muggers and murderers, who could leap out on him without warning at any time. We pulled over. He spotted us and climbed into the back seat next to me.

'Good morning gentlemen,' he said, his jowly face contorted into a yawn.

'Sorry, am I keeping you up?' I asked.

'Not at all dear boy, as ever I am hanging on your every word. I'm just a little pooped, that's all,' and he yawned again, 'a late night,' and he smiled enigmatically, 'with a friend.' Then he elaborated, 'It was Vaughan Williams at the Sage.'

'Good was he?' asked Kinane.

'What?' Baxter didn't do anything to hide the incredulity in his voice. Kinane just assumed he hadn't heard the question.

'Vaughan thingy; was he any good?'

'You're not serious Joe? The man's been dead for half a century.'

'Eh?' it was Kinane's turn to act confused, 'well I don't know who he is, do I? I was only asking.'

44

At this point Baxter should have shut up, but he carried on digging and I let him.

'Don't tell me you've never heard of him, that's tantamount to an impossibility. He was the greatest English composer of the twentieth century . . .'

'Listen Baxter,' interrupted Kinane. 'I don't have the time to listen to some poncin'arsed, classical shite like that. I like proper, non-wanky stuff; Dire Straits and Sting and a bit of Fleetwood Mac,' before adding, 'something you can tap your fingers against the steering wheel to when you're driving, like normal people.'

'Alright lads,' Palmer said, 'don't get your knickers in a twist. We picked Baxter up for a reason and it wasn't to talk about concerts.'

'It's done,' Baxter told us curtly.

'What is?' I asked him.

'That which you asked me to do.' He had clearly gone into one of his sulks. 'A cast-iron, fool-proof and entirely legal . . . *ish* . . . cash transfer that has enabled us to place a very significant amount of money beyond the grasping arms of Her Majesty's Inspectors of Revenue, ergo the tax man, into an offshore account at a highly-accommodating little bank in the Cayman Islands.'

The Caymans was invented for people like us. The place is the fifth largest financial centre in the world after New York, London, Tokyo and Zurich, holding assets of eighteen trillion dollars on deposit. Why? Here's a clue; in the capital, George Town, there are eighteen thousand corporations registered in one building alone. They don't even try to look legitimate. And who is responsible for ensuring the Cayman Islands plays fair and doesn't launder money? Well, the place is still an overseas territory of the UK.

'You've done it then?' I asked Baxter disbelievingly.

'Yes,' he told me smugly, as he awaited my congratulations.

'No hitches?' I asked.

'None.'

'The entire five million?'

'The whole bloody lot.'

'Well done,' I told him. This was good news and I felt in need of some, 'Palmer, turn the car around and head for the Quayside.'

'Where are we going?'

'For lunch,' I told them, 'at Café 21.'

CHAPTER 6

I never tire of Café 21, even with Baxter as a lunch companion. Maybe it's because I don't own the place, so I can relax there.

Baxter was characteristically verbose throughout our meal but he'd earned the right to be pleased with himself and regale us with tales of his life before joining our firm. He liked to tell the story of his difficult childhood; how he struggled to fit in as a boarder at his famous, old public school. The way Baxter told it, he was a precociously gifted child, a sensitive soul who was bullied relentlessly because of this obvious potential for greatness. From there it was an upward trajectory that took in Cambridge, then the City, where his genius for numbers was ruthlessly harnessed until he was deemed surplus to requirements and 'cast adrift' as he put it. He was actually arrested for embezzling millions of pounds of client money, in a fraud so Byzantine in its complexity it was only discovered at all because of the credit crunch. The old, long-established broking house he worked for was running out of cash. They had to resort to digging into their reserves to fund them through the crisis, which was when they realised there was a large black hole. Henry Baxter got six years and did three.

I'd read about the case in the papers but it was Amrein who really put me onto him, when Baxter was about to emerge from prison. The complex nature of Baxter's fraudulent transactions, coupled with the extraordinary web of companies he managed to set up to launder his ill-gotten gains, making them virtually tax free, made him just the kind of man I was looking for. I needed someone who could move money around and Baxter could do it with not a little élan. Palmer called Baxter a math-magician, a phrase our accountant loathed, which is why Palmer kept on saying it to his face.

I doubt Baxter would have signed up with us at all if it wasn't for the ARA. The Assets Recovery Agency took him apart and clawed back virtually everything he had stolen. He couldn't have been more bitter about that.

'So you know all about this smoke and mirrors, city-boy, swank-wank stuff then, do you Baxter?' asked Kinane.

'If you mean, can I explain the difference between a collateralised debt obligation and a credit default swap then yes, I can,' he smiled, 'whether you will be able to grasp that difference is another matter.'

I interrupted before things got more heated. 'Perhaps, Baxter, your time would be better employed explaining to the boys exactly how you lifted five million of our ill-gotten pounds out of the country, cleaned it, laundered it and only paid three per cent tax.'

'Three per cent?' asked a baffled Palmer.

'It's very simple dear boy,' explained Baxter, 'I merely adapted a model already favoured by some of the super-rich in our country,' and he waited till he was sure he had our full attention before continuing, 'I set up a partnership trust and registered it in Jersey. The partners in the trust, who just happen to be us, meaning subsidiary companies we own that operate under a variety of names, all contribute sizeable sums of money, totalling five million pounds, which amounts to the combined profits of our legitimate businesses, with a very sizeable chunk of illegitimate takings thrown in.'

'You mean the drug money,' said Kinane.

'We then take that five million and invest it into our partnership trust, which buys a dividend from an offshore company we already control. That dividend actually costs fifty million pounds because it is worth fifty million . . . only it isn't, because it is entirely fictitious. That's the bit of the scheme I adapted.'

'Come again?' asked Palmer.

'You spent five million pounds on something with no profit?' asked Kinane, who had already lost the thread completely.

'It isn't real,' confirmed Baxter, 'nor is the forty-five million pound loan we took out to buy that fake dividend.'

'So it's a fake loan, with fake interest and fake repayments to purchase an imaginary dividend.' I explained.

'I don't get it,' said Palmer, 'if it's all fake then what do we get out of it?'

'Tax relief,' I told him.

'Is that all?' asked Kinane.

'Is that all?' snorted Baxter, 'we have just laundered five million pounds into an offshore account and it cost us just one hundred and fifty thousand pounds tax, plus transaction fees, meaning we keep four million, eight hundred and fifty thousand pounds, which is now nestling in a bank account in the Cayman Islands.'

'If we'd paid Corporation Tax at twenty-four per cent, it would have cost us one-point-two mill.'

'So Baxter just saved us over a million quid?' asked Palmer.

I raised my champagne glass to Baxter, 'hence lunch at 21.'

'So how does that work then? Why would they let us get away with it?' added my head of security.

'Because we are claiming tax relief on the cost of buying the dividend,' said Baxter, 'exploiting a loop hole on the benefits from that dividend,' he explained, as if it was obvious.

'I don't get it,' said Kinane.

'And there was I assuming you would,' Baxter's tone was dripping with sarcasm, 'but this is my area Joe. Yours is breaking arms.'

50

'And I'll break yours if you talk to me like that again.'

'Simmer down lads. This should be a day of celebration,' I reminded them, 'it doesn't get much better than this. Baxter did a good thing for the business.'

'Why don't they clamp down on these tax dodges?' asked Palmer, 'you're a clever man Baxter but you can't be the only one who's spotted this one.'

'I'm sure I'm not but loopholes are like mole hills,' explained Baxter, 'you stamp on one and there'll be another one on your lawn in the morning,' he took a reflective sip of his wine, 'besides no government really has the appetite to tread on the rich these days. Look how many millionaires are in the cabinet. They tend to hang out with other millionaires.'

'Wait a minute though, who are we paying the fees to?' asked Palmer.

'To the company that oversees the tax avoidance scheme,' I explained, 'it's their cut for sorting out the deal.'

'But the deal is fake,' said Palmer.

'Then it was easy money, wasn't it?'

Palmer and Kinane looked at me like I'd gone a bit nuts and was talking to an imaginary friend, so I put them out of their misery, 'the two hundred thousand pounds in fees gets divided between the four main board directors of Barrack Road Investments, which means fifty grand each for

Henry Baxter, David Blake, Nick Palmer and Joe Kinane. I mean to say, with a tax avoidance scheme of that complexity and cunning, I'd say they've earned it, wouldn't you?'

There was silence for a moment and then Palmer chuckled and it turned into a laugh, 'back of the net,' he said.

I didn't feel guilty about the money we'd shoved away. There were a lot of people on my payroll and I had to stump up the cash for them week in, week out. There were also the 'drops' to various fixers, problem-solvers and intelligence-gatherers, not least Amrein and his highly shady and very expensive organisation, who effectively legitimised us in the criminal world. Amrein's outfit gave us permission to control the city and, in theory at least, ensured no one else could take it away from us. All of this was a form of tax and I didn't want to be shelling out millions more for the government to waste it on Enterprise Zones or the Big Society. Magicians use distraction, misdirection and sleight of hand to make people look the other way while they get away with their trick. We are just like magicians, only on a much larger scale.

Some of our legitimate businesses still paid tax of course. It was great cover and we are not entirely hard hearted. Besides, we weren't the worst offenders. The biggest money launderers are the banks. Standard Chartered, a noble old British bank, was forced to pay a fine of $340 million to the US government because it laundered two hundred and fifty billion dollars of dirty Iranian money through its marbled corridors. That pales compared to the $1.9 billion dollars HSBC was fined for laundering drug money for criminal cartels. I don't see Britain's biggest bank mentioning that on any of their uplifting TV commercials.

Big corporations have been moving profits abroad for years. In their world it's simply clever accounting. The billionaire retailer Philip Green avoided a £285 million pound tax bill by making himself an offshore resident of Monaco, then putting his company in his wife's name. The government came after him straight away but only to seek his advice. The Prime Minister got him to conduct a review of government spending. You honestly couldn't make that shit up.

We talked all afternoon, until Baxter inadvertently stumbled on a thorny topic. It was strange that among the millions we'd laundered it was a few grand that caused the falling out.

'Three per cent tax?' Palmer said, as if he still couldn't get his head around it, 'normal people pay way more than that.'

'And there'll be plenty left over for a sizeable donation to the Conservative party,' Baxter told him.

'A donation?' Kinane was incredulous, 'to the fucking Tories? Are you having a laugh?'

'If we drop fifty grand into Tory coffers they'll leave us alone,' explained Baxter, 'they'll be too embarrassed to catch us, if they've got to admit they took money from us. It's a self-fulfilling prophesy; they only take money from legitimate businessmen therefore, in taking our money, we must be legitimate businessmen.'

'But we're not legitimate, we're bent and everybody knows it. SOCA will warn them off us,' said Palmer.

SOCA or the Serious Organised Crime Agency was tasked with bringing down drug smugglers, money launderers, armed, violent criminals and people traffickers. We'd never trafficked human beings but we ticked every other box on their wish list and always had to assume they were keeping an eye on us.

'SOCA would warn them about taking money from Gallowgate Holdings, but they know nothing about Barrack Road Investments.' I informed him, 'and our real names aren't on the founding papers.'

'But are there not rules about political parties taking money from offshore companies?' Palmer asked.

'Barrack Road Investments has a UK-based sister company, for want of a better phrase, with a discreet, private little office in London from which we can donate to whoever we please. In reality it's little more than a PO box.'

'I don't like it,' Kinane's mood had soured, 'giving money to the Tories? Might as well give it to the IRA or the Taliban.'

'Oh don't be ridiculous Joe!' mocked Baxter.

'Why not?' Kinane protested, 'they've both done less damage to the north-east than the fucking Tory party,' and he folded his arms defiantly.

'Let's talk about it later, eh?' I suggested. 'Nothing's been decided.' I had been hoping for a calm and pleasant day for once, but this wasn't going to be it. What should have been a celebratory lunch ended on a tense note.

CHAPTER 7

That night I went looking for Vince. He was an unassuming lad who kept his head down and his hands clean but could be relied upon to manage a handful of our bars and clubs in the Bigg Market and the Quayside. This time of night he would normally be down at Privado, our low-rate lap-dancing bar. We didn't spend any money on fancy trimmings here. All we needed was a couple of poles and a glitter ball, then we turned the lights down low and we were in business. The lasses here made their money persuading the punters to shell out for a private dance. They would pay to see them topless and give more to get them fully nude but it would all be over in the time it took to play two tracks. Then another lass would come over to fleece them out of more cash. I've seen drunk guys walk out of there hundreds of pounds down, with absolutely nothing to show for it but the hazy drunken memory of a bit of naked flesh.

There was never any shortage of lasses willing to give it a go. I didn't know what the guys who came here thought of the girls after they left but

I knew what the girls thought of the men; mugs, every last one of them.

I'd not been in Privado for a long time. There was no need. Vince ran it and the place virtually looked after itself. I had bigger things to care about. Big Auty was on the door, as always, with one of the younger lads from Joe Kinane's gym.

'Evening Davey,' he said. I'd known 'Big Auty' for years, ever since I was a kid in fact. He was a legend on the doors of Newcastle and he had a sideline as corner man for our boxing prospect, Phil 'The Warrior' Watson. His hair was silver now but he was still one of the toughest guys in the city. When he was on a door for us there was never any trouble.

'Evening Auty,' I said, 'Vince around?'

He nodded, 'I'll get him.'

I followed Big Auty into Privado and stood in the bar while he went out back to find Vince. The first thing that struck me was how dead it was. Either the economy really was beginning to bite or men had finally realised that going to a lap-dancing bar was about as sensible as keeping a bonfire going all night with ten pound notes. I could only see two punters. They were outnumbered by twelve girls in lingerie or skimpy dresses.

A voice from the bar said, 'Look what the cat dragged in.'

I'd hoped that Michelle wouldn't be in Privado. I figured she'd surely quit the business by now. She was sitting on a bar stool in an old-fashioned cocktail dress, the ones with the split up the side that go right up to the hip. A couple of the other girls looked a bit uncomfortable, because they knew who I was, but I ignored Michelle's comment. She wasn't going to let me off that lightly. 'I thought you'd forgotten all about us.'

'No,' I told her quietly, 'but I lived abroad for a while.'

'So I heard,' she said, way too brightly. She would also have heard I was shacked up with Bobby's daughter and a father to boot. I made sure I kept eye contact with Michelle, so she understood she couldn't push me too far. I knew why she was annoyed at me. We'd had a night, just the one, and I hadn't bothered to call her for a repeat performance. At the time I was newly broken up with Laura and trying very hard not to climb into bed with Sarah, because I knew Bobby would never have tolerated that. Michelle was single and seemed the ideal solution but she woke up in the morning acting like I was her new boyfriend, while I couldn't wait to get out of there.

Under normal circumstances, I would have made more of an effort to ensure there was no lingering bitterness between us. I would have at least called her, or bought her some dinner and explained I was just not ready for a commitment right now, but they weren't normal circumstances at the time and I had way too much to deal with to worry about her hurt feelings.

Before she could think of anything else to say in

front of the other girls I said, 'I didn't expect to see you still working here Michelle. I thought you'd have graduated by now.'

When I first met Michelle she was always going on about how she was only doing the lap-dancing short term and part-time. All of the money was going towards her student debt. She told everyone that, as soon as she graduated, she'd be off.

'I did graduate,' she told me, 'ages ago, but there's a recession on out there, or haven't you noticed?'

'Certainly is,' I agreed, 'but I'd have thought a bright girl like you wouldn't struggle too long to get a job.'

This made her flush even more. 'Maybe not,' she admitted, 'but graduate jobs don't pay half as much as I can earn here,' and she waved her hand at the room airily, 'when it's not dead.'

'Of course,' I agreed, 'and it's amazing how quickly you get used to a certain standard of living.' I didn't point out the obvious; that another year or two working in Privado full time would render her qualifications irrelevant. A little further down the line and she'd be stuck here, competing for tips with twenty-year-olds who had firmer tits and fewer lines on their faces.

'Anyway,' she said, 'my boyfriend's cool with it, so . . .' That last comment was for my benefit.

'That's handy,' I said, then I spotted Vince walking towards me, 'lovely to see you again Michelle.'

'Yeah,' she said and gave me a forced smile, 'you too.'

'Sorry to keep you,' said Vince, 'I was sorting the books out.'

'No problem,' I said, 'can I have a word?' And I led him away from Michelle, who went back to propping up the bar.

To begin with, Vince had agreed with me, 'they're all dead aren't they? There's only Joe Kinane left from Bobby's inner circle but it's a bit before his time. I can't think of anyone who'd go all the way back to . . . when was it again?'

'My father left Newcastle back in '72 and kept in touch with me ma for another four years or so. There was no more contact after about 1976.'

'Bloody hell, that was an age ago,' Vince started to drum his fingers on his desk like he was thinking, then he suddenly said, 'have you tried Jinky Smith? He's about the only one of the old 'uns left, I reckon.'

'Blimey. I'd not thought of Jinky,' I admitted. 'He hasn't been in the firm for years though. You sure he's still alive?'

Vince nodded, 'he still gets around, just.'

'How can I find him?'

'I haven't seen him in a while,' he said, 'we don't encourage the old lags to pop in. We'd soon lose our licence if some toe rag was doing coke deals in the bogs or nicking wallets. We get enough grief about having full nudity.'

'But you've seen him around?'

'Well, yeah, he pops in the bars occasionally but he's not a regular.

'So where does he live?'

Vince thought for a while, then finally said, 'I seem to remember he's got a flat in Benwell or Fenham or some other shit hole, poor bastard.'

I suppose I couldn't expect Vince to know the address of every down-at-heel ex-member of the firm. I'd have to get Sharp onto this one.

CHAPTER 8

I'm a very light sleeper, but nobody could doze through the sound of a front door coming violently off its hinges. I was out of our bed before it hit the ground, even as Sarah was waking up with a start and screaming for me. I reached the landing and leaned out over the stairs in time to see armed, uniformed police officers crashing through the broken door into our home. I was relieved it was only them. The alternatives would have been far worse. One of them spotted me and shouted for me to stay where I was. I ignored him. Instead I turned back to Sarah who had come out onto the landing looking panicked.

'It's okay,' I assured her, 'it's nothing. They are just taking me in but they've got nothing.' We had often talked about me being lifted by the local police or SOCA and we had both agreed that Sarah would stay calm and call the lawyers, but she didn't look calm right now.

The police had come straight through the heavy front door like it was balsa wood, but they'd failed to take a more simple obstacle into account. I could hear one of them swearing as he tugged at the stair gate we'd installed to ensure Emma didn't fall down the stairs. Someone shouted at him to go over it and he cursed again as he tried to vault the little metal gate and couldn't manage it first time.

I looked at Sarah again and repeated, 'they've got nothing. You hear me?'

'Yes,' she said and I couldn't think of anything more reassuring to say because, whatever the police thought they had, it was strong enough for them to arrest every man protecting our property, before smashing my front door down and dragging me from my bed in the middle of the night. That worried me more than I cared to admit. What the hell was this about?

Having finally navigated the stair gate, the police came thumping up the steps, their heavy boots making a din. They were shouting, and Sarah and I both instinctively looked through the opened door of Emma's bedroom. She was sleeping through the entire thing. Even a busted door and a half dozen burly, armed police officers bursting into our home couldn't disturb my little girl.

The lead police officer looked on edge. He had his pistol aimed right at me, 'David Blake?' he screamed.

'Yes,' I said quietly, even though I hate having guns pointed at me, particularly by people who looked as stressed as he did.

'Don't move and put your hands in the air!'

I was tempted to point out that I could hardly

do both, but instead I slowly raised my hands, then I put the palms on the back of my head, which seemed to calm him. 'Okay,' I said, 'it's fine officer, I'm happy to assist you with your enquiries. There's just two little things.'

'What?' he barked, straightening his arm and pointing his gun more firmly at me in emphasis.

'Let me put some clothes on,' I told him, because I was standing there in just my boxers, 'and shut the fuck up.' He looked startled by that. 'We have a small child sleeping in there.' I indicated Emma's room with a faint movement of my head. He stared at me for a moment like I was trying to distract him and might attack if he took his eyes off me for a second. I must have looked pretty harmless though, standing there in my underwear with my hands behind my head, because he finally stole a quick glance through the open door, saw Emma and realised I was telling the truth.

'Okay,' he said in something between a gasp and a whisper. 'Sorry Miss.' Sarah gave him a murderous look and went to check on Emma.

'You know why you are here,' the detective told me for the third time.

'I have no idea why I am here,' I answered. *Here* was the police station on Market Street, a grey, grim, sixties-built, flat-roofed box of a building. The interview room was just as stark; a table, some chairs, two filing cabinets in the corner, a DCI questioning me, three more plain clothes in the room to make sure I didn't deck him and run off.

'Are we going to mess about all night?' asked Detective Chief Inspector Hibbitt, a man I had never clapped eyes on before, until he snarled an introduction at me five minutes earlier. He was the SIO or Senior Investigating Officer in the case I was about to be questioned over, he told me, with barely disguised contempt, while strangely neglecting to inform me what that case was, hence his rather ridiculous statement that I knew why I was here. 'See if you can work it out,' he added, 'go on, give it a go.'

Behind him, a Detective Sergeant, who was equally unknown to me but apparently went by the name of Fraser, paced up and down behind him looking like a caged tiger. I had never seen police officers looking so wound up before. They were treating me like I was the mastermind of some terrorist outrage, not their local, friendly drug-dealing, money launderer gangster. I'd been offered a lawyer but I find these chats about crimes I have been linked with tend to go better if I let the police feel they are more in control. I let them ask their questions and deflect them. Then they let me go home and that is usually the end of the matter. If I involve my lawyer it tends to mean a protracted stay at the station and a tedious impasse, which leaves the police frustrated and angry because I didn't cooperate. There isn't much good-will directed at me from the local plod but Sharp has told me that I get a few Brownie points for at least allowing them to have their little talks with me unencumbered by a posse of lawyers.

'Night shift a bit dull, was it?' I asked, 'and you wanted to liven things up a bit?'

'Carlton,' he said.

'I might have known,' I replied. Carlton was behind this, 'DI Carlton's been my biggest fan for a while now. He seems to think I'm a criminal mastermind, not a respectable north-east business man.'

'We know all about you, Blake, so there's very little point in pissing us around,' the DCI told me, 'you used to work for Bobby Mahoney and he has been missing, presumed dead, for years now. He might be on a tropical island somewhere but more than likely he's buried in the foundations of one of those yuppie apartment blocks you built on the Quayside. You've been doing very well since then, haven't you? Well,' he added, 'you *were* because we've never been able to prove anything,' then he continued, 'but that's all about to change.'

Then Hibbitt put his palms on the table in front of me, stretched across it, leaned in close to me and hissed, 'there is a line, Blake, and you just crossed it. You are going down for a very long time.'

'Is this the bit where I get to say something like, "I have no idea what you are talking about, Inspector", because I *really* do have no idea what you are talking about, Inspector.'

66

'Carlton,' he said again, but he didn't tell me more.

'What about him? Is he here? I don't know what he thinks he has got on me but it's nothing. You are going to look very stupid when my lawyer tears you apart and sends you the bill for my front door.'

The DCI shook his head, 'You can't just do anything you want, hurt anyone you want. Don't you see that? Sooner or later . . .' his words tailed away and he shook his head in something like bemusement. He was looking at me like I was shit on his shoes. He stepped back from the table.

'Shall we start again?' I asked, 'perhaps you can tell me what it is that you or Carlton think I have done? Would that make sense? You are supposed to do that; under your own code of practice from the Police and Criminal Evidence Act, you are meant to let me know why you have brought me here.'

The DS, who had been watching me intently, suddenly lost control and let out a roar. He marched up to my table with a ferocious look in his eye and smashed his fist down onto it hard.

'You fucking bastard,' he hissed at me while he tried to regain control. I just stared at him, wondering what the hell he was on to make him act like this, 'you . . . evil . . . fucking . . . bastard. You are gonna pay! I promise you that!'

'Look,' I said, in as reasonable a voice as I could muster, 'there's obviously some kind of mix-up here. I haven't done anything . . . out of the ordinary.' I was choosing my words carefully, abandoning the pretence that I was a law-abiding citizen for a moment.

The DS ignored this. 'Carlton is a good man,' he told me, 'he's worth a hundred of you.'

I frowned at him, 'What's happened to Carlton?' I asked. 'I haven't seen him in weeks.'

'He was close,' the DCI interrupted, 'very close, so he said. He was going to nail you and you knew it. You just couldn't help yourself, could you, you fucking low-life.'

'Wait a minute,' I told them both, 'has something happened to Carlton, because it has got nothing to do with me. You lot have your jobs to do and I might not like you for it but I understand and grudgingly respect it. I've never come up against any of you like that. If Carlton has taken a kicking, if he's fallen down the stairs or been hit by a car, gone missing or stubbed his toe on the pavement, I repeat, it has nothing to do with me.'

'Got an alibi, have you?' asked the DCI, as if I was pulling the other one. 'Got your men to do the dirty work? That's how people like you operate isn't it? You're not hard, Blake, you'd be nothing without men like Joe Kinane to back you up.'

'Neither I, nor anyone who works for me in any capacity, has done anything to hurt or harm DI Carlton,' I told him, 'and if you think we have, you are definitely on the wrong track.'

'Leave me alone with him for just five minutes,'

DS Fraser was virtually frothing at the mouth now, 'I'll get him to talk.'

'Oh please,' I told him, 'you're acting like an idiot.' And that's when he went for me, launching himself across the table and swinging a haymaker at me that caught me off balance, even though I saw it coming. I ducked, but he still connected with the top of my head. It wasn't a crashing blow but the intent was there and the two DCs who'd been standing to one side had to drag him off me. They managed to haul him away but I didn't get an apology.

Instead the DCI just said, 'You killed Carlton's daughter, you murdering bastard, and if it was down to me I'd bundle you in a car, take you out into the woods where they found her and beat you to death, because I wouldn't waste the cost of a bullet on you.'

'What? Are you out of your mind? I didn't kill his daughter. I didn't even know he had a daughter. Who the fuck told you that?'

He leaned in close again as he relished giving me the answer. 'He did.'

CHAPTER 9

I listened in shock as they told me. Gemma Carlton, eighteen-year-old daughter of DI Robert Carlton, had been murdered and her body dumped in woodland. They'd kept her name out of the papers for now but there would be a press conference later that day, without Carlton, who was in no fit state to appear before the public. Instead, Gemma's uncle would appeal for witnesses.

Carlton was being treated for shock and grief and whatever they called it nowadays when your mind shuts down, because you've been driven out of it by something so bad you just can't even begin to process it. At some point though, he had been lucid enough to speak to senior officers. They had gently coaxed from him whether there was anyone who held a grudge against him or Gemma, anybody who could have killed the girl because of it. He told them that person could only be me.

Gemma was sweet, she was innocent and kind and could never hurt a fly, she loved her mum, respected her dad, didn't even have a steady boyfriend. The only possible motive for killing

Gemma would be to stop her dad from functioning as a police officer, preventing him from closing that big case; the one he'd been working tirelessly on. He had told everyone he was close to breaking the old Mahoney crew and bringing down their boss, David Blake.

I didn't say much. I just sat there and listened and figured now was probably the right time to ask for my lawyer. They'd got it all so wrong but couldn't see it and there was no way I was going to convince them. I was the devil right now. Carlton was going to put me inside so I killed his daughter to derail him. It was outlandish, it was ludicrous and completely untrue but they weren't in any mood to be convinced.

'If you really believe I am capable of this, if you actually think I ordered it, or could ever persuade any of my men that it was a good idea, then nothing I can say will alter your view, but I did not kill this poor girl. Now I want my lawyer.'

'You can have your lawyer,' said the heavy-set man, who had silently entered the room while I was speaking, 'but first I'd like a word, if I may.'

I had never met Detective Superintendent Alan Austin but I knew of him and he was fully aware of me. I recognised him from TV footage of police press conferences, like the one they were about to have for Carlton's daughter. He turned to the DS who had attacked me, 'I could hear you all the way down the corridor, Fraser,' he told the man calmly, 'go and get yourself a coffee,' then he added pointedly, 'in the canteen.'

DS Fraser grudgingly left the room and Austin picked up a chair and brought it with him.

'Get him his lawyer,' he ordered the DI. 'And give us five minutes,' he added. 'Well, go on,' he said, and all of them slunk reluctantly from the room.

'Perhaps they think you might try to kill me,' said Austin, who rightly assumed he did not have to introduce himself to me, 'or they reckon I'm on your payroll. That's the rumour, you know. That you've bought and paid for half of the CID round here.' I didn't answer. I just let him say his piece. 'Now then, this is a right horrible mess, isn't it?'

'You don't seriously think I would kill a policeman's daughter just to stop him from investigating my company?'

'No, I don't,' he admitted, 'but there are a large number of people here who do because Carlton told them it was you. Some of them are very senior indeed.'

'Jesus Christ!'

'On the record, we are exploring several lines of enquiry.'

'And off the record?'

'It's all about you. The brass have got it into their collective heads that Gemma Carlton was most likely killed because of her father's investigation into an organised crime firm.'

'That is fucking preposterous. Whatever you might think about my company, we are not the Cosa Nostra.'

'I know,' he told me, 'I have explained that I do not think you, or anyone linked to you, is likely to have committed this crime, but that is not a popular view here right now. The word has gone out to investigate Gemma's murder and to find a link with you. You have a motive, all they need is the evidence linking you to Gemma and they *will* find it.'

'Manufacture it, you mean. They have already made up their minds,' his silence confirmed this.

'It's not a question of manufacturing anything,' he informed me, 'you know how this works. There is always plenty of evidence out there, some of it cast-iron, a lot of it circumstantial, but if there is a political will from the CPS to build a case and present it effectively to a jury of laymen . . .'

'Meaning thickos and simpletons they've dragged in off the street.'

'. . . then they will get their conviction. You know that's how it can work.'

'I do,' I conceded, 'so why are you here? What do you expect me to do about it?'

'That's up to you but, if you really want them to stop thinking you had anything to do with Gemma Carlton's death, then I'd say it is fairly obvious what you have to do.'

'Find the real killer?'

He nodded.

'And just how do you expect me to do that?'

'Use the men in your . . . company,' he told me, 'they can go places we can't, talk to people who might not normally be too forthcoming to police officers. They might find it easier to persuade people to be more open, but I'm not going to tell you how to go about it. I'm just asking you to help me find the man who killed a young girl I have known her whole life. We are all hurting very badly right now. I have my own private view of you and your organisation Blake, and you probably wouldn't care to hear it, but I don't believe you are stupid enough or so far beyond redemption that you would arrange to have an innocent girl murdered to throw my colleague off your scent.'

I didn't answer him for a while. Instead I tried to think of ways I could persuade the police I had nothing to do with this girl's death, without actually investigating the case myself, but I couldn't come up with any.

'Alright,' I said, 'give me everything you've got on the poor lass that I don't already know, anything that could help me find the man who did this. My guys will look into it,' he nodded his agreement. 'I'll find the killer and bring him to you.'

'Make sure you do,' he cautioned, 'he's not much use to us dead.'

'He'll be no use to me at all if he's dead. I want him breathing and talking. I need him to explain this had nothing to do with me.'

'One last thing, Blake,' he told me, 'no patsies,

fakes or mentally-ill suspects, no losers coerced into confessing to a murder they didn't commit because you put pressure on them or their families. We'll see straight through that and you'll have blown your last chance of salvation. I kid you not.'

I noted he was fond of biblical terms like salvation and redemption and wondered if that was significant. Was Detective Superintendent Austin a bit of a bible basher? 'Just leave it with me,' I assured him.

CHAPTER 10

By the time they released me, it was getting light. I called Sarah and told her not to worry. 'It's all a bunch of nothing.' I'm not sure she believed me.

I called Sharp and got him out of bed. I arranged a crash meeting with him, then got Palmer to come and pick me up. My head of security drove me quickly out of the city, heading north, glancing into his mirrors now and then to make sure we weren't being followed by any plain clothes plod. When he had convinced me we were alone, I got him to turn the car around and drive south until we reached the Angel of the North. Palmer stayed in the car. Sharp was already waiting for me and he wasn't happy to be there.

'It's a bit bloody public this, isn't it?' he hissed, as he filed in next to me and we began a slow walk towards the two hundred tonnes of rusting steel that constituted the Angel. His eyes were all over the place, as he checked out the bushes for surveillance teams, but we were virtually alone here at this hour. It was a cold, misty morning that would deter any but the most hardy.

'Yeah, you're right,' I said, 'that old bloke with the flat cap walking his dog has got to be with SOCA. Get a fucking grip, Sharp, it was your idea for us to meet here in the first place.'

'That was ages ago. Before I was convinced the bastards were out to get me.'

'The bastards are out to get all of us,' I informed him, 'and this time it's me they're after, not you, so listen up, because this is important.'

We stood a few yards from the Angel, which towered sixty feet above us, and I briefed Sharp on everything the Detective Superintendent had told me about the murder of Gemma Carlton; including the police assumption that I was responsible for her death.

'But that's crazy,' Sharp said, 'you'd never be that daft.'

'Or that evil,' I reminded him, 'you forgot that bit.'

'Aye, well, that too,' he conceded.

'I'll need you on this big style.'

'I'm on it already, and so are forty other detectives, but nobody told me they were linking you to it. Jesus,' he shook his head, 'they know, don't they? They know I'm your man on the inside. That's why they're not telling me anything.'

It was a possibility, but I couldn't allow Sharp to be deflected by self-doubt. 'That's bollocks. They only hauled me in last night and they didn't get any sense out of DI Carlton until recently. You'll be briefed. I've no doubt about that. You'll be expected to come up with the evidence to put me away.' Then I told him about Austin's request for me to investigate the case in parallel with the police operation.

'That's a bit unusual isn't it?'

'Highly unusual, but Austin is worried they only have one line of enquiry and he doesn't believe we did it. He thinks the real murderer is going to walk. He might hate us but he doesn't want the girl's killer to get away with it, does he? I want you to straddle both investigations; ours and yours.'

He didn't say anything to that and I could sense there was something else. 'What is it?' I asked him.

'It might be nowt,' he said, 'but the timing's interesting.'

'What?'

'Henry Baxter was arrested last night.'

'Was he? For what?'

'Careless driving and driving with excess alcohol.'

'He was pissed?'

'Well, he was over the limit.'

'Is this legit?' I was asking Sharp if Baxter really had been drink-driving or if it was some ruse by the police to bring him in and question him about me.

'Seemingly so; I made enquiries and he was pulled over by uniform for driving erratically. It's a bit of a coincidence him being taken in like that and you getting dragged there a few hours later though.'

'Maybe that's all it is. I can't see Henry Baxter disappearing into the witness protection programme because he's been pulled over for drink-driving, can you?'

'No,' he admitted, 'but stranger things have happened. Anyway, he'll be bailed later.'

'I'll keep an eye on him,' I promised. 'Oh, and I nearly forgot. There's something else you can do for me. I need to find a man called Jinky Smith.'

'Who the fuck is he when he's at home?'

'One of the old guard, like you suggested, so ask around. Start earning your money.'

'Yeah, alright,' he mumbled, 'but if I run out of luck I might not get to spend any of it.'

There wasn't much more to be said and we both fell silent as the old guy with the walking stick finally drew level with us. His progress up the hill had been tortuously slow and he looked incredibly weary. I knew how he felt.

With everything that was going on I could have done without the next meeting I'd arranged, but I'd promised Joe Kinane, and I didn't piss that man off lightly. Today we were going to sit down with his eldest lad.

Kinane had three sons, all of them carved out of something like granite, and each one of them named after a famous Newcastle United player; Kevin, Peter and Chris; Keegan, Beardsley and Waddle, though he regretted that when Waddle eventually signed for Sunderland. He even attempted to use

Chris' middle name for a while, but unsurprisingly it didn't stick. He had a daughter too. She was married with kids and had nothing to do with our business.

'What did you call her then?' I asked him once, 'No girl ever played for the Toon.'

He laughed, 'I suggested Jackie, after Jackie Milburn, but wor lass went mental at me,' and he grimaced at the memory. 'We called her Carol in the end.'

Kevin Kinane was an enormous bloke whose fearsome appearance was enhanced by his smashed-in teeth. A while back he had been set upon by some heavily-armed thugs who worked for a dealer of ours who had gone decidedly native. Braddock's men couldn't resist smashing the unarmed Kevin in the mouth with a gun, leaving him with a hole in his teeth and earning him the nickname 'Christmas', as in 'all I want for Christmas is my two front teeth.' He had a couple of false ones fitted but didn't take to them, so he simply discarded them and went around with a gap instead. When Kevin smiled it made him look even more sinister than before.

I had been giving Kevin Kinane more responsibility lately, to see if he could handle it. He had gone from overseeing our distribution of H at the Sunnydale Estate to effectively controlling the entire operation across the city. I could trust him because he was Kinane's eldest son and as close to family as I had working for me.

'Our Kevin wanted a word,' Joe told me as they sat down in my office at the Cauldron. I could see the impatience in Kevin's eye. Already his dad was interfering.

'Let him speak for himself, Joe.' I said, and Kinane sat back in his chair looking edgy, like he was itching to put words into Kevin's mouth for him. Kevin shot his father a glance that clearly meant 'back off and leave me to it'.

'What did you want to see me about?' I asked, though I knew already.

'The future,' he told me, before quickly adding, 'of the firm. If you ask me, H has had its day. There's no profit growth potential there. We've bottomed out and it will never get any bigger. We should be concentrating our efforts in other directions.'

'Such as?'

'More coke, some ketamine, a bit of E, but mostly it's the coke. Blow is where it's at.'

'I agree with you. So what does that tell you?'

'Give up the heroin. It's high risk and the profits aren't big enough to justify the jail sentences that go with it. The estates are beyond saving, so cut the dealers adrift and let them fight it out between them till there's a top dog. You don't need the hassle and we can always wholesale to whoever's left standing.'

I watched Kevin Kinane intently. There was intelligence there. His dad was a powerful force but he didn't have the smarts of his three sons.

81

Maybe they'd actually attended school or perhaps they got it from their mum. More than likely they'd had to live by their wits on the streets for so long they'd developed a natural instinct for this kind of thing.

'You are right Kevin, H is pretty much dead. There's no real future or growth there and we should concentrate less on it. We can scale down, take an arm's length view and put our mind to other areas where we see long-term potential. That's smart thinking.'

'Cheers,' he said.

'But you are only half right,' I told him, 'we need to keep control of the heroin trade in Newcastle and it worries me that you don't understand why.'

'To keep order,' interrupted Joe Kinane, and we both gave him a look this time.

'I'll come back to that,' I told them. 'Firstly, we still get valuable revenue from H and we can't do without it yet. We are not a PLC and we don't have to have growth every year to keep share-holders satisfied. H is still a high-profit, sizeable revenue business in this city. Why give it to someone else when it took us so long to nail it down in the first place?'

'We can still make money out of the wholesale, without getting our hands dirty,' Kevin told me. 'I thought that was what you wanted.'

'I do want that, but I know I can never have it. If we wholesale to whoever is left standing, as you put it, we'll end up with another Braddock running the place, not paying us on time, buying from other firms when it suits him, and his boys will be running riot. Joe is right, we have to keep order on those estates. They might be absolute shit holes but not everyone on them is vermin. We have to stop teenagers from hosing each other every time there's a trivial argument about respect or we'll end up like those estates in Peckham and Hackney. They've got kiddy gangs doing stabbings and drive-bys instead of business. We still have some rules; no crack cocaine, no getting kids high, no pimping girls out to pay for their habits, no unnecessary violence for the sake of it and no mindless killing. This is one of the main reasons the police tolerate us. They don't like us. They will lock us away if they can get the evidence but always, at the back of their minds, they know we keep order and they ask themselves what would emerge in our place if they took us all down tomorrow.'

'I didn't think of that,' he conceded, and I liked that he hadn't tried to pretend he knew it all.

'Then there are more sentimental reasons. I still love this city and I don't want Newcastle turning into the South Central Projects.'

'Fair enough,' he had conceded my point, but I could tell he was deflated. Kevin thought I didn't value his opinion, but only a fool wants to be surrounded by 'yes-men'. Where was the value in that? I needed people who would challenge me about the best way to run the firm, as long as they did what I told them once I'd made up my mind.

83

'You've done a good job for me, Kevin,' I told him, 'you deserve a bigger role in the firm. I want you to take on more responsibility for me.'

'Just name it', he said, and I could see the look of quiet satisfaction on Joe's face. He'd got what he wanted. I didn't mind that at all because Kevin Kinane had potential.

'I will,' I told him, 'we'll talk again soon. There is one thing you can do for me today though; get the lads together at the Mitre tonight,' he nodded, 'and leave us to it for a bit will you. I need a word with Joe.'

CHAPTER 11

The whole firm turned up at the Mitre. We filled the upstairs bar of that old pub and the ancient floorboards creaked under the weight of so many huge blokes. We opened the bar so they could all have a few pints and Vince was in charge of the ancient vinyl jukebox. That used to be Hunter's job. Once, we'd have been treated to a diet of eighties rock, which never let up. Now that he was gone, Vince had assumed the mantle of DJ and his choices were just as archaic, though different to Hunter's. You wouldn't think it to look at Vince, with his suit and tie and permanent presence at our bars and clubs, which churned out endless R&B, that his taste was really indie, bordering on Goth. That evening, while we waited for all of the lads to turn up, we got Echo and the Bunnymen, Teardrop Explodes, The Alarm and Hazel O'Connor. Then he started cranking out the really Suicidal Sid stuff with The Sisters of Mercy and The Mission before The Smiths finally took the biscuit with *There Is A Light That Never Goes Out*.

Finally, when Spear of Destiny's *They'll Never*

Take Me Alive faded away, I gave Vince the nod. Everybody had assembled by now so he turned off the jukebox. I needed to speak before they all got too pissed to listen. I drew the lads in close and held up the black and white, ten-by-eight that Austin had given me so they could all see it.

'This is Gemma Carlton,' I said.

'Nice,' answered Peter Kinane approvingly.

'She was.'

'Oh.' That shut him up.

'Two nights ago she was killed. This poor lass was murdered and her body dumped.'

I told them everything I knew about the manner in which she died, described the location of the body and gave them all the relevant information. Once they'd digested the fact that a pretty, young thing had been senselessly murdered, I dropped the bombshell.

'There's one other thing. Gemma Carlton was the daughter of Detective Inspector Robert Carlton.'

I watched them all for their reaction. They all knew DI Carlton and what he was trying to do to us. I wanted to be sure that none of them had a fucked-up idea of what constituted justice in our world and had taken matters into their own hands. Instead all I saw was a sea of shocked faces.

'I want this picture circulating. I want everyone to see it. You ask around. This isn't about business, so the normal rules do not apply. It doesn't matter what you have heard about her old man or what he has said about me. I don't care that he wants to put all of us away for a long time. His daughter didn't deserve this and neither did he. No one does. You got that?'

There was some unintelligible mumbling at that but they were all in agreement.

'I want you to find the fucking low-life who did this thing. Firstly, I want this done because it's the right thing to do and that ought to be reason enough.' I let them digest that and, when there were no dissenting voices, I continued. 'Right now the Polit are all fired up and they want to crack heads. They are bad enough when someone comes after one of theirs, so you can imagine what they will be like when it's the only daughter of one of theirs. They are short on brains and common sense at the best of times and they are not thinking straight. They have no leads so they've got a very foolish idea into their empty heads. They think that, since Carlton was investigating us, maybe we were somehow responsible for this evil thing.'

My lads are pretty hard to shock, they've seen plenty of stuff between them, but you could tell they were floored by this one. There was a sound like a collective sharp intake of breath. Then all of a sudden it was like I was a politician being heckled from the floor, but it was only the competing cries of, 'No fucking way!', 'Hadaway and shite man!', 'Have they gone fuckin' mental like?' and a half dozen other similar shouts that were lost in the angry din. They were furious and resentful, as I knew they would be, and I ran the risk that this would weaken their determination to find Gemma's killer, but I needed to let them all know exactly what was at stake here.

I had to hold up my hands to restore order, 'I know,' I assured them, 'I know, and I share your anger and disgust, but they are hurting right now and not thinking clearly. So it's our job to find the real killer and hand him over.'

'Fuck that,' said Kinane, 'when we find the cunt, we'll slice him to pieces.'

'No Joe, we won't. You're not thinking either. How is slicing him up going to persuade the police we had nothing to do with it? No, as much as it might disgust us, we hand him over and give them their man. He'll get a life sentence and it will be hard time, the hardest there is. They'll realise we are not the men they think we are, for what that's worth. and it's not much. Like it or not though, until we catch this sick bastard, normal business will be impossible for any of us, so that's another reason we need to clear this up, and fast. That, and the fact that someone has put a poor, young lass in the ground and is still out there somewhere. Let's make sure she's the last one he kills.'

There were murmurs of agreement at that one. 'You work your districts, you ask around and I want someone on this twenty-four-seven who can feed all of it back to me.'

'I'll do it,' replied Kevin Kinane without a second's hesitation, 'like you said, we can't do any normal business till it's sorted and we don't want some sicko out there walking around our city.'

I admired his eagerness to take this on for me and I knew that might be worth something. I figured this would require leg work and tenacity. It needed someone with the energy to keep at it and Kevin Kinane wanted to prove himself to me. This was his chance.

'Good lad Kevin,' I said, 'you meet me daily until this is over. All of you, I want every scrap of information feeding into Kevin. We've some bent law on our books that'll help but they need leads and we are the people to provide them.'

Joe and I left the Mitre and drove back into the city together. 'What do you reckon?' I asked him.

'Not a glimmer.'

'There's nobody?'

'Every one of them was shocked rigid man,' he assured me, 'as I told you they would be.' There was indignation in that last bit.

'Yeah, okay, you were right. I'll give you that, but our boys aren't saints so I needed you to look them in the eye while I spoke to them, but if you are telling me there is no one . . .'

'Listen to yourself man,' he snapped at me, 'this is us. We are not some drug cartel from Bolivia, we have rules, remember? They might not be written down anywhere but we have rules and everybody knows them.'

'Yeah,' I admitted, 'you're right,' and when he

said nothing in reply, I added, 'I'm sorry. I am. I didn't really think any of our crew was capable of . . . but I had to be sure. That's why I asked you, because I trust your judgement. Remember Joe, I have to think the unthinkable sometimes.'

'Yeah,' he answered, 'I s'pose so.' But I could tell he still had the hump with me.

'Let's get a drink Joe,' I suggested, 'after that I need one.'

CHAPTER 12

The next week was one of the longest I've ever experienced. We got more police harassment in seven days than we'd had in the previous three years put together. Some of our guys were lifted off the streets of the Sunnydale estate, on suspicion of dealing, even though we never kept the money or the stash anywhere near the man, so there was no real evidence. It didn't matter. They were held overnight so they couldn't do any business.

Two of our pubs had their licences rescinded on trumped-up accusations of exceeding their licensed hours and providing illegal gambling on-site. Even our sports injury clinic was closed down on suspicion that it may have been providing sexual services in exchange for money; something that everyone in the city already knew and hadn't cared about for years. The massage parlour had been ticking over nicely without offending anyone in authority but now the police were hitting everything they knew about. I could get all of them back up and running soon enough but it was a hassle and I realised that Austin was right. This would only end if I found the real killer.

My meetings with Kevin Kinane took on extra significance and he didn't disappoint me. At first we had to filter a lot of crap about the girl, taking no time at all to dismiss outlandish theories, which ranged from her being a notorious five-hundred-quid-a-night hooker who'd upset an obsessed client, to her dad being her actual killer because he'd been sexually abusing her for years and she was about to tell her mum.

'I reckon it's all bollocks,' Kevin assured me and I was glad he wasn't taken in. 'Sharp says there's nothing to any of it.'

'What kind of person makes this shit up?' I asked when we'd discussed yet another stupid theory. 'Did Sharp speak to the brother?'

'Yeah but he didn't have any ideas. He's devastated apparently and he seems normal, if that's what you're asking?'

'That is what I'm asking,' but I didn't really expect to learn that she'd been topped by her own brother.

'Sharp says he's clean,' he informed me.

'That's good enough.'

It took Kevin a few days to come up with anything we could actually trust. 'Some of the lads on the doors do remember her,' he told me. 'You know how we rotate the boys around our places. More than one said they'd seen her.'

'They recognised her?' This seemed strange, considering she was only a young lass and hardly a veteran of the club scene.

'Yeah, so I checked on our newest places first, the ones the young lasses like. I started with Cachet. They remember her down there.'

I didn't want to hear that. 'Shit, really? We get bloody hundreds in Cachet every weekend. Are they sure about her?'

'I checked. She was a regular, down there most nights, mid-week as well as the weekend.'

I couldn't believe what I was hearing. This meant that Gemma Carlton really did have a link to me, however tenuous, and the police would soon pick up on it, if they hadn't done so already. 'How the bloody hell could a student afford to pay her way into Cachet every night?'

'That's just it,' he seemed reluctant to give me the bad news, 'she didn't. They used to wave her through into the VIP lounge. She had one of our passes with her name on it.'

'Fuck. Who gave her that then?' This was getting worse.

'I checked the register and her name was on our records as a platinum card holder but it doesn't say who signed it out to her. We've been slack at that,' he admitted, 'I've given them a bollocking.'

'Jesus, did Danny not know her?'

He shook his head.

'Find out who's responsible for this. Somebody

must know someone who knows something. Keep at it.'

'Will do boss.'

I drove home from one difficult conversation and straight into another. I was late, I was tired, worried and preoccupied and the last thing I needed was Sarah in the mood to talk.

'I'd like to speak to you,' she said, as soon as I walked through the door and she looked serious.

'Can I get a drink first?' She nodded and I poured my drink while she waited for me to sit down with it. 'What is it?'

'I've been thinking,' she informed me, 'a lot.'

'About what?'

'My dad.'

'Oh, I see.'

'And I think I'm ready to hear it. I think I need to hear it, in fact.'

'Hear what?' I genuinely had no idea what she was going on about.

'What happened to him?'

'Eh? What do you mean?' This was the conversation I had always dreaded. 'You know what happened to him.'

'I don't, not really. I only know what you told me.'

'Which was?' I knew what I'd told her but I was stalling.

'That he was gone,' she reminded me, 'that he was never coming back.'

'What else is there?' I asked dumbly.

'I know it was hard for you,' she admitted, 'you were there. I know how difficult that must have been.'

'I don't think you do,' I snapped and realised I was taking stressed gulps of my drink. It was half-gone already.

'But it has been hard for me too,' she continued, 'I never got to see him, to say goodbye. I spend so much time thinking about him and sometimes I feel like he isn't really dead and . . .'

'He's dead Sarah,' I assured her, 'believe me. Your father is dead and he isn't coming back. You don't need to know anything more than that.'

'What happened Davey?' she asked me. 'You say I don't need to know, but I do.'

'You do know. Alan Gladwell happened. He bundled your dad and Finney into a car and he took them away.' I held up my hands so she knew that was all there was to it. Just talking about this was enough to make me feel sick. I hated lying to Sarah, but what choice did I have? I couldn't tell her the truth.

'I want to hear it all,' she said.

'No, Sarah, you don't, trust me on that.'

'I didn't know why I'd been feeling the way I was but then I saw a documentary about families who had lost loved ones in Afghanistan and Iraq and how they needed to hear the details from the friends of the dead soldiers or their commanding officers. They couldn't move on until they had the image of what actually happened in their heads. They wanted closure.'

I suppose I should have made something up real quick, but I just couldn't do it. God knows I'd had enough time to prepare myself for her questions but I had always hoped they might never come.

'Closure?' I asked her lamely. 'That's just some psycho-babble American bullshit.'

She flared at that. 'No David, it's not. I need you to tell me what happened to my father. That's not bullshit. It's real.'

'Yeah, well, it's a bit too fucking real.' I went to take another sip of my drink and realised it was empty. 'I was there, remember?'

I got to my feet and she watched me with a hurt look on her face. I needed to get out of there. I needed to leave that room and it had to be now, but I didn't have a good reason so I had to make one. I decided to look shocked and upset, which wasn't hard because that was exactly how I was feeling inside.

'I can't believe you just sprang it on me like this with no warning,' I rounded on her, 'like you just expect me to relive the whole thing because you are suddenly ready. Well I'm not.'

She got to her feet too but I was already out of there. 'Where are you going?' she called after me.

'Out!' I managed and if she did reply I didn't hear the words because I was too busy slamming the door behind me, glad to be outside in the cold and breathing in great gulps of air as I headed for my car.

I didn't go home that night. I stayed in our hotel on the Quayside. I didn't really sleep though. I spent most of the night lying awake, wondering why Sarah suddenly wanted to know all the details of her father's death. Occasionally I heard raised voices from the street down below, as clubbers stumbled out on to the streets looking for taxis and couples had half-hearted drunken arguments they'd have forgotten about in the morning. I envied them that. I knew I should have spun Sarah some yarn about Bobby dying bravely in a hail of bullets, or collapsing of a heart attack after a beating, but I just couldn't bring myself to do it. Did I believe Bobby Mahoney would somehow be looking down on me from wherever he was, judging me while I lied to his only daughter? No, but it just didn't feel right.

The next morning I went straight to the Cauldron. I didn't call Sarah because I didn't know what the hell to say to her.

CHAPTER 13

The Cauldron wasn't open to the public but the lads were lounging about in the bar. Soon they would have things to do and debts to call in. This was the calm before the daily storm.

Peter Kinane is a nice enough bloke, for a thug, and he's bright too, despite inheriting the brawn of his dad, but sometimes I think he's too sensitive to operate in our world. Peter had just been dumped by some lass he'd been shagging for a while and he was gutted. He'd been stupid enough to admit it too and the lads began to taunt him mercilessly. He hadn't yet learned the golden rule about our world. You've got to be able to take it, no matter what they say to you.

'I'm telling you man, she was a munter,' Kevin Kinane announced when the subject of his brother's ex came up in conversation again.

'No she wasn't,' Peter protested weakly from a seat in the corner of the bar. Joe Kinane was watching it all with detached amusement, his other son Chris, the quiet one, sitting next to him.

Palmer, Vince and some of our more established faces were all enjoying the sledging.

'She had a canny pair of tits on her,' conceded Kevin, ignoring his younger brother. 'If you could have transplanted them onto a skinny bird, Keira Knightley maybe, then they would have looked good, but on her, well, they were a waste of a nice pair of puppies, if you ask me.'

'Oi!' warned Peter, 'I am *in* the room!'

'BOBFOC,' said Palmer quietly.

Peter rounded on him and demanded, 'What's that supposed to fuckin' mean?'

Palmer shrugged, 'body off *Baywatch*, face off *Crimewatch*.' He then repeated the word, 'BOBFOC', to ensure Peter took in his meaning. Peter Kinane looked like he was about to start throwing punches.

His elder brother Kevin was gleeful. 'He's been upstairs in his room for weeks now, wank-stalking his ex on Facebook.'

'No I fucking haven't!' replied Peter Kinane, seriously flustered now.

'I caught you looking at her pictures on your laptop the other day, admit it man.'

'So what,' said Peter, 'I was only bloody looking. It's not a crime is it?'

'No Peter, to be fair it's not,' I assured him because I was thankful for the distraction of this banter and when his face brightened a little I added, 'it's just a bit pathetic.'

'Hey, howay man, don't you start an' all,' he told me.

'How long's it been Peter? Since the break up?' asked Palmer rhetorically, 'three weeks? Oh well, never mind eh, because three weeks is the critical point.'

'How's that like?' asked Peter, as Palmer reeled him in.

'Well, if she really wasn't shagging someone else behind your back when she dumped you . . .'

'She wasn't,' Peter assured him.

'She will be by now.'

'Fuck off! Will she shite. She's not like that.'

'Yes she is Pete,' said Vince, playing along with it.

'They all are,' announced Palmer solemnly, playing the wind-up to perfection, 'you might think your lass is made of sugar and spice and all things nice but right now, even as I speak and you're fretting about her, some big, hairy-bollocked bloke is up to his nuts in her.'

Peter launched himself at Palmer then, knocking the table between them to the ground, upending our beers in the process. We were creased up and we carried on laughing as an enraged Peter Kinane chased Palmer round the room, throwing haymaker punches that my bodyguard would have dodged easily if he hadn't been laughing so hard himself.

In the end Peter managed to connect with one and Palmer was knocked off his feet. I'd never seen that before. Peter moved in to give Palmer a proper kicking and we all jumped in to restrain him, but Palmer was back on his feet already and he hit Peter Kinane with a supreme upper cut that rocked the younger man back on his heels and followed it with a martial-arts-style kick to the belly.

They both had venomous looks in their eyes now, so I shouted, 'Pack it in, you two fairies!' as the rest of the lads grabbed them and pulled them apart.

Palmer swore at Peter Kinane and I shouted at him, 'shut the fuck up Palmer! You deserved that smack in the mouth, so take it like a man!' and he gave me a sheepish look that seemed to acknowledge I might be right. Then I turned to the younger man, who was red in the face and panting, like he didn't know how to even begin to quell his rage.

'Calm down Peter,' I told Kinane junior, 'it's just banter. Learn to dish it out and take it, if you want to stay up late with the grown-ups.'

'Aye, aye, alright,' he said, brushing away the arms that were restraining him. He took a moment to calm himself, 'but he knows he was out of order. If he had said that about your lass, *you'd* have bloody punched him.'

Everybody went quiet then and Peter Kinane instantly realised he was out of order for daring to equate a lass he had been shagging for three months to my long-term partner, the daughter of the legendary Bobby Mahoney. I could see in his face he immediately recognised that fact and was worried.

'No I wouldn't,' I assured him solemnly, 'I'd just have him killed.' And everybody fell about again.

My mobile rang then and someone said 'saved by the bell'. The tension broke and everyone started to get their crap together and move away. I took the call.

'I found him,' said Sharp, 'the man you've been looking for.'

CHAPTER 14

'**B**enwell's not the smartest part of Newcastle,' admitted Kinane, with something like under-statement, as he drove the car along one of its side streets with boarded-up shop fronts, 'but it's not as bad as they say.'

'Bits of it I wouldn't walk around on my own,' I said, and he grunted a begrudging agreement to that, 'loads of druggies and alkies who'd rob you and give you a serious kicking for the spite of it, there's dog shit everywhere, the lasses are all pregnant by the time they're thirteen and none of them ever know who the father is,' he grunted at that too, 'and then . . . there's the rough part.'

'Fuck off,' but he was laughing when he said that.

'And unfortunately for Jinky, that's the bit he lives in.'

I remembered Jinky from the very early years of my involvement with Bobby's crew, when I was just a nipper, long before I officially joined the firm. I was little more than an errand boy. I was handy for certain low-risk, low-consequence jobs and didn't cost much. They were a source of pocket money and made me feel like I belonged somewhere when my ma was usually working at two, or even three, jobs at a time, some of them in Bobby Mahoney's pubs, and my older brother didn't want to look after me.

Unsupervised, I took to hanging round anywhere I reckoned I could make myself useful to Bobby or his main men. Some of them, as you might expect, were horrible to me. The last thing they wanted was a runty kid cramping their style. Others tolerated my presence and some were pretty decent. I knew that if I kept my mouth shut and did what was asked of me, I'd occasionally get some extra grub or some cash. Nobody in Bobby's crew was ever broke. They were always flush with money and they liked to spend it, or even give it away, to show how minted they were. Some weeks I'd take home almost as much as my mum. I'd give most of it to her and when she asked how I'd got it I'd say, 'running errands for Bobby' and she'd snap, 'make sure that's all you're doing'. But she never stopped me from going there and I think I knew why. My mother was honest all of her bloody life and look where it got her. She never had jack shit. The husband ran off and left her in the lurch, with two boys to bring up on her own and Our young'un was a bloody tearaway. He was uncontrollable at that age and she'd already credited me with having more sense than him, even then. I think, in the end, she didn't have the energy left to argue with me about hanging around with Bobby Mahoney's crew. Maybe she just thought I'd be safer if I was with them than on the streets on my own or as part of a gang. The older kids didn't bother to pick a fight with me because they knew I was in with Bobby. He never tolerated drugs either, which was something my mother and he could agree upon.

'Jinky' Smith's real name was Jimmy Smith and he shared the same name as a legendary footballer from the seventies. The real Jimmy Smith was a flair player with bags of style on the pitch who was called 'Jinky' off it. That sense of style seemed to sum our Jimmy Smith up, so he got landed with the same nickname and it stuck, long after the player had left St James' Park.

Jinky was what members of our crew would nowadays call a 'fanny rat'. He was a ladies man, who could charm the birds off the trees, though I remember my mother being less than impressed by him. 'He's all wind and piss,' she said once and I was sufficiently shocked by her extremely infrequent use of a swear word to recall the cause of her scorn. 'He thinks he's God's gift to women, does Jinky Smith. Well, if he is, I hope they remember to keep the receipt so they can take him back to the store.' And I realised that whatever charms Jinky had in the eyes of other women, she could see right through him. He drove her home from the club a few times, after she finished her shifts behind the bar, but I suspect that was on Bobby's orders and she never once let him in the house.

Then one day Jinky was arrested, charged and sent down for being part of an armed robbery Bobby had organised. He kept his gob shut and ended up doing nine years. When he came out it was obvious he was a changed man, by which I mean he had lost his nerve, along with his good looks, and it was clear he had no part to play in the firm any more. This was in the late eighties. His era was over before mine had even properly begun. Bobby paid him off. Knowing Bobby it would have been a generous settlement for his loyalty, knowing Jinky it wouldn't have been enough. The proof of that was here in front of me now; the ground floor flat I wouldn't have housed an Alsatian in.

Kinane waited outside. He made himself visible and stood by the car so nobody had any foolish notions about damaging his precious Lexus. He was one of the few people in the city who could stand calmly next to a posh car in Benwell without either the tyres or the owner being slashed. A gang of teenagers watched him from across the road, but they didn't make a move and he wasn't the slightest bit bothered by their presence.

I hadn't seen Jinky in a long while and I knew he would have changed a hell of a lot, but even I was surprised to see the state he was in. The man who answered the door took a long time to reach it. I could hear him shuffling about inside the tiny one-bedroom, ground-floor flat, then he called out 'just a minute' in a weak and raspy voice. The effort required for that set him off on an exhausting, phlegmy coughing fit. He was still hacking it up when he pulled the chain back on the door and opened it to squint out at me. While he frowned, probably wondering if I was a council official, a policeman or a debt collector, I took in the stooped and prematurely aged former jack-the-lad. The famously luxuriant hair was long and straggly, the face lined and haggard and the eyes grey and watery. For a man still in his sixties, he didn't look great.

'Fuck me senseless,' he finally muttered, 'it's only Davey Blake,' and then he laughed like he couldn't quite believe it. 'Come in, man.'

I stepped inside. There was a smell of burnt onions and sour milk coming from a tiny galley kitchen, which was separated from the living room by a sliding door. There was a sofa, but it was covered in black bin bags, which I hoped were full of old clothes, rather than rubbish.

'Would you like a drink?' he asked me. 'I must have something in here,' and he headed for the kitchen.

'No need,' I told him and I took the whisky bottle out of the bag I was carrying.

'Eeh, you're a grand lad,' he said and he shuffled off to get us a couple of glasses. They were just about clean enough, so I poured us both a generous measure. I chose a rickety wooden dining-chair and it wobbled on loose legs when I sat on it. He settled into his one grubby, green arm chair.

'I'd have cleaned up a bit if I'd known you were coming like,' he assured me, 'but it's the maid's day off and the butler must be shagging the cook 'cos I haven't seen either of them all day.' Then he laughed at his own joke and I smiled gamely.

'It's nae bother Jinky,' I told him, 'how are you keeping?'

'I'm grand,' he said, despite the evidence of my own eyes. 'Newcastle manager's been on the blower, wants me to play centre forward on Saturday. I've said I'll think about it.'

This was the Jinky I remembered, always joking, always taking the piss, usually out of himself, 'I don't go near the ground these days mind, on principle,' he was absolutely serious about that, 'it used to be a cathedral but that fat man's turned it into a whore house. You should send that Joe Kinane round to have a word.'

'He offered to do it.'

'Aye, well, he should then,' he conceded, 'but I know you wouldn't want anyone's name in the papers.'

'We were always too professional for that Jinky. Leave the headlines for the hard men who like to fight and feud with each other, while we hold the real power. That was always our way.'

'That's what I always liked about working for Bobby. We were a classy bunch,' and when I gave him a look, he chuckled, 'well, for villains,' then he was serious for a moment. 'I was sorry to hear about your ma,' he told me solemnly, 'truly sorry,' and he looked like he meant it, 'she was a touch of class that one, a cut above every other woman who worked in any of Bobby's places and none of us ever forgot it,' and he chuckled to himself. 'None of us dared swear in front of her. She was a proper lady and we'd mind our manners when she was around, even Bobby . . . especially Bobby.'

'Thanks Jinky,'

'So,' he said, 'what can I do for you?'

I took my time and explained why I was there. Jinky listened intently and screwed up his face like he was trying hard to recall long-forgotten events. When I finished, he said, 'Well he was always there, your dad, hanging around, and then one day he wasn't. It wasn't so unusual back then, for people just to go off and do something new, even if they did have a wife and bairns. There's always easier money to be made some place else,' he chuckled, 'you've seen *Auf Wiedersehen Pet*. This has always been a place people left to go and do other things. I love it here,' he assured me, 'couldn't live anywhere else me, but it isn't exactly the land of opportunity. Geordies are like the Irish, we're scattered all over the world. Your dad probably opened a bar in Marbella or somewhere and just never came back.'

'He did do that,' I said, 'not the bar in Marbella. I'm talking about the leaving for work. My ma told me all about it. He'd been working away for years, but then she went to see him to talk about their future together. He was in London and they were going to work it all out between them. We were going to live down there, but it never happened. He wrote to her for a while and phoned her. One day the letters and the calls stopped. I wasn't that old when she told me he probably wasn't coming back. I don't even remember him.'

'Aye, well,' he said, looking a bit uncomfortable at what probably sounded to him like a sob story. 'Look on the bright side,' he added, 'if you'd have gone down there all them years ago you'd probably be a Chelsea fan by now.'

'Aye,' I said, 'and think of all the glory I'd have missed out on.' I didn't want to stay too much longer in Jinky's flat. It was a depressing place to call a home and I wondered why he'd allowed himself to end up like this. 'What about you Jinky? Didn't fancy the married life?'

'No, not me. It's a mug's game. Women are more cunning than any man and I ought to know,' and he chuckled to himself, 'if it wasn't for other men's wives, I'd still be a virgin.'

'They're not all like that Jinky.'

'Tell any woman what she wants to hear and she'll climb into bed with you, whether she's single, courting or married,' he told me earnestly, 'and by the time she's climbed out again she'll have convinced herself it was all her fella's fault, so she won't even feel guilty about it.'

'I thought I was a horrible old cynic Jinky, but you take the proverbial Garibaldi.'

'I'm telling you man. There's only two kinds of blokes in this world; the ones who do the shagging and the poor mugs who know nowt about what's going on behind their backs. Make sure you take wor lass out before some other man does . . . er . . . no offence like.'

'None taken,' I told him, 'just don't go round my house while I'm out or my lads will have to have a word.'

He started laughing heartily at that and the laugh became a spectacular coughing fit. I realised that poor old Jinky had become the victim of his own success. He'd been so adept at charming neglected lasses into his bed that he was left with an inbuilt distrust of all women. But look where that had got him, a loveless existence, in a squalid little flat. There was a certain cruel irony in that.

'Do you want us to ask around, quiet like, to see if anyone knows anything about your dad? I see a lot of the old guys in the club.'

'Cheers Jinky, I'd appreciate that. I figure someone might know what happened to him. Tell them there's a few quid in it for them if they have information I can use,' and I reached inside my wallet and took out a ton. He made a half-hearted attempt to wave it away. 'You'll need to buy a few pints if you're asking around on my behalf,' I said and I left the hundred quid on the little table next to his half-filled whisky glass.

Then I wrote my mobile number on the top of his *Racing Post*.

'It's been canny craic,' I told him, as I picked up the bottle and poured him a larger measure.

'Thanks bonny lad,' he said as I left him with the bottle and his memories.

CHAPTER 15

Long gone were the days when we recorded CCTV on grainy videos to be wiped and recorded over, until all you could see was a snowstorm of white flecks on the screen. These days Robbie had it all linked in to a digital network. At the offices of our watchers, in a former call-centre, he and his team could summon up footage from any one of dozens of cameras that covered our sites, twenty-four-seven, all over the city.

'Robbie, I need you to take a look at the CCTV footage for Cachet, inside and outside the building,' I ordered, as I handed him the ten-by-eight of Gemma Carlton.

Robbie was a slight young man with an old-fashioned, straight haircut that looked like his mother had combed it for him that morning. 'What am I looking for?'

'Any sign of the girl. I've been told she used to go there. I want it confirmed. Find out who arrived with her and, more importantly, who she left with.'

'What timescale are we looking at here?'

'I don't know. Start with the past month.'

'A month? That's a lot of footage. Any idea what nights she went out? Just weekends?'

'No, she was a student, so it could be week nights.'

'Shit.'

'What's the problem?'

'That's a lot of footage. Say four hours a night, six nights a week for a month. That's a hundred hours of tape on one camera alone and we've got a dozen, looking for a single girl among a shed-load.' He picked up the ten-by-eight, 'and she looks like a hundred other girls we get in there every night. Do we know what she was wearing when she went to Cachet? That might help narrow it down, a bit.'

'No,' I told him, 'but we think she was a regular and we've seen her name on the guest list for the VIP lounge, so concentrate on two cameras for now. Get your lads to look out for her in the queue at the main door. You take the one that faces the lift to the VIP area. You can go through it at twice the normal speed and just pause it . . .'

'Every time I see a fit, young brunette stepping into the VIP lounge?' he said dryly. 'That won't take long.'

I was starting to get pissed off with Robbie's attitude. I paid him very good money that nobody else would have given him, not after his prison sentence. We'd rescued Robbie through the Second Chances centre and handed him the opportunity to make more than an honest day's pay for some

114

dishonest work that did not involve getting his hands dirty. He was a computer whiz kid, an IT geek who could summon up a live feed from any CCTV camera in Newcastle because he had hacked into the city's main frame, but I needed to remind him who paid his wages.

'Have I given you anything else to do, Robbie?'

'What?'

'Is there somewhere else you would rather be right now?'

'No,' he protested, 'it's just . . .'

'What job do I employ you to do?' I interrupted and he froze. He could tell I was pissed off with him.

'IT sp . . . sp . . . specialist,' he stammered. Robbie had a stutter, but it only showed when he was nervous.

'No Robbie, not the one on your business card,' I told him, 'your real job.'

His voice was a squeak, 'I'm a watcher,' he managed, 'for the f . . . f . . . firm.'

'So get on with it,' I ordered, 'and stop moaning.'

'I'm not moaning,' he protested, 'I'm just saying . . .'

'And of course, the quicker you start . . .' I prompted, 'or do I have to ask Kinane to come up here and keep an eye on you to make sure you're not slacking?'

'No, no, I'm on it,' he assured me, simultaneously tapping away at his keyboard so he could summon up the necessary footage, but then he remembered the other part of my instruction and he called, 'Mark! Get over h . . . h . . . here . . . now. I need you to plug into the footage for camera s . . . s . . . seven on the main door of Cachet. We're looking for a g . . . g . . . girl.'

Mark ambled over and said, 'A girl? In Cachet? That doesn't narrow it down.' He'd obviously not heard a word of the conversation I'd had with Robbie, who quickly interrupted him.

'Sit down, log on and shut up,' and he slid Gemma Carlton's photograph over to the desk he wanted Mark to occupy, before adding, 'just g . . . g . . . get on with it. It's important.'

Mark looked a bit startled, but when he saw the look on my face he did exactly what he was told.

'Call me when you find something.' I ordered and I left them both tapping away furiously on their keyboards.

'How's Biggus Dickus?' asked Palmer, when I joined him outside. That was his affectionate name for Robbie after the friend of the Roman with the stammer in *Life of Brian*.

'He's not moaning,' I told him, 'he's just saying.'

'Oh,' he said, 'I assume you put him straight.'

'You protected him while he was on the inside, he'd never get another job anywhere else and we reward him handsomely for his expertise, so this is payback time. I expect him to come up with something. Otherwise what is the point of having him?'

Kinane was up before the magistrates that morning and he was still baffled by it. 'I don't understand,' he told me in the corridor outside the courtroom, 'I thought you'd just fix this.'

'I tried,' I told him, with what I hoped sounded like exasperation at the judicial process, 'but it's not as simple as that. There were too many witnesses for this to just go away. You did torture the bloke in broad daylight on the hard shoulder of a busy main road. The police have a queue of people who ID'd you and none of them reckon it looked the least bit like self-defence.'

He looked chastened at that, 'Yeah, I know but . . .'

'There isn't a but,' and I sighed, 'you're going to have to plead guilty. You won't be doing any prison time, that's all been worked out, but it's the best deal I could get you under the circum-stances and, if you moan at me about it, I'll withdraw my help and you can take your chances on your own.'

'All right, okay,' he held up his huge hands, 'I'll plead guilty.'

The public gallery was surprisingly busy that morning. I put in an appearance even though I don't normally go anywhere near a court when one of my lads is up on a charge but I wanted to see this. Palmer was with me, plus Vince and a couple of the other members of the crew, including Chris, Peter and Kevin.

The bloke I'd hired was one of Susan Fitch's colleagues and he did a good job. 'Joseph Kinane is a hard-working, family man with no previous convictions,' he told the Magistrates confidently, because the record of Kinane's short jail sentence in the seventies had mysteriously failed to reach the Magistrates, thanks to the help we'd enlisted from the Court Clerk. Magistrates are all amateurs so you don't really have to buy them. They rely on the Court Clerk for all of their legal advice, including sentencing guidelines, so if you can get at the clerk you're half way there and we knew a couple who were malleable.

'He was unreasonably provoked, then attacked by two young men with a string of convictions between them,' added the solicitor, 'both of whom, I should add, were driving without the usual impediments of road tax, insurance or even a licence between them.'

That got a frown from the bench. 'There has also been some considerable doubt cast as to who exactly grappled with the young man who then fell and sustained a broken jaw. Witnesses have described another man who left the scene suddenly without waiting for the police to arrive.'

I didn't mind him saying that because no one really got a good look at me, and Kinane had already sworn blind he was the only one in the car that day. 'I was on my way to visit my elderly mother,' he had explained, 'who has been quite poorly lately.'

'The final factor I wish you to take into account,' the lawyer instructed the bench, 'is the failure of either of the young men who claimed to be victims of the alleged assault to take the trouble to attend today's proceedings.'

'Someone must have had a word,' Palmer whispered to me.

Kinane pleaded guilty to the less serious charges and the Magistrates accepted this, which meant he didn't have to go to Crown Court. He waited for his fine to be handed down but I knew that would never teach him a lesson, so I'd arranged a more suitable punishment.

Kinane looked almost bored as the lady magistrate, a dead ringer for Margaret Thatcher, lectured him on the importance of personal responsibility in a civilised society. Magistrates are like politicians, you have to distrust the motives of anyone who actually wants the job and I could tell she was enjoying every minute of this. I don't think he heard a word of it until she reached the bit about the sentence. At this point he straightened, so he could hear how much he had to pay.

The Thatcher clone told him, 'We have decided not to hand down a custodial sentence Mr Kinane . . .'

'Right,' he said, 'thanks.'

'. . . conditional upon your agreeing to attend a minimum of ten sessions of anger-management counselling.'

Kinane quickly interrupted, 'Do you not want a fine like?' he asked her, 'I've got money. I'm not a doley, I can pay yer knaa.'

'No,' she told him witheringly, 'we do not want a fine Mr Kinane. We want you to seek professional help in order for you to be better able to control your temper.'

'Mr Kinane accepts this gracious offer,' the lawyer quickly responded on his behalf before Kinane lost that famous temper once again. At that point he looked over at us and realised we were all desperately trying to keep control. Palmer was doubled up and laughing silently, his body shaking with mirth. Vince had a grin on him like a Cheshire cat and I just about managed to stifle a smirk, but he knew he'd been had and he scowled at us all.

'That will fucking teach you,' I told him, as I handed him his pint in Rosie's bar afterwards, 'not that ten hours of anger management is ever going to cure you of being a cunt.'

'Bastard,' he muttered, as he took the pint, 'you're all bastards, in point of fact'.

I had known that the worst punishment that could have been handed down to Joe Kinane, aside from prison, was one in which he was forced to sit in a group, while admitting out loud that he had anger issues and it all stemmed back to his childhood because his mummy never cuddled him. This would be a form of living hell to a man like Kinane, who had bottled up every negative emotion he'd had in his life and thought the only proper way to handle a problem was to 'fucking deal with it'.

The wind-ups and piss-takes would have gone on a lot longer if Palmer hadn't walked back in at that point after taking a call outside in the street. He looked at me and shook his head, which could only mean one thing; more bad news.

We stood outside Rosie's bar, which sits in the shadow of St James' Park, the huge, white foot-balling cathedral right in the middle of our city.

'What is it?' I asked him.

'It's Baxter,' he told us, 'he's been arrested.'

'Again?' I couldn't believe it. 'What's he done now?'

'Fuck me,' snorted Kinane, 'doesn't put a foot wrong in years and now he's picked up twice in seven days. The man's a one-man crime-wave. What are they gonna charge him with now? Littering with intent?'

'Murder,' said Palmer.

Sharp had learned his lesson from our last meeting. This time, when I called him, he didn't grumble. He met me in the small apartment block we keep in the city, to accommodate guests of the firm and for crash meetings like this one.

'Tell me about Henry Baxter,' I said, 'that's my prime concern right now.'

It was pretty amazing to think that being wrongly accused of the murder of a detective's daughter could actually be priority number two, but I was having a very bad week.

'When Baxter was arrested for drink-driving they did all of the usual stuff for someone as far over the drink-drive limit as he was,' Sharp explained to us. 'They breathalysed him, finger-printed him, then took a buccal swab from his mouth before they let him back on the streets. It was purely routine, and so was the cross-checking of the DNA sample. We do it for everyone because it works. We had one guy who was picked up after a brawl in a pub car park. It turned out he'd done an armed robbery fourteen years back and left his DNA at the scene when he'd given the building society manager a smack in the mouth to make him behave. He must have cut his hand on the bloke's broken teeth because a tiny smattering of his blood ended up on the counter top. We matched the samples and now he's doing sixteen years for it.'

I could see Kinane looking uncomfortable. I knew he'd be recalling all of the armed robberies and punishment beatings he'd been involved in over the years. There were probably microscopic traces of Joe Kinane's DNA all over this city.

'That's fascinating Sharp, but what has that got to do with Baxter and a murder?'

'Sorry,' he said, 'but it's the same thing. When Baxter's DNA was taken it was matched by the computer to a cold case. They reckon he's the perp. He must have done it. The odds against it are millions to one.'

'Baxter? A murderer? I seriously doubt that,' I told Sharp.

Kinane chipped in then, 'Who'd he kill? A tax inspector?'

'No,' answered Sharp, 'a little girl.'

CHAPTER 16

To my complete disbelief, Henry Baxter was placed on remand in Durham nick, to await trial for the murder of a thirteen-year-old girl named Leanne Bell. He soon got word to us.

'I am not going anywhere near Durham nick,' I told Palmer. I was about to meet the owners of that York hotel I wanted to buy. The heat might have been on us since the death of Gemma Carlton, but we still had to keep the business going. They were due at our Quayside restaurant and I didn't need the prospect of a cosy prison visit at the back of my mind. 'I have to put as much distance between me and that child-murdering prick as possible, particularly now. Surely you understand that?'

'Course I do, obviously.' Palmer looked like he was about to continue but Kinane cut him off.

'If it was down to me, we'd have him shanked in the showers,' my enforcer told me, 'and not like Toddy. I'd get someone to fillet him, so he died slow. I'd want him screaming in agony when he finally went. He deserves it for what he did to that girl.'

'Careful Joe,' Palmer chipped in, 'we don't know for sure that he's guilty.'

Kinane gave Palmer a vengeful look.

'We really don't,' my head of security reminded him, 'all we know is he was picked up for drink-driving, they took a DNA swab and let him go, we hear nothing for days and the next thing we know he's lifted off the street on a ten-year-old murder charge and banged up in Durham.'

'Sounds pretty straightforward to me,' grunted Kinane.

'So you are one hundred per cent certain this isn't some crafty SOCA plot to get Baxter to come over all supergrass, are you? Because I'm not.'

Kinane snorted like he thought that was ludicrous, but he didn't say anything more. Palmer continued, 'He knows stuff, Joe. Baxter knows damaging things about us, so the last thing we should do is cut him adrift. What else has he got to bargain with?'

'Palmer's right,' I admitted reluctantly. Kinane turned to face me then, with anger in his eyes. 'He is,' I assured him, 'we can hate Baxter all we like but we shouldn't cut him loose completely. Not yet. We need him to keep thinking we are on his side while we quietly dismantle everything he set up, so nothing can be traced back to us. Then, once we have done that, we'll drop him like a hot rock and he can rot in prison for the rest of his miserable life.'

'I'll drink to that,' Kinane nodded, finally getting my point.

'So you'll go and see him?' asked Palmer.

'No I won't, not personally' I told him, 'I thought I'd spelled that out.'

Palmer nodded, 'You did, but he's having none of it, and he knows where all the bodies are buried. You just admitted as much yourself.'

'So I have no bloody choice?'

'That's about the size of it,' he confirmed.

Durham jail is a Category B closed prison, which means the inmates are not the highest risk, but escape is meant to be made very difficult for them. Men like Henry Baxter, who are on remand awaiting trial, are usually held as Category B prisoners. Durham is no cake-walk though. A decade ago its seven wings had the highest suicide rate of any prison in the country, and there are more than nine-hundred inmates housed within its walls.

We drove up to the huge nineteenth-century building with trepidation. Not because I was scared of the place. It was our link with a probable child killer that was alarming me. It was all I needed right now with the murder of Gemma Carlton hanging over us.

'You'd better wait here,' I told Palmer, as I surveyed this forbidding building. 'If I know

126

Baxter he'll be jumpy enough as it is without seeing you.'

Baxter was scared; terrified in fact. I could see it in his podgy, sweaty face and piggy eyes, as he walked into the stifling room, uncombed hair sticking up in a Tintin quiff.

'There's no one else here,' I assured him, 'except him.' Baxter glanced over at the tame prison guard who stayed a discreet distance from the table I had chosen. We were in the visitors' area, but visiting hours were long over. I didn't want my conversation with Baxter to be public.

We used Amrein to get me some private time with Baxter. Prison officers are pretty easy to buy. They earn fuck all, so they are particularly susceptible to a little extra bunce for a seemingly innocent bending of the rules. That's how you start them out, by giving them a few hundred quid to turn a blind eye to some weed or a mobile phone being brought in. What they usually don't realise is that, once they are on the pay roll, it's impossible to come off it. If they've broken a rule, they are ours. When they try to duck the next favour we need, we remind them they've already broken the law by accepting our money and how easy it might be for someone to find that out.

Baxter sat down opposite me. I glanced at our tame warder and he backed away, ambling over to stand in a corner. Now we could talk freely. Baxter looked as if he expected me to start things off; ask about his well-being perhaps, make sure he was getting three squares a day and his copy of the *Telegraph* delivered each morning. I wasn't about to do that.

'You start,' I told him, then I stayed silent, while he gathered his thoughts.

'You've got to get me out of here,' he told me, then he waited for my response.

I couldn't help but laugh at that one. 'Sure I will Baxter,' and I nodded at the screw. 'I'll get him to have a word with the governor and he'll let you out. You'll be back in Newcastle in time for afternoon tea at the Copthorne.'

'Stop pissing about,' Baxter hissed, 'this isn't funny. You don't know what it's like in here. You don't know the way I'm being treated. Like an animal.'

'Oh sorry, I didn't realise. That was insensitive of me.' He looked a bit baffled by that answer. 'Though maybe, just maybe, you should have thought of that before you raped and strangled a thirteen-year-old girl. I had you pegged as a lot of things, Baxter, but a nonce wasn't one of them.'

He opened his mouth to reply and I braced myself for the denials. I wondered what tactic he would choose. It wasn't me, it was someone else who looked like me, the DNA test was wrong, it's a set-up, she was fine when I left her. Instead Baxter surprised me with a half-snort, half-laugh.

'Rape?' and he shook his head as if that was the

funniest thing ever. 'Ha, you've got to be joking,' then he rolled his eyes, 'not with that one.'

I was side-swiped by that answer, like I'd been hit with a sucker punch I didn't see coming. It took a moment to recover my train of thought. Whatever morals I had left, and I didn't have many, Baxter had managed to offend them.

'You're saying the girl was willing?'

'I'm saying it wasn't rape,' he told me impatiently, through gritted teeth.

'Well either it was rape or she was willing Baxter. There's no in-between.'

'Course there is,' he told me firmly, 'there just comes a point when all the cock teasing has to end, when all the treats and the attention has to lead to something in return. She understood that, at least that's what I thought.' He even managed to sound indignant.

'Oh I get it Baxter. You gave her some sweeties, maybe a bit of pocket money and that entitled you to have sex with her, even though she was only thirteen?'

'Yes, well,' he looked a bit uncomfortable at that, 'that one was thirteen going on . . .'

'Fourteen?' I offered. 'Fifteen maybe? Or was she thirteen going on sixteen, so you got it into your head that she was fair game did you? How old were you at the time? Forty-five? Not exactly *Romeo and Juliet*, is it?'

'I'm saying that age is no real indicator,' and he jabbed his finger at the table-top, 'and this one was older than her age. You know what they say,' and he arched his eyebrows at me, 'if they are old enough to . . .'

'Complete that sentence and I swear I will smash your sick face into this table and I will keep on doing it.'

That shut him up. I glanced at the prison guard. 'By the time he legs it over here to save you, you'll be a fucking vegetable, eating puréed meals for the rest of your sad, child-raping life. You got that?'

He eyed me carefully like he was wondering whether I was just bluffing, but whatever he saw in my face made him back down. 'There's no need for threats,' he told me quietly.

I had to take a deep breath to control my anger and remind myself where I was, before I continued, 'Let's just pretend for a moment that you haven't committed rape or, at the very least, even using your version of events, statutory rape. Shall we do that, Baxter? Even then, there is one obvious flaw in your defence.' He looked at me like he couldn't quite see it. 'You killed her,' I reminded him quietly.

He looked like he was struggling to control his emotions then but I didn't see guilt or shame in his eyes, only anger and spite.

'She was going to tell. The silly, little bitch was crying and she wouldn't stop and she kept saying "I'm going to tell" over and over again. She said it to me,' he paused to let that sink in, 'so what choice did I have?'

I looked at the man I'd had on my payroll for nearly three years and decided there and then to forget about everything I'd said to Palmer and Kinane. Baxter may have known a lot about my organisation but we would just have to live with that, because I'd made my decision.

'You're on your own, Baxter. From now on you can take your chances with the state-appointed, fresh-from-his-law-degree, apprentice lawyer they are going to give you, then you can stand there in the witness box and you can explain to those twelve jurors that the little girl you raped was just a cock tease. Then you can tell them how you had no choice but to kill her because she was going to tell on you and we'll see what happens shall we? Good luck with that, you sick sack of shit.'

He didn't like that, and his face took on the look of a spoilt child who's just had his toys taken off him. I'd already reasoned that the police would be more interested in sending a child-killer down than giving him a deal in return for information about me and, no matter how much he hated me now, Baxter wasn't about to trade that for nothing in return. He'd stay quiet out of spite.

'If you were in our lock-up right now I'd let Kinane sort you out with his tool-box and he'd give you the full treatment. He'd keep you alive for days. You'd better hope they lock you up in solitary forever because if you ever get out I'll make sure that happens, and do you know what, the police wouldn't give a shit. The Chief Constable would probably shake me by the hand. They wouldn't waste a minute trying to track down your killer. Not one. Jesus, you don't even know how sick in the head you are, do you? That's the really sad bit.'

It took a considerable effort, but I got to my feet. I was intending to lamp Baxter round the head for good measure before I walked away. I'd have to apologise to the screw and give him some extra wedge later, for the embarrassment I caused him, but I was pretty sure he could pass it off as an assault by another prisoner and I was relishing the fact that I was about to inflict some pain on this bastard.

'Sit down!' he barked at me, 'you're going nowhere,' and the shock of his certainty deflected me from thumping him, at least for the time being. Then he said, 'Not unless you want to kiss goodbye to your five million pounds.'

I took a long hard look into Henry Baxter's eyes, so I could tell if he was bluffing, then I sat back down again.

CHAPTER 17

'I am going to stay quiet and calm while you explain to me exactly what you have done, Baxter.'

'It's very simple, he said, 'I knew they would come for me, as soon as they got my DNA because of that stupid driving offence. I knew they would be back. I went to a lot of trouble to evade that same test ten years ago when they did it on every man for miles around.'

'I'll bet you did Baxter. Did you pay someone off or just disappear for a while? Actually, don't tell me, I don't want to know.' Baxter was lucky he did time for fraud back when they weren't big on taking DNA from everyone who went inside. He was a white-collar criminal who stole some money, not a high-risk danger to the public.

He chose to ignore me. 'I knew I'd have at least a week before the results came back but I had nowhere to run to and no real money. I wouldn't last six months on the lam in any civilised country with an extradition treaty, and men like me weren't built to live in mud huts halfway up the Amazon. It would be worse than this place.

So I needed a little life insurance policy; something that would get your attention and secure your help. I changed the access information for that bank account in the Caymans. Your money's still there, but you can't get it. Not without my help.'

'Your money is perfectly safe,' Baxter continued, 'but I am the only one who can release it for you, which I am prepared to do,' he pronounced the last bit like he was doing me a huge favour, 'in return for something from you.'

'Baxter you are going to give me my money regardless of whether I help you or not, because we both know that I could have you killed in here.'

'I actually seriously doubt that,' he said, and when I gave him a look he continued, 'you're hardly going to murder me here in front of your tame prison officer and, in case you have forgotten, I am a Rule 45, segregated prisoner. I'm in solitary. That's what they do to the "nonces".' Baxter did that stupid thing with his fingers that denotes speech marks and rolled his eyes at the absurdity of his prisoner classification as a sex offender.

'You *are* a nonce Baxter,' I told him, 'you raped and murdered a little girl. There's not a man in this nick that wouldn't torture you and kill you for the fun of it. They hate cunts like you in here and, come to mention it, people aren't too fond of your sort out there either. You wouldn't last ten minutes outside these walls. Solitary is the only place where you are safe, for now.'

He gave me a sour look, 'And that's my point. While I'm locked up on my own in a wing that is wholly populated by sex offenders, none of your usual contacts can get to me. Because, forgive me if I've misread this situation, the firm does not tolerate nonces and won't do business with them. Frankly, even if you did, there's no one on my wing more than five foot six. Have you seen them when they line up for their lunch? All of them; pathetic, seedy little men,' and he looked disgusted, as if he himself was excluded from that group. 'I know the firm has people in here but they're on C wing with all the other killers, armed robbers and enforcers. I also know you've paid people to get rid of men you don't need any more but I'm no Toddy, oh yes, I've heard that story. He didn't see it coming did he? But I do see it coming and I don't care, because you are not going to kill me, you are going to get me out of here, otherwise it's bye-bye five million pounds and, oops, I seem to have no more money to pay my suppliers, or the men on my payroll, and you wouldn't want that, would you? If that happened, you'd be about as popular in Newcastle as I am.'

I was hating this and hating him. Partly because of what he had done but mostly because he was right. I wasn't sure I could get at him on a solitary section of a sex offenders' wing. That was the whole point of separating the nonces in the first place and, even if I could have Baxter killed in here, it would lose me my five million. Without that money I wouldn't be able to trade for very long before I was struggling to meet our commitments and I dealt with people who were a hell of a lot scarier than the tax man.

'You're going to get me out of here,' he told me. 'How?'

'That's your problem, but you'd better work it out and fast. That five million is locked up safer than the Bank of England and if I go down you'll never see a penny of it.'

'You killed her. You just told me that and there is DNA evidence linking you to the dead girl.'

'I've admitted nothing, not to the authorities and that's what counts. To them I have denied everything except teaching the girl to play the piano. I gave her a few unofficial lessons and I could easily have come into contact with her then. You can pass on your DNA by shaking hands.'

'Not that kind of DNA, Baxter. Not the kind they are going to cite in court.'

'Then find a way to discredit them, Blake. Get me off and get me free and I'll be out of here. Then I'll give you your money back. You have my word.'

'Your word?'

'Yes,' he assured me, 'I am a man of my word.'

'Of course you are,' I said, 'how could I forget that? You're a proper English gent.'

'Don't take the moral high ground with me Blake. I may have killed a girl but not because I'm sick in the head. I'm not a psychopath. She was going to tell the police and get me locked up for a very long time. You, on the other hand, have had numerous people killed for exactly the same reason. It's all about self-preservation in the end. We are just two sides of the same coin, you and I. We both dare to do what is necessary to survive.'

'Don't compare yourself to me Baxter.'

'Why? Because it hurts? It's true, isn't it? How many people are in their graves because of you, Blake? Why don't you admit you have killed people when it proved necessary? Or do you struggle to look at yourself in the mirror these days? Is that why you are so bloody coy?'

'Shut up!' Before I had even thought about it consciously my fist shot out in a jabbing motion and crashed hard into his nose. He'd been leaning forward too far and I hit him with a blow that was packed with anger. Baxter's head jerked back and he let out a high-pitched cry as it fell forward again and he put his hand up to his face. He looked down in horror at the blood on his palm – more was pouring from his nose.

The prison officer rushed towards us in a panic. 'Get back there,' I ordered him angrily and he froze in his tracks, unsure what to do.

'You'll pay for that Blake,' Baxter told me, his voice a nasally whine, as he wiped the blood and snot from his battered nose. 'That'll cost you fifty grand; to get me back on my feet when this is over.'

He got out of his chair and walked to the door that would take him back to the safety of his cell in solitary, then he turned back and reminded me, 'You think about everything I've just said. It's not as if you have any other option.'

CHAPTER 18

'How did it go?' asked Palmer as I climbed back into the car outside Durham nick. 'Great,' I said, 'we had a lovely little chat.'

'And we're cutting him off,' he reminded me, 'once we unravel everything?'

'It's not going to be that simple.'

Further discussion was interrupted by the sound of Palmer's mobile ringing. He answered it, grunted and handed the phone to me. 'It's Robbie.'

'We've been through the CCTV footage,' he said, 'hours of it.'

'And?'

'She's on there alright. A few t . . . t . . . times.'

I had mixed feelings about that. On the plus side, at least we might pick up some clues about who Gemma Carlton had been hanging out with before she died, but confirmation of her presence in our club linked her to me, however loosely. It could be claimed I'd met her there or seen her across a crowded room and realised she was Carlton's daughter, which would be one more piece of circumstantial evidence to add to the police case that was doubtless building against me.

'What did you see?' I asked Robbie. 'Was she with someone?'

'Er . . . you need to come over and take a look at something.' He seemed reluctant to tell me more over the phone.

'What have you found Robbie?' I demanded.

'A smoking g . . . g . . . gun.'

I picked up Kevin Kinane and arranged for Sharp to meet us at the old call centre. We huddled around the monitor as Robbie tapped away at his keyboard and brought up the right images. 'Mark found this from the camera on the main door,' he tapped another key and up came black-and-white footage of the scene outside Cachet on a busy Friday night. 'It's from the night before the girl was killed.'

There was a queue of youngsters waiting patiently to get in. Because the club was doing so well, it would have been a long wait but our doormen kept everybody in line and anybody who acted up would be refused admission, so the line moved forward slowly and steadily but in good order.

'There,' said Robbie, as a group of girls was allowed in and the two behind them were asked to stand and wait their turn at the front of the queue. One was tall with long dark hair and the other was a petite brunette in a white coat, wearing a short skirt. I looked closely at her face. From the photographs I'd seen, this looked like Gemma Carlton to me

'What do you think?' I asked.

'It's definitely her,' Kevin Kinane replied.

The girls were finally permitted to enter and they disappeared off the screen. 'Now we go inside,' said Robbie. He tapped his keys again and up popped a view of the interior of the club. He paused it and said, 'There'. We watched the girls squeeze through the crowd. 'We keep losing sight of them,' he told us, 'but I've tracked them using all of the cameras in Cachet and I spliced the footage together.' It was like watching a film edited to show only the two leads. The girls slowly made their way through the club, 'they don't go to the bar,' and we watched as they walked around the dance floor, 'they don't hit the dance floor,' he explained pointlessly, 'then we lose them again until . . .' We cut to a view of the VIP bar. The camera that pointed down on to the lift which transported guests away from the great unwashed to the VIP lounge showed it slowly rising, the door opened and the two girls emerged with big excited grins on their faces.

'So they went up there on their own, but who were they meeting?'

'The whole VIP bar is a blind spot,' Robbie told me. 'I know, I know, I'm having it looked at. There'll be a new camera there tonight,' he assured me, 'anyway, you have to wait a while for another sighting, two hours to be exact,' the view changed again.

It was the same scene by the lift door, but with different people standing around chatting and drinking. Robbie pointed at the screen again. Sure enough, Gemma's friend came into view, a little unsteadily. She turned back towards Gemma, who was following her, but she wasn't alone. Gemma Carlton had her arm linked with a man's and she was laughing like she'd had at least a couple of bottles of our finest. I couldn't see his face though.

'Who's that?' asked Sharp and we continued to watch as the three of them walked towards the lift.

'His back's to us,' I said, and for a moment I thought we'd never see the face of the man Gemma left Cachet with, but then the lift doors opened. The group waited for it to empty and they stepped inside. Then they turned around so they were facing outwards. Gemma reached forward to press the lift button and then finally we saw the face of the man she left our club with on the night before she died.

'Jesus,' I said, 'that's Golden Boots.'

CHAPTER 19

Things had not been going all that well for Golden Boots, not that you'd notice it from the way he carried himself. As far as he was concerned, he was still Billy Big Bollocks, an unlikely media darling with legions of Twitter followers, a blog and a weekly tabloid newspaper column, ghost written of course. He never had to worry about having enough time for all of this verbal diarrhoea, because he rarely played any football these days. If he wasn't suspended for kicking, punching or head-butting opponents on the pitch, or his own teammates on the training ground, there were always the scuffles with members of the public he met on his regular nights out.

On the rare occasions that Golden Boots was not in trouble of one sort or another he was injured, his ageing joints struggling to cope with the wear and tear of a decade of top flight football and a history of poor refuelling choices; mainly a preference for beer and cocaine over fruit juice and pasta. His long-suffering club had grown tired of paying the man eighty thousand pounds a week to not play football and were desperately trying to offload him to anyone who was willing but, amazingly, there were no takers.

When I went round to see Golden Boots, I took Joe Kinane with me. I knew that would concentrate what little mind the Premiership's finest possessed, because he was shit scared of Kinane, with good reason. A little while back, our late but legendary enforcer, Finney, almost broke both of his legs because he tried to get violent when we interrupted a minor drug deal he was doing with Billy Warren, one of our dealers. Now, by way of making amends, he 'does a bit of business' with us, as he puts it, selling heavily-cut cocaine at ludicrous prices to a group of his Premiership mates.

We both get something out of this; we get the money, for Golden Boots it's the chance to pretend he's a gangster in his spare time and he loves the kudos that comes with being a 'face'.

The guy who answered the door didn't look like an athlete. He was sporting a three-day stubble and, even at this hour of the afternoon, he looked a bit out of it. His eyes were glassy and he was sniffing, but he didn't have a cold. As usual, he pretended to be pleased to see us but I knew he dreaded our little visits. He showed us into his cavernous house.

'What do you reckon?' he asked, all smiles, as we stopped before the centrepiece that dominated the huge hallway in his new home; it was a statue of himself. The sculptor had carved him life-sized, in bronze, kitted out in the England shirt he had worn just once during his mockery of a career.

'How much did that cost you?' I asked him.

'Forty grand.' He said it like it was nothing.

'It's fucking hideous, even by your standards.'

Golden Boots laughed nervously because he thought I was joking. 'I like it. I think he's caught me just right.'

'You're s'posed to be dead before they put a statue up,' said Kinane menacingly, 'them's the rules.'

'Yeah, well, I ain't dead yet, am I?' answered Golden Boots and Kinane just narrowed his eyes and smiled at that, which made the footballer look even more nervous.

We sat on huge leather sofas in his games room, which was the size of most people's houses. There was plenty of space for the ubiquitous snooker table and a bar. He didn't deny knowing Gemma Carlton when we questioned him and admitted he had heard about her death.

'I can't believe it,' he told me, 'murdered like that,' but I couldn't say he was exactly grief stricken.

'I saw her on the Friday night,' he confirmed, 'down at Cachet. I remember that and I remember her. She was a hottie and she knew the score. We had a couple of bottles of the good stuff in the VIP bar then I took her and her mate back to mine for the party. In the end I chose her. Her mate wasn't too chuffed about that but I doubt she'd have killed her over it.' At least his ego didn't extend quite that far, 'I mean there are always plenty of lasses around but I figured this one was worth the effort.'

The effort? He probably only had to beckon her to his table and he was halfway there. These young, local lasses would arrive at his house with eyes like saucers, not realising it wouldn't actually gain them much, except a few minutes of Golden Boots grunting and sweating on top of them, before he got them a lift home and never saw them again.

'So you slept with her?' I asked.

'Not slept with, no,' he answered. 'I shagged her, but she didn't stay the night.' He meant he wouldn't have allowed it. 'I got one of my lads to run her home.'

'One of my lads' meant a member of his increasing entourage, a bunch of blaggers and hangers-on who 'looked after him' as he put it.

'Did you see her the next night?' I asked pointedly, 'the night she died?'

'No,' he said, 'I had another party but she didn't turn up. At least I didn't see her, but there were a lot of people here, so she could have been around.'

'Then someone might have seen her?'

'I s'pose,' he conceded, 'but no, I'm pretty sure she wasn't here.'

I didn't think he was the most reliable witness, not these days. He was using more coke and booze than before and I reckoned a girl he'd shagged could walk right past him and he might not notice her.

'Speak to your lads,' I instructed him, 'ask them if they know anything about her, including whether she stopped by on the night she died, even if it was only for a while and you didn't see her. Maybe someone gave her a lift home. Hey, maybe she wasn't there at all. Perhaps she was over you by then.' He just stared blankly at me. 'This is important. We need to know what happened to this lass, understand?'

'Because she's a copper's daughter?' he asked.

'You've read that much in your comic then? Yeah, there's a lot of heat on this one. Until it's resolved nobody will be able to do any business. Have the law been to see you about her yet?'

'No,' he said.

'They will,' but I didn't tell him it was me that would be grassing up his intimate knowledge of Gemma Carlton to the police. I needed to give them something and this was all I had, for now.

'That's all I need,' he said, 'the law sniffing around me.'

'Welcome to my world,' I told him.

When we left Kinane asked, 'Why didn't you let me sweat him a little. He'd have spilled.'

'Because there's nothing to spill,' I answered, 'Golden Boots is a terrible liar. We can spot it a mile off when he's hiding something and he's terrified of you. He knew the girl, he shagged the girl, end of. Maybe his lads will tell him something, but I doubt he'll ask them properly, so we'll get your Kevin to have a word with them instead, shall we?'

It had been a few days since my meeting with Jinky Smith and I was driving through the city when I took a call.

'Is that David Blake?'

'Yes,' I waited for the next words and when none came, asked, 'who's that.'

'Never mind,' his breathing was audible, as if the speaker had damaged his lungs and every breath was a struggle, 'I hear you're after information about your fatha.'

'Who told you that?'

'Jinky passed us the word.'

'And you have some?' I asked, 'let's hear it then.'

'It'd be better face to face. I could meet you,' another raspy breath and he added, 'Jinky said there was some money in it like.'

'There might be, if what you're peddling is worth it.'

'I think it is.'

'Then come and see me,' I told him, 'you know the Cauldron?'

And the breathy rasp turned into a choked chuckle. 'I don't think so. I'll not see you behind closed doors, no offence, but I'll meet you out in the open.'

'Where then?'

'On the Blinky Eye Bridge.'

'When?' I asked, worried it might be a set up.

'Tomorrow lunchtime. Twelve o'clock.'

I hesitated, but only for a second. I didn't think anybody would be daft enough to try to shoot me there on a lunchtime, and this fella sounded old and tubercular.

'Alright,' I said, 'I assume you know what I look like. How will I know you?'

'I know you alright,' he wheezed, 'and you'll know me when I come up and start talking to you.'

'Okay, but I hope you're not a time waster.'

'Oh no, divvent worry about that. What I've got to tell you is gold.'

CHAPTER 20

The Blinky Eye Bridge stretches across the River Tyne, linking Newcastle's Quayside to Gateshead's posh end; the bit with the Baltic contemporary arts centre and the seventy-million-pound Sage building. The Blinky Eye is designed for pedestrians and its official name is the Millennium Bridge. The kid in me still thinks it looks like the jaw bone of a giant whale with one bit sticking up and the other half resting on the ground. It gets its nickname because the top half can fall back and the lower bit flip up, so that both parts are out of the way when ships want to pass through it. Then it drops neatly back down again to let the common folk walk over it once more. Since it weighs more than eight hundred tonnes, that is no mean feat of engineering.

Because the bridge is more than a hundred metres, from one side of the river to the other, the mystery man couldn't have picked a more out-in-the-open location to meet me than this one. He was late though, and I spent my time scanning passers-by to see if I could clock him. Palmer watched over me from the Newcastle side of the bridge, just in case.

From his wheezy voice and the fact that he was likely to be a contemporary of Jinky's, I was expecting an older man and that's exactly what I got. I spotted him a mile off and immediately relaxed. His progress across the bridge was spectacularly slow, each step measured, like a child pacing out a treasure map. He straightened when he finally reached me and I let him catch his breath. I was no doctor but I reckoned he had a year, at best.

'Fags,' he said and, for a second, that looked like all the explanation I was going to get, 'fucked me lungs up,' he added. 'I'm only bloody sixty.' He looked like he was having trouble dealing with what he knew was inevitably coming his way.

'If they don't get you, the booze and the birds will,' I said and he let out a grim laugh at that.

'True enough.'

'You've got some information for me,' I reminded him, 'we can start with your name, if you want paying that is?'

'Alreet,' I could tell he was reluctant to concede even that, 'it's Paul Armstrong.'

'Sit yourself down man,' I told him and he sank gratefully into one of the metal bench seats on the bridge.

'So, what do you know?'

'I worked for your old mate, Mickey Hunter, when he had the garage, the one he peddled his used motors out of.' Every few words he took a breath and I could tell each one hurt him, so he was economical with them.

I nodded, not because I knew the place but I was aware of Hunter's dealership. The cars were so hot they virtually drove themselves out of there. He had it for years and it was a classic front for all of his other business, but it was gone by the time I really knew the lads in the firm, replaced by the old body shop he kept underneath the railway arches that knocked dents out of cars and acted as a front for his real role as quartermaster to our firm. After Hunter was killed we never left the job of supplying our weaponry to just one man any more. It was another area of security we had tightened up. I couldn't run the risk of one guy knowing everything we'd been up to.

'So you were with the firm?' I asked.

'Not really,' he admitted, 'I mean we all were a bit, you had to be, but I was on the outside looking in. I did some stuff for Bobby now and then but nowt that would really get me into bother with the law. I remember your dad though. I remember him well.' And, just when I thought all I was going to get was some pointless reminiscences he added, 'And I saw him the day before he disappeared. I reckon I must have been one of the last to see him in fact and it was all very strange like.'

He had to stop for breath again – the delay was frustrating.

'What was so strange about it?'

'Your dad bought a car from Hunter. He went from being broke one day to minted the next but there was nothing unusual about that, if he was in on one of Bobby's jobs.'

'My father never actually worked for Bobby,' I told him, because that's what everybody had always told me.

'He was never a full member of the crew, but he did jobs.'

'You reckon?' I wasn't so sure about this, but he was.

'I'm telling you man. He did stuff for Bobby, on and off like, that's how he started people out, to see how they got on. You didn't just sign up overnight. You had to prove yourself before you got the big wedge.'

'How do you know all this, if you weren't a full member of the crew?'

'Because Hunter was my gaffer for years and I saw them all come and go.' It was a reasonable enough explanation but I had still never heard anything about my dad working for the firm before.

'So what did he do for Bobby then?'

'Whatever needed doing. You ought to know what that means.' I did and didn't need it spelling out. 'Anyway, your dad bought the car from Hunter but when he headed south the next day, he left it behind.'

'Eh?'

'It was a Cortina Mark 2, only a couple of years old. Nice motor for the time. He paid cash. I was there and I watched Hunter count it out, then they shook hands on the deal.'

All of a sudden he seemed to be finding his breath. It was as if the excitement of telling his story had overridden his condition for a while.

'Alan said he would come back and collect it later, because he had some business to sort out in town first, but he never came back for the car. It stayed on the forecourt. Later on, everybody was saying that Alan Blake had left the city and gone down south for a job in London. Didn't even stop long enough to collect his wife and bairn he was in that much of a hurry.'

'If he'd done something for Bobby, summat worth the cost of a car, the law could have been sniffing round,' I offered, 'maybe that's why he left so quickly.'

That would explain why my dad skipped town and left ma and Danny behind and why he might have had to stay away for a couple of years, if it was something serious.

'But here's the bit that doesn't ring true. They said he went on the train. Now, if he was planning a new life, with or without his wife and bairn, would he really buy a Ford Cortina one day and a train ticket the next, no matter how flush he was?'

'No,' I said, 'he wouldn't. What happened to the car?'

'It stayed on the forecourt for weeks, then Hunter sold it.'

'You mean he sold it again?'

'Aye that's exactly what I mean.'

'And there's no way my da could have returned later and got his money back?' I knew Hunter well enough to know that last bit was unlikely.

'Hunter? No chance, he was tight as arseholes,' he shook his head. 'I worked there all day and he never came back. I thought it was odd when he didn't collect his new car because the next day was a Sunday. You weren't even open on a Sunday. You weren't allowed to be, back then.'

'And you never said anything at the time,' I asked, 'to Hunter, I mean, or anybody else who was spreading this story about my dad leaving on a train?'

'I did ask Hunter about it, yeah, stupidly.'

'Why? What did he do?'

'Nothing,' he replied, 'but then that nutter Jerry Lemon came up to us the next Saturday neet when I was having a few pints in town, he telt me I had a big mouth. He said "Careless talk costs lives", you knaa, like that old poster in the war. He telt me to remember that, if I wanted to keep my teeth.'

Jerry would often go around threatening people on Bobby's behalf, so this fella asking questions about my dad's car must have meant something. Maybe that was why he had to leave Newcastle. Had he upset Jerry Lemon or did he somehow manage to tread on Bobby's toes? Whatever happened it can't have been too serious but it was

155

big enough for him to quit town in a hurry, and for him to stay away for a good while.

'So you stopped asking?'

'God yes,' he said, 'it was none of my business.'

'No,' I said, 'I suppose it wasn't, but Jerry Lemon's long dead.'

'Aye, well, if he wasn't, I wouldn't be standing here talking to you now, would I?'

'Fair enough,' I told him. 'Is there anything else you want to tell me?'

'Well, it's obvious isn't it,' he said, then added, 'they must have killed him.'

'That's one way of interpreting it,' I admitted, but I knew what he didn't. My dad had fled the city right enough and now I was closer to understanding the reasons why, but he had still been in contact with my ma for years after. I wasn't even born when my dad jumped on that train and headed south, but the old timer wasn't to know that.

'Can you think of any reason why he might have fallen out with Jerry?'

He opened his mouth to speak, but his breath caught in his throat again and the coughing started up once more. I waited and tried to be patient but I wasn't expecting much from him if I was honest. The business with the car was intriguing enough but the old git didn't have the full story, so I doubted he would shed any further light on the mystery.

When he finally finished coughing he told me, 'Aye, I knaa all right,' and he seemed puzzled that I didn't.

'Well,' I told him, 'out with it then.'

'It was 'cos of the job they did together. The one that went wrong.'

'The one that went wrong?' I repeated dumbly, trying to get my head round it, 'what job was that then?'

'The robbery of the Stuart & Brown payroll,' he said, 'haddaway man, you must have heard of that one? You know, the engineering company?'

I shook my head. 'So you're saying my dad was in on a wages snatch?' He nodded. 'And it went pear-shaped?' He nodded again.

'Well, you could say that.'

'How do you mean?'

'It was 'cos of your dad,' he told me.

'Why what did he do?'

'He buggered off, didn't he?' the old bloke told me, 'and he took all of the money with him.'

CHAPTER 21

I just about managed to get the words out. I managed to say, 'Thanks, that's useful.'

'Useful enough?' he asked me, his eyes pleading.

'You'll want paying for it,' I said. 'I don't have it on me but you'll get some bunce. If you think of anything else to tell me then you've got my number.'

'Champion,' he said.

I kept the presence of mind to tell him who to see for his money. He seemed satisfied with that and shuffled away. I gave Palmer the nod so he knew it was all okay and I walked off too, crossing the bridge until I was on the Gateshead side. Palmer would follow me at a discreet distance, but he knew when to leave me alone.

I walked slowly up to the Baltic Mill. Normally, I like this lovingly-restored building, but today I barely glanced at it. I bought a ticket and walked inside, mooching around in there for a while, pretending to look at the paintings while I thought this through.

If it was news to me that my father might have

done a job for Bobby Mahoney, it was an even bigger shock to hear he had taken all of the cash. If that was true, it was no wonder he had to leave the city in a hurry, but why hadn't Bobby tracked him down if he stole from him? Why would he keep employing my mother afterwards, unless he thought my dad might come home for her one day and he would be waiting, keeping her close to him like that, so he could spring a trap? Shit, why would he ever trust me? Didn't it worry him that I could be a chip off the old block? It didn't make any sense.

I knew my father had left Newcastle on a train two years before I was born and now I knew why. I also knew he had managed to keep the contact with my mother going for more than four years before disappearing forever. I'd always thought he was a low-life who didn't give a shit about my brother and me, but maybe his final disappearance was more sinister than I had realised. Did Bobby trick an address out of my ma, or did my father put his head above the parapet by stupidly coming home and Bobby finally reckoned with him. This wasn't what I was expecting to find when I first started digging into my father's life. That old guy had given me a hell of a lot to think about.

'Have you considered my offer?' asked Henry Baxter, as if his proposition was a perfectly reasonable one. We were back in the visiting area for another private audience, while the prison guard watched me nervously. Baxter's nose was bruised and swollen where I'd punched him.

'Yes.' I felt sick inside having to eat humble pie in front of this twisted man.

'And?'

'I'll do my best to get you out,' I told him, 'but only to get my money back. Just so we understand each other.'

He pondered this for a moment.

'No apology, I note,' he told me sniffily, as if he really thought I was going to say sorry for bloodying his nose, 'but there is one final thing. It's quite important actually.'

'What is it?'

'You don't think I'm just going to walk out of court and go off with you and Kinane so you can torture me into giving you the passwords and account numbers you need, then kill me, do you? That's not the way it's going to work. You are going to let me go and when I have left the country, only then will I send you the information you need to access the . . .'

'Not a chance. There's no way I'm letting you leave the country, or even this city, without giving me access to the money. I want to see proof that we've retrieved it before I let you go. Then you can disappear forever for all I care.'

'Then we have a problem, because I obviously

don't trust you to let me go. I suspect that once you have your money, you will allow Kinane to kill me.'

'That's a risk you'll just have to learn to live with, if you want my help.'

'No.'

'Then you'll stay here and rot.'

'And you'll lose five million pounds. How long will you be able to continue to pay your suppliers, or the men who work for you, with a hole that size in your accounts?'

'Then we both have a problem.'

He went quiet for a moment, as if he was thinking it all through, then he said, 'Are you a superstitious man, Blake?'

'Not especially.'

'But you're a father and you care deeply about your daughter? I mean you wouldn't be human if you didn't. Don't look at me like that. I'm merely stating the obvious. If you wish me to leave the courtroom with you when this is over, to give you the information you require, then I need you to swear an oath.'

'What kind of oath?'

'I want you to swear that neither you, nor any of your men, will attempt to kill me or harm me in any way, that you will release me once you have the information you need and leave me to my own devices.'

'Fair enough.'

'And I want you to swear this on the life of your infant daughter Blake. If you are prepared to do that then we might just have a deal.'

I walked out of that nick feeling like I needed to take a long, hot shower. Is this what it's like when you make a pact with the devil, I wondered?

There was one more thing that was troubling me.

I had absolutely no idea how to get Baxter off his murder charge.

None whatsoever.

CHAPTER 22

We were sitting in Susan Fitch's smart, Grey Street office, surrounded by leather-bound law books, the musty smell of them filling the room, when she asked me, 'You want my firm to represent Mr Baxter?'

'No, Mrs Fitch,' I answered, 'I do not want your firm to represent Baxter.'

I was surprised when she exhaled in relief at that.

'Thank heaven for small mercies,' she said, 'right now that man's name is poison. But, if you don't want us to represent him, then what do you want?'

'I want you to get me someone who will. This must be at arm's length,' I explained.

My solicitor sat back in her chair and thought for a while. I could tell Susan Fitch spent money on her clothes and hair but she was starting to look a little weathered these days. Her face was lined and pale from a life spent too much indoors, poring over the books that imprisoned her. 'Tall order,' she admitted, 'but I could probably find someone somewhere who's desperate enough.'

'Not just someone. Baxter has to be acquitted.'

'Tall orders I can do, but miracles are not my forte, Mr Blake.'

'Why is it so hard to get him off?'

'A number of reasons,' and she began to count them off on her fingers. 'Your employee knew the girl and the police can prove that; he lived near her at the time of her murder and gave piano lessons to a number of other young girls in the area. The police have established that, as well as a roster of regular clients, he had unofficial sessions with a number of young girls, including some of the victim's friends and they think that Leanne Bell may have been one of them. Now that he is under arrest, they will be interviewing every girl he has ever spent a moment with and something will come up, be under no illusions about that. If Baxter gave them sweeties or booze in return for the tiniest glimpse of their training bras then he is irredeemably and deservedly fucked. If they were promised money or weed, if he so much as looked at a girl in a funny way or set his hand gently down upon her knee, to show his approval at a nicely-rendered bit of Debussy, then he is doomed.'

'You could be right.'

'Then there is the man himself. I have met your accountant on a number of occasions and he is not the kind of fellow who instils confidence, nor can I imagine him charming a jury. Baxter is a rude, arrogant, bigoted, singularly unattractive man. I found him dirty, vulgar and sleazy and he sweats a great deal. Frankly, he *looks* like a child killer, or a jury's idea of one, and that's how they are likely to regard him. But that's just my opinion and none of that matters too much when set against the big, clinching factor.'

'The DNA?'

'The DNA,' she agreed, 'most people only have to hear there is DNA evidence linking someone to the scene or the victim and that's it; the prosecution gets their conviction. Most jury members won't have the faintest clue about the science. They don't know and they don't want to know. If there's a professor on the stand with some letters after his name, telling them the mathematical odds against DNA evidence being incorrect are immense, you can almost see them nodding in agreement.'

'And the odds are?'

'Hundreds of millions to one,' she assured me.

'So how do you challenge that kind of evidence?'

'You don't. As far as I'm aware, you can't, and I wouldn't be willing to try. This is a no-win case if ever I saw one.'

'So what's the good news?'

She shrugged, 'Accountants are ten a penny.'

'Like lawyers?'

She gave me a humourless smile, 'And gangsters.'

'This one is special,' I told her and she gave me a quizzical look. 'Not the man. Baxter is vile and deserves everything he gets but the information he holds is . . . valuable to me. I want it back. I need it back, in fact. Without it my entire organisation is in considerable jeopardy.'

'I see.' She seemed taken aback.

'I hope you do,' I assured her.

'Then you are going to need a very good lawyer indeed.'

'One of those dispassionate, messianic types with the super-keen intellect who believes the system owes every man the right to a fair trial,' I suggested.

'Yes,' she said, 'all that and a monstrous ego.'

Things had been strained with Sarah since she had asked me to tell her about her father's last moments. She had actually apologised for springing that on me but, if I thought I'd heard the last of her questions about Bobby, I was sadly mistaken. She tried raising the matter with me again, more than once. She explained that it was important for her to know exactly what had happened to her dad. She drew parallels with my own search for the truth about my missing father, which I didn't thank her for.

'I want to know if my father is still alive Sarah, that's all,' I retorted. 'I just want to understand why he walked out on us all those years ago, so I know how to answer Emma's questions when she gets older. You want to hear details I'm not comfortable discussing with anyone, let alone you.'

I managed to avoid the subject or curtail the conversation each time she raised it with me until it began to drive a wedge between us. Eventually it became a real source of friction, until one day it erupted into a full-blown row.

'I don't understand why you won't even talk to me about it. I have a right to know.'

'And I have a right to choose not to relive the worst day of my life,' I countered.

'I don't need you to paint me a picture Davey, I just want you to fill in the gaps.'

'What gaps?'

'I don't know!' she shouted at me. 'That's the fucking point!'

'I'm not discussing it with you anymore and that's it!'

'What? The conversation's over because you decide it is?'

At that point, Sarah looked like she was about to explode and I was spoiling for a fight as well. It was the sound of Emma crying upstairs which brought us back to reality. I think we both thought we'd woken her at first and we stopped shouting and listened for a second.

'Nightmare,' I said and she got to her feet. 'I'll go,' I told her, 'you've had her all day.' When I reached Emma's room she was tearful and sitting up in bed. As soon as she saw me, she opened her arms wide, as if only a hug from her daddy could banish the monsters from her world.

'Come here, sweetie,' I told her. She looked exhausted, so I picked her up and carried her into our room.

'You lie in mummy and daddy's bed for a while.' I put her under the covers and tucked her in. She fell asleep almost instantly. I lay down next to her and closed my eyes for a moment.

When I opened them again I realised I'd dozed off. I checked my watch and found I'd slept for nearly three hours. Emma was still asleep in the bed beside me. Sarah must have given up on us both and gone off to sleep in the spare room.

I still wasn't sleeping well and I woke as soon as it was light outside. I got up and left early, careful not to wake Emma. A couple of hours later I was sitting in my office at the Cauldron when Susan Fitch called me.

'You remember we talked about the type of man you need; the dispassionate messiah with the monstrous ego?'

'Yes.'

'I think I may have found him.'

Julian Aimes was an arrogant, overgrown public school boy with an overriding belief in the unending power of his abilities. He was very tall, which meant that he literally looked down on people for much of the time, and frowned when he asked questions, which made him appear challenging even when he wasn't trying to be. Baxter would have liked him.

His chambers were in Durham, but we met him in the coffee house on the Cathedral Square, so I didn't have to go to his office. I kept my voice low, so the tourists couldn't hear us discussing a child's murder while they sipped tea and ate walnut cake. With the help of Susan Fitch, I outlined the key points of the case to him, we described the challenging character of his potential new client, the circumstantial nature of the supporting evidence, which included the proximity of Baxter's home to the girl's and the fact that he had served prison time in the interim for unrelated charges, which we hoped would be kept from the jury. Then, as if we were consciously saving the worst till last, we told him about the DNA evidence.

'I'm not inexpensive Mr Blake,' was all he offered when I was done.

'I'm not unaware of that, Mr Aimes,' I replied.

'Good,' he answered, 'I find it practical to get the vulgar subject of money out of the way early. It saves my time and the client's embarrassment,' he brought his fingertips together in front of his face, then stared at me thoughtfully, 'but have you told me everything I need to know?'

'There's one thing you haven't asked me,' I said, unsure if I was impressed by his bluntness or not.

'And what's that?'

'Whether Baxter is guilty or not?'

His eyebrows knotted together quizzically and he stared at me in puzzlement.

'Oh, I see. You know do you or, should I say, you think that you do? Mr Blake, were you there when the girl was murdered?'

'No,' I admitted.

'So you didn't witness the act being perpetrated?'

'I think I just answered that question.'

'Indeed,' he said, 'then we must both acknowledge at least a modicum of doubt as to Mr Baxter's guilt. From what you tell me, there were no witnesses to the actual killing?'

'That's correct.'

'Therefore, whether you view the man as innocent or guilty is entirely irrelevant.'

I was beginning to feel like a school pupil being chastised by a master.

'If you believe him to be innocent that is of no practical use to me whatsoever. The judge and jury will see you as wholly biased, your assertion being based, as it is, around your professional relationship. Frankly, there isn't a man convicted of murder who has not had at least one friend, partner, colleague or mother who was willing to swear they never could have done such a thing and it counted not a jot in their favour in the end.'

I was about to reply to this, but he continued,

'conversely, if you believe him to be guilty, then this can only be based on your, again, wholly biased view of his character while he has been in your employ. The only other alternative is that the accused man has confessed to this heinous act but has chosen not to repeat said confession to the relevant authorities and, officially at least, resolutely maintains his innocence. I must also therefore continue to assert it. Also, he may not have been of entirely sound mind when he uttered this purely hypothetical confession, of which I wish to know nothing. Is that understood?'

'Entirely. I only asked so I could be sure you had no qualms about representing someone accused of raping and murdering a child because, if you do, now is the time to mention it.'

He gave me the schoolteacher look again. 'Whether I have personal feelings, either now or at any time in the future, about the victim of this crime, they are of no consequence when compared to the greater imperative of upholding the judicial system of this country and its first principle; that every man, no matter how wretched, be given the opportunity of a fair trial with the best defence he is able to procure. Without this, we may as well simply present the facts to a judge, allow no reasoned argument as to a man's guilt or innocence, then let said judge pronounce a verdict without the complication of a jury.'

'Fair enough,' I said, 'then you will take the case?'

'I will accommodate you,' he answered, as if he was being extremely gracious. 'For now you will have to excuse me,' he added, 'I am late for a meeting at my chambers. We will talk again in due course.'

'Thank you,' I said, 'you'll need to discuss the case further with Mrs Fitch . . .' but I was already talking to his back. I watched him walk from the coffee house and stride purposefully away across the quadrant.

'Told you he was messianic,' said Susan Fitch when he was gone.

'And has a monstrous ego.' I reminded her.

After the meeting with Aimes I went straight down to the prison where Henry Baxter was waiting for me. It was time for another cosy chat in the visiting room.

'The prison chaplain loaned me a Bible,' Baxter explained, 'nice chap, someone you can have a conversation with. Not like everybody else in here. So, if you could place your hand on it, we can begin.'

'I'm not remotely religious, Baxter.'

'Humour me,' he replied.

'Why?'

'Because I suspect that even an irreligious cut-throat like you might baulk at placing his hand on a Holy Bible, then swearing on the life of his infant daughter and going back on his oath. I think even you would be a little superstitious about that.'

He was right. I was. Baxter may have been a child-murdering sicko but he'd read me correctly. No way was I going to tempt fate with my little girl's life by breaking an oath stacked against it, whether a Bible was involved or not.

'Do you swear that you will do everything in your power to get me out of here in return for access to your money?'

I put my hand on the bible, 'I swear.'

'Do you further swear that, having secured my release, you will neither kill me nor order my death at the hands of anyone in your organisation, and I include contract killers in that equation obviously, or anyone else you might choose to hire.'

'I swear.'

'And do you also swear not to harm me nor allow anyone else in your organisation to torture or injure me in any way.'

I sighed, 'I swear.'

'Don't take this lightly Blake,' there was a flash of anger. 'I'm not.'

'Neither am I Baxter, believe me.'

'And do you finally swear to release me within twenty-four hours of my acquittal, which as you know will be more than ample time to transfer the funds back to you?'

'I swear.'

'And do you swear all of this on the life of your infant daughter, Emma Blake?'

'I do.'

'Say it then.'

'I swear all of it on the life of my infant daughter, Emma Blake.'

Baxter scrutinised me for a second, as if he feared I'd somehow fooled him, then he nodded.

'Good,' he concluded, 'then we are back in business.'

CHAPTER 23

Iknew Joe Kinane would go loopy at the prospect of helping a nonce, and I wasn't wrong about that, but I felt trapped by Henry Baxter's blackmail and couldn't see any way out of it.

'I don't understand!' Kinane bellowed. 'How are you somehow beholden to an oath you've made to a child killer? If he's done this thing, and it sounds like he has, then get him off the charges, get your money back then kill the sick twat.'

'I don't understand either,' admitted Palmer.

'You're not a father,' I told him, and that shut him up, 'and you are,' I reminded Joe, 'so let's hear you take an oath on your sons' lives and see how lightly you take it.'

Any further discussion was cut off by Fallon's arrival. He'd called a meeting and I was hoping it wasn't trouble – but that was exactly what I got.

'Someone put one of my guys in the hospital yesterday.'

He was pacing the office floor in the Cauldron, looking like he wanted to rip somebody's arms off. Fallon was one of those old-school Glasgow enforcers who looks like he came out of his mother's womb fully formed, clutching an iron bar. We were allies these days, thankfully. We bankrolled Fallon in Glasgow when he took control of the city from the Gladwells and we shared responsibility for the Edinburgh drug trade jointly, taking over when there was a power vacuum after Dougie Reid was sent down for life.

'Which guy?' I asked.

'Tommy Law.'

I knew Tommy, or I should say knew *of* him. Whoever gave him a beating must have been rock hard or mob handed, possibly both.

'I fought the law and the law won,' I offered, 'but not this time.'

He didn't look amused.

'Was this about territory?' I asked, because Tommy Law oversaw a good chunk of our Edinburgh operation.

'Aye, he was warned off,' confirmed Fallon, 'while they were breaking both his arms and legs and smashing his jaw in.'

'Jesus, who did it? Do we know that much at least?' I couldn't imagine who would have the sheer brass balls to come up to Fallon's patch and beat the shit out of Tommy Law like that.

'According to Tommy, they're Eastern Europeans.'

'Eastern Europeans? Could he not narrow it down a bit?'

'Oh aye,' he told me, flaring, 'it was easy to

narrow it down because Tommy speaks fluent Serbo-Croat and, from their accents alone, he could tell exactly where they were from. They're either Russian, Polish, Czech, Serbian, Croatian, Ukrainian or Albanian. Basically, from what he was able to mumble through his broken jaw, I'm fairly certain they are from some place east of Newcastle, get my meaning?'

'Alright, alright, I hear you,' I replied, 'it was a stupid question. The only thing we should really be discussing here is our response.'

'Agreed,' he said, 'but I want to hang fire a wee while on that.'

I was impressed by this uncharacteristic restraint. 'That's unlike you Fallon.'

'I've got my reasons.'

'Which are?'

'McGlenn's disappeared.'

'Oh.'

'So has his stash and all of the money.'

McGlenn was a dealer who worked for Tommy Law, 'and you think it's the same guys but you're not sure yet. You're wondering if McGlenn is involved and put them up to it?'

'I've not known McGlenn as long as my Glasgow crew. He's an Edinburgh lad. Maybe he got greedy and stupid and flew off to Ibiza with it all. If he has then we'll find him and deal with it separately.'

It didn't much matter for McGlenn whether he had been killed by the Eastern Europeans, or cut a deal with them to take down Tommy Law, then done a runner with Fallon's money. You didn't steal from Fallon. Either way, McGlenn was a dead man. It mattered to Fallon though. He wanted to know exactly what had happened to his dealer, because he was wondering if we were already in an all-out war. Me? I couldn't believe it. Things had been quiet for so long and now, all of a sudden, everything was erupting around me.

'Keep me informed.' I said. I needed Fallon to handle this one on his own. I had enough shit to juggle.

'Of course.'

While Fallon was briefing me, Palmer had walked away to the window, his lack of attention irritating me.

'What is it Palmer?'

'It might be nothing,' he said it so quietly I could barely hear him, 'just a guy I've seen a couple of times now. He walked by the Mitre the other day when we were coming out and he went past here too as we were walking in.'

'Can you remember everyone who walks by one of our places?' This seemed barely credible.

'Not everyone,' he admitted, 'but I remembered this one.' His tone made me take him seriously.

'What was he like?'

'Tall, stocky, middle-aged, dark brown hair, dressed in one of those old green Army jackets that were popular years ago.'

'So, apart from the crap fashion sense, what

offended you about his presence? Seeing him twice in two days?'

'It's a big city,' he told me. He meant the odds were pretty long on that happening.

'A professional?'

'Didn't look like a pro but maybe that's cos . . .'

'He's a pro?'

'Exactly.'

Kinane couldn't deal with a conversation as opaque as this one.

'You're saying he looks like a pro,' he challenged, 'because he doesn't look like a pro?'

Palmer snorted at the absurdity of his own argument. 'That's one way of putting it.'

'Jesus H Christ,' and Kinane shook his head, 'you'll be seeing spies on every street corner.'

'But it might be nothing?' I countered.

Palmer shrugged. 'It's probably something.'

'You are itching to get out there,' I said, 'so go on.'

'I will,' he said simply, 'just to have a nose.'

While Palmer was gone, Kinane, Fallon and I continued to discuss what should be done when Fallon found out who was behind the attack on Tommy Law, but my mind wasn't fully on this localised Edinburgh dispute. I was just waiting for Palmer to come back into the building, probably with an unconscious, army-jacket-wearing, thug hanging over his shoulder.

When Palmer did return, fifteen minutes later,

he looked troubled. I gave him a look. 'No one out there,' he said.

'You sure?' I asked him.

'As sure as I can be,' he answered.

'Meaning he could be out there,' offered Kinane, 'he might just be better than you.'

'Thanks for that comforting thought Joe.' I told him.

I was sitting in The Strawberry pub with Palmer waiting for Kevin Kinane's latest report when Maggot showed up, with his usual great timing. I like The Strawberry, which uses its location as the closest pub to the football ground as a fine excuse to paper its walls with framed and signed portraits of Toon legends old and new. I've been drinking here since I first blagged my way in as a teenager, in an era when its windows were nearly always boarded up. Like me, it has moved with the times and gone up in the world. I like the place, but I don't like Maggot.

'Bloody hell,' I hissed, 'that's all I need.'

'What the fuck does he want?' asked Palmer.

Maggot pretended not to have noticed us at first, even though I had seen him clock me as soon as his ferrety eyes came around the corner. He went into an elaborate routine of looking down while he walked towards the bar, patting the pockets of his crumpled denim jacket, looking for cigarettes, a lighter and his wallet, all of which he took out one after the other, as if to reassure himself that they were still there. Then he stopped, looked to one side, clocked us, as if for the first time, feigned surprise and came over with a big false smile plastered all over his grubby face.

'Alreet Davey,' he said, like he was thrilled to see me. 'How are you doing?'

'Canny,' I told him, 'at least I was.'

He ignored this and asked, 'Are you wanting another one like?' as he nodded hopefully at our nearly-full glasses.

'Yes please Maggot,' answered Palmer, 'that's very good of you.'

But that wasn't what Maggot meant, and we all knew it. Instead he just stood there looking part hopeful, part disappointed.

I took a twenty out of my wallet and slid it over the table towards him. 'Get them in then.' And those rodent eyes lit up.

Maggot bought the three pints and carried them unsteadily back towards our table, clasping them together with yellow, nicotine-stained fingers, spilling some of our beer in the process. I didn't ask him for my change and he didn't offer any. It must have slipped his mind.

'So come on, out with it,' I demanded, as he took his first deep gulp of beer, 'what is it you're wanting?'

'Eh?' he said, all innocence, 'oh no, I was just passing.'

'Fuck off Maggot. You were looking for me, you

found out we were in here and you tracked me down, so what's it about?'

He looked a bit worried, but immediately turned my accusation into flattery. 'Eeh there's no fooling you Davey Blake, sharp as a tack, that's why you're the boss, it's just a little loan like.' The words came out in a self-conscious rush.

'Another one? Christ what is it this time? The horses or Sticky's card game?'

'Aye, well, a bit of both,' he admitted.

We paid Maggot well, considering all he ever did for us was run the Sports Injury Clinic, our dodgy massage parlour on the outskirts of the city, yet he pissed away most of his wages on beer and betting. Maggot was a low-level operative in the firm and Bobby only kept him on the payroll because he was always loyal to members of his crew. He did have one skill however, and it had nothing to do with his day job. He had the uncanny knack of knowing virtually everything that went on in this city and that made him useful on occasions.

'How much is it this time?' I asked.

'Five grand,' he told me, with an apologetic shrug.

'Which must mean you owe about three and you want the other two to try to win it back.'

From the look on his face I knew I was near the mark. 'So I'll let you have three and a half. That way you can pay your debts and survive until pay day.'

What was I thinking? Maggot was the kind of guy who lived off tins of beans and fried eggs, mopped up with slices of cheap, white bread. Every spare penny went down the bookies or the boozer. I knew he'd be betting that extra five hundred before the day was out.

'Cheers man Davey,' he said, 'I owe you.'

'You do,' I told him, 'but you've got to earn it first.'

'Oh hey man, please. Sticky's looking for uz, says I have to pay him today or . . .'

'He'll break one of your arms.'

'So he says.' Maggot looked worried, and he had cause to be if he owed Sticky. This was a high-stakes, illegal poker game we got kick-backs from. You didn't go into that game without proper money behind you, unless you were as dumb as Maggot.

'He'll lay off you if I tell him to,' I said, and Maggot grinned. 'I might not tell him though,' the grin vanished. 'Like I said, you've got to earn it. Now, what have you heard about this copper's daughter.'

'Just the usual,' he said.

'Fuck off Maggot. I know you. You'll know something none of us knows, so what is it.'

He thought for a long while. I knew Maggot well, he would be desperate to please me to get his money but he wouldn't dare make something up. 'Just that . . .' he hesitated.

'Out with it.'

'She did a bit, you know,' he said.

'A bit of what?'

'Just that she liked a bit of blow, you know.'

'And who told you that?'

'Just someone I know,' he mumbled, 'he knows all the footballers, says she used to go to their parties and that.'

Maggot was worried I wouldn't believe him. The poor young copper's daughter had been painted as a blushing virgin in the Press and he was saying the opposite, but the link to the footballers corroborated what Golden Boots had told us. Doing a bit of coke tended to come with the territory when he was involved.

'And how could she afford that, I wonder?' I asked him.

'Well I don't think she had to pay for any of it, but she was a game girl. She knew how it worked.'

'Now then Maggot!' shouted Kevin Kinane, slapping a huge hand down on the older man's shoulder 'when did you crawl out from the U-Bend?'

Maggot hadn't realised Kevin Kinane had crept up behind him and he jumped out of his skin

'Fuck off, Kevin!' he retorted, without thinking it through, which was a stupid move because I knew Kevin wouldn't let that one go. He would wait till Maggot was on his own one day and give him a slap.

'Why don't you make me, you fat bastard? Look

at you,' and Kevin curled his lip at Maggot, 'you're like a sleazy little pork scratching on legs.'

'Both of you shut up,' I ordered, 'this isn't a playground. It's a shrine,' I indicated the pictures on the walls, 'now show some respect. What have you got for me Kevin?'

Kevin Kinane looked uneasy.

'It's alright, he's family.' Maggot was many things but he wasn't a grass and none of this was too sensitive. We were looking into the case at the request of the police anyhow, but Maggot gulped down his pint as quick as he could, burped and said.

'I've got to be off anyhow. You'll have a word with Sticky for us?'

I nodded and Maggot slunk away. Once he was gone Kevin gave us an update.

'Okay, I caught up with some of Golden Boots' lads,' he said, 'they're practically a fixture at Cachet, so we know them all. They all remember Gemma and they saw her at the party on the Friday night. She walked in on Golden Boots' arm. A bit later he took her to the bedroom. A very short while later he came out and he pretty much ignored her after that. You know what he's like.'

Kevin took a sip of his pint and continued, 'She hung around for a bit. Eventually he gets one of his lads to drive her and her friend Louise home and we know she got there safely. Here's the interesting bit, I spoke to all of his friends and some of them say she wasn't at the party on the Saturday night but a couple of them reckon she was. She tried to see old Golden Boots again but he was busy.'

'Meaning he was shagging another lass?'

'Yep.'

'How did she take that?'

'Not well, apparently. She got pissed and started saying stuff about him.'

'What sort of stuff?'

'Tiny cock, shit in bed, that kind of thing.'

'So what happened?'

'Eventually she fucked off, but nobody knows when she went or who with. I've asked everyone. Most of them don't remember her at all. You know what his parties are like? Stacks of people, everyone high or pissed, dozens of strangers mixed in together in that big house of his, people coming and going all night. All we've got is a couple of folk who remember a brunette with the hump at Golden Boots. One minute she's there and the next she's gone.'

'What about his entourage? Anyone give her a lift home this time?'

'They all say no,' and he cut me off before I could question him, 'and I didn't ask them nicely. They'd have told me. Someone could have driven her though. He's got nine cars and the keys are just lying around, plus there will have been a dozen other cars on the driveway or in the grounds and taxis coming and going all evening. Who's going to remember one young girl?'

'Alright, thanks Kevin. Let's hand that over to Sharp and he can take it from there.' Kevin nodded, then he went off to the Gents. I was pleased with his efforts. This was just what I needed; a plausible explanation behind the death of the young lass that didn't involve me. She'd attended a party, she'd got the hump, maybe there'd been a row, she was drunk and vulnerable. Perhaps she tried to walk home on her own and was offered a lift by some predatory bloke, who drove her out of there while no one was looking. It was enough to take the heat off me and get the police looking in a different direction. They could untangle the rest.

'So poor little Gemma Carlton liked to do a bit of blow and shag footballers,' I said when he had gone, 'not quite the innocent little copper's daughter we thought, eh?' but Palmer didn't seem to be listening.

'A pork scratching on legs,' he said quietly, 'that's priceless, that is.'

'Finish your pint,' I told him, 'we've got work to do.'

CHAPTER 24

I had never seen the man before, but we picked him up on CCTV easy enough. It was Palmer's army-jacket guy. My blokes stopped him before he got too close to the main door of the Cauldron. Vince took their call, listened for a moment, then lowered the phone so he could speak to me.

'There's a fella downstairs says he wants to see you. The boys told him to fuck off but he said he knew you were here and he wouldn't leave till you heard what he had to say. They threatened to kick the shit out of him and he just laughed, said he didn't care what they did to him.'

'Bloody hell,' commented Kinane, 'he's either nails or he's as mad as a badger.'

'Who is he?' I asked.

'He says his name is Bell, Matt Bell,' answered Vince.

'Do you know who he is?' asked Kinane.

'Yes,' I said, finally understanding, 'he's the father of Leanne Bell, the little girl Baxter killed.'

'Jesus,' said Kinane.

'What do you want me to do?' asked Vince.

I didn't want to turn the poor bastard away, but

I was pretty sure I wouldn't want to hear what he had to say to me. In the end I said, 'They'd better bring him up.'

Two of our guys escorted Matt Bell into the room. I noticed that they stayed close to him but I had two guys from the door, plus Palmer, Kinane and Vince with me, so I didn't feel in any danger. The man before me must have been in his late forties, but you could see in his eyes that he'd been through something resembling a hell on earth. Our guys were all big, hard blokes, but he didn't seem remotely intimidated by them. I watched as he glanced at Kinane, Palmer and Vince, then finally his eyes fell on me.

'David Blake?' I nodded. 'My name is Matt Bell,' he told me, 'do you know who I am? Why I have come here to see you today?'

'I think so, yes.' He dipped his head slightly, as if to acknowledge that I hadn't bothered to lie to him. 'Take a seat,' I told him.

'I'm fine standing thanks,' he replied then, without preamble, he began. 'There's a man being held on remand in Durham jail called Henry Baxter. I understand you know him?'

I couldn't see any point in lying about that, 'I do. He has worked for me for a while.'

'Then you know what he has done to get himself in Durham nick?'

'I know what the police are telling me he's done, yes.'

'Baxter murdered my daughter, Mr Blake.' He said it with a conviction that was absolute, then his voice cracked, 'My little girl'. He cleared his throat, then he continued, 'Sorry,' he said, 'I promised myself I would say my piece and get out of here without making a bigger fool of myself than necessary, but it's hard. It was ten years ago, but I think about it every day, so it doesn't feel like ten years to me,' then he balled a fist and planted it firmly against his chest to indicate his heart, 'my grief is still fresh.'

'I understand.'

'Do you?' His tone made it clear that he seriously doubted that. 'I assume the police are telling us both the same thing, that there's no doubt Henry Baxter is the man who murdered Leanne. Baxter raped and strangled a thirteen-year-old girl, then he drove her out into the country. He dug a ditch at the edge of a field and he dumped her in it, so we couldn't find her. Two months, Mr Blake. That's how long it took for the police to discover my little girl's body. For eight weeks my wife and I clung to the slim belief that she might still be alive, somehow, that maybe she'd just run away, even though that hope was chipped away with every freezing night that passed until they found her.' My crew stayed silent while he said his piece, everyone afforded him that respect. 'All those days spent knowing our baby was most likely gone forever but, until we knew for sure, we would allow ourselves to hope that she could be alive somewhere and we might get her back one day.'

'Then the police told us they'd found her,' he paused to let that sink in, 'after two months,' then he looked at me closely before telling me, 'I had to identify her. I couldn't put my wife through that.'

'I'm very sorry,' I said, 'for what that's worth, and I know it isn't much.'

'I don't suppose you can imagine how that felt?' he asked me.

'No,' I replied truthfully, 'I can't.'

'And you don't want to?'

'No,' I agreed, 'I don't.'

He seemed relieved that I hadn't tried to bullshit him and he sighed, 'Nobody does. I can't say I blame them. They feel for you but they don't know what to say. What is there to say? We didn't get invited to too many parties after.'

'They were all there for the funeral mind,' he continued, 'I'll give them that; all the friends and relatives. The church was packed. Loads of people we didn't even know turned up that day. My wife thought that was lovely. Lots of strangers outside the church to pay their respects. I thought they were ghouls, grief-tourists intruding on our pain. I wanted to scream at them to piss off, but I knew it would upset my wife, so I stayed silent. My little girl's funeral was on the evening news. The presenter was very solemn, for about a minute, then they cut to the football results, like everything

191

was alright again. I couldn't believe anyone could actually care about the football when my Leanne was lying cold in her grave and her killer was still out there.'

I didn't say anything. I knew he wasn't done yet.

'When the funeral was over, we gradually lost touch with the friends and the neighbours. They didn't want to come round any more. The ones with kids must have felt guilty that it wasn't their little boy or girl, or maybe they thought our bad luck would rub off on them. You know the worst part? I used to lie awake at night and wish it on them instead. Isn't that awful? I used to wish that sick man had taken another little girl, anybody's, I didn't care whose, just not mine. I'd see lasses in the street about the same age as Leanne and I'd resent them because they were still walking around when she couldn't and I'd dream about another reality where it was one of my neighbour's kids whose funeral we'd all attended.'

'My wife wanted to try again, after a while, for another child I mean, but I just couldn't. I felt like we were trying to replace Leanne, betraying her somehow and I wouldn't go along with it. Eventually she wanted to tidy all of Leanne's things up, put them in boxes and "move forward" as she called it. Even the counsellor said that might be for the best, that it might stop me from living in the past. I wanted to smash his face in for saying that to me.

'It was never going to work for my wife and me

after that. She once told me, after the divorce, that every time she looked at me, my face reminded her of Leanne and it broke her heart,' and he gave me a humourless smile. 'What chance did we have, eh?'

'I can't imagine what you have been through, Mr Bell, I really can't. None of us can. But I know you came here for a reason, so what is it that you want from me?'

'Henry Baxter worked for you.'

'Yes, but obviously I never knew . . . please believe that. I would never have . . .'

'You never knew that he was a child murderer, you mean?'

'Of course not.'

He shrugged. 'How could you know? They're not like the psychos on the films, are they? Child killers look quite ordinary. Otherwise we'd see them coming and warn our children to stay away from them, but we certainly didn't see him coming. He lived a few streets away but we didn't know what a monster he was. The police didn't even bother to interview him at the time. I'd lie awake at night knowing he was out there somewhere, whoever he was, getting on with his life, unpunished, enjoying himself, perhaps even planning to do it again.'

I could have told him that Baxter served prison time for fraud since then but I didn't think he'd view that as any form of justice, so I kept silent.

'Baxter is no friend of mine, you can be assured of that.'

'But he has hired a new legal team,' he told me, 'expensive ones, the best. The police were surprised he was able to do that. They thought you might have had something to do with it.'

'I don't know why they would think that. He's not been with me that long.'

'Can you look me in the eye and tell me you are not the one paying for the fancy lawyers, Mr Blake? Can you do that?'

'I don't wish to offend you, Mr Bell. You've been through a great deal and every man in this room feels for you, but I don't have to look you in the eye and say anything.'

'No,' he admitted, 'I suppose you don't. I would like to ask you for something though . . . I know you don't have to do anything you don't want to but . . .'

'I'll help if I can.'

'Don't protect Henry Baxter. He killed my daughter. The police know it, the CPS know it, I know it and you know it too. The DNA evidence proves it and I want justice for my darling girl. She was thirteen years old when Baxter murdered her, she'd have been twenty-three now, married maybe, perhaps with a kid of her own. I might have been a grandfather. I understand you are a father too, Mr Blake. The police told me you have a daughter, so now I am appealing to you, as one father to another, not to help Henry Baxter. Please, I'm begging you in fact.'

I knew that every eye in the room was on me. I could feel Kinane staring at me intently and Matt Bell's gaze didn't leave mine for a moment.

'Family money,' I told him, 'that's how he can afford his fancy lawyer, Mr Bell. Henry Baxter will get no help from me,' I assured him and felt one step closer to hell when that poor man's shoulders slumped in relief and he thanked me.

CHAPTER 25

I don't think I had ever needed a drink as much as that night. We started in the Bigg Market and worked our way down towards the Quayside, stopping in all of the old pubs I used to drink in when I was younger. I didn't want to think, I just wanted to drink and talk about anything other than the man who had just called to see me. Palmer must have sensed that so he stayed off the topic.

'What was it like growing up around here?' he asked, while we sank a couple in the Duke of Northumberland. 'It must have been hard if your ma was on her own?'

'It was, I suppose. My mum never really had much. Not material stuff. She didn't want for anything later in her life though. I made sure of that.'

'Must have been good for her to have you around,' he said.

'She could be a difficult woman to help. She wouldn't let me give her money and if I bought her stuff I could tell she didn't like it if it wasn't Christmas or her birthday.'

'Then one day I had a great idea. Mum was looking tired. So I hired a cleaner to help her round the house. I thought she'd be chuffed. She didn't say much about it at first but I assumed she needed time to get used to it and she'd come round in the end, once she felt the benefit of all the hours she saved. Instead the cleaner called me up after a few weeks and told me there was no point going round anymore as the place was always spotless.

'I went straight round to my ma's to have a go at her. "What's the point in me paying someone to clean your house if you just carry on doing it yourself?" I asked her.

'My mum looked a little flustered, but she shouted back at me, "well I don't want her thinking I live in a pig sty, do I?"'

Palmer chuckled. 'How did a woman like that end up working for Bobby Mahoney?'

'Well, it's not as bad as it sounds,' I said, 'she never actually killed anyone. Bobby just used her on the door of the really rough clubs and she'd do the occasional armed robbery.'

He laughed at that image. 'You know what I mean.'

'I do, yes,' and it was something I'd thought about over the years and never really got to the bottom of, 'my mother always struggled to get by, she always had more than one job on the go because, even when my dad was around, he couldn't hold one down. She lost count of how many places he worked. Somehow she must have met Bobby or someone who worked for him and got a job behind the bar in one of his boozers. I think steadily, over the years, she did more and more work for him and less for other people so, by the time I can remember, she was full time at his places. I think he liked her, they all did apparently, she had something about her, didn't take any shit from any of them. It made them respect her. It kept them on their toes.'

'So is that how you got into this then?' he asked me, 'because of your mum?'

'God no, she'd have freaked if she thought I'd end up like them. I mean she knew I worked for Bobby but I always gave it a bit of spin. She was the main reason I used to have those business cards with 'Sales & Marketing Director – Gallowgate Leisure Group' written on them. It gave me a veneer of respectability.'

'Do you think she fell for that?'

'Not deep down, but I think it helped her deal with it and she knew I wasn't muscle, so maybe she thought I wouldn't be in harm's way. If that makes her sound naive then so was I. I used to believe it too, remember?'

'I remember.'

'I didn't sign up for Bobby when I was a bairn. They would tolerate me in the bar between opening hours, if she was tidying or helping the manager clean the lines. She knew the cellar work better than the men. So I'd sit there at one of the tables when the pub was closed in the afternoon, drawing or playing with soldiers, until she was done. Bobby and the crew understood she had to keep me with her. There was no one else. He didn't seem to mind. He was a big, scary bloke, particularly for a nipper like me, but if he saw me sitting there he'd come over and give me a stern look and say "Your mother's working, so make sure you sit there quiet like and divvent work yersell.""

'What's that mean?'

'Basically, behave. So I'd nod my head and he'd just go, "good lad; help yourself to a bag of crisps, just the one, mind," and I'd get to go behind the bar and get my crisps. When I think now of all the stuff I've seen and done, good and bad, since that time, I still look back and think that was the ultimate. I mean I was getting free crisps from the man himself right, from behind Bobby Mahoney's bar and he was letting me. It didn't get better than that.'

'So how did you start working for him?'

'It was a few years later and it started when I saw something I shouldn't. He used to have this old snooker hall, it's not there anymore. It was cheap and anyone could play down there. I was in with a friend once, messing about. We were so small we virtually had to stand on a box so we could reach the tables and we could hardly pot a ball, but we were learning and thought we were cool and grown up, you know. Anyway, one day we were playing on a table that a flash twat called Harry Cassidy liked to use, so he kicked us off. He was a local hard knock who didn't work for Bobby and he didn't ask us nicely. My mate was daft enough to complain that we'd paid for the table so Cassidy cuffed him one and he went off crying. The old man who ran the place made himself scarce because he was frightened of Cassidy. For some reason I stayed. There was this massive open cupboard set back in the far wall where they stored all of the old kit that was falling apart; cues, triangles, bits of broken cushion, so I just climbed up there and sat it out until they were done, so I could get back on the table later, all the while looking daggers at Cassidy. I wanted to be the next Hurricane Higgins and Harry Cassidy wasn't going to stop me. Anyhow the place emptied because of Cassidy, so he was there with his mate, who was a sort of poor man's enforcer.

'Next thing, two blokes walk in. I knew from being with me ma that they were members of Bobby's firm. Jerry Lemon and Jinky Smith. Both tough guys, but Jerry was a fucking psycho. Not a big bloke, but he had that menace, you know.

'Now Harry Cassidy is a villain but he's not daft, he knows who these guys are, so he's immediately wondering if they are after him but they just nod and grunt their hellos and start setting up on the table next to him to play a frame, so he relaxes and so does his minder. They must have been playing fifteen minutes or so, Cassidy and his minder on one table, Jerry Lemon and Jinky on the next one and, even at my age, I must have only been eight or nine, I had an instinct that it was about to kick off. I don't think Cassidy did, which is one of the reasons you've never heard of him.

'Jerry Lemon is bent over his shot and I can hear him even from my little cubby hole in the far wall. He's chuntering on to Jinky, "Eeh you've left us nowt man, you spawny bastard," that sort of thing. He goes down on the shot then he comes back up again, takes another look, shakes his head, goes down again, comes back up. While this is happening, Cassidy's minder bends down on a shot and Jerry suddenly flips his cue around and brings the thick end down hard on the back of the bloke's head. He goes down like someone just pulled the plug on him, out like a light. I'd never seen anything like it before. I'd witnessed a few fights in the school playground, obviously, but not violence like that. It was shocking but somehow exciting too. Before the bloke has even slumped to the floor, Jerry is after Cassidy shouting "Come here you!" and Cassidy tries to leg it but he can't, because Jerry is coming for him one way and Jinky from the other side of the table. He's trapped then, down on the floor on the blind side of the table, where I can't see him anymore, but Jerry and Jinky gave him a good kicking while Jerry explained the reasons for his beating. I didn't hear

201

it all but I do distinctly remember the words "Bobby" and "Mahoney" being mentioned as the kicks went in on this helpless bloke. He looked in a right mess when they finished and do you know what I was thinking all the while they were doing it?'

'What?'

'Good,' I admitted, 'you hit my mate, you fucking deserved that. I think I even had this confused thing going on in my young mind where I actually thought they were giving him a kicking because he'd hit my pal, like Bobby was a good guy beating up a villain for hurting a kid, as if he was Batman or something, only he sent his men to do it instead.'

'Anyhow, when the beating was over, Jerry turned round and finally spotted me sitting at the back of this dark cupboard, watching it all.'

'Oh dear.'

'Oh dear, is right. I was the only witness and I was terrified. "What you doing there?" he starts shouting at me but thank god Jinky was with him because he said, "That's Tina Blake's kid, isn't it?" and that took the wind out of Jerry's sails, because me ma was family and he knew Bobby liked her. They made me climb down out of the cupboard and Jinky took me away from Jerry and explained how Cassidy was a very bad man who was going to do some really bad things and hurt people, so they had to hurt him first to stop him. I lapped that up because it went along with my

Bobby-Mahoney-as-masked-vigilante theory. Next thing, Jinky has taken a pound note out of his pocket and given it to me. A quid note was a lot back then. He tells me that's for being brave and a reward for never saying anything to anyone about this, then he gives me a message and tells me to run to the club and give it to Bobby. He tells me "If you dae it right, Bobby will give you another pund." So I run off to deliver the message. I can't remember the words but it was something vague like, "the problem's over". I see Bobby and tell him. He smiles at me, ruffles my hair, says I'm a good lad and, true to Jinky's word, gives me another quid. It was a grand day's work.'

'I can see how that might have started something,' Palmer admitted.

'They knew they could trust me after that. I started running errands, simple stuff, messages for other members of the crew. At first I didn't understand the messages I was given but, as I got older, I worked them out. It didn't matter. I was practically family and I wasn't going to tell the police anything, was I?

'Bobby kept telling me to "stick-in" at school, so I could go off and do something with my life. When I came back in the holidays he gave me bar work, which I was glad of. It was only when I finally left college and wanted to come back to the north-east that I seriously considered working for him. Times were changing and I knew he could use someone with half an ounce of brain; he was being advised by the likes of Jerry Lemon and Finney and they weren't the brightest. Bobby was sharp as a razor, but he needed someone he could trust to hear him out and give him that second opinion.'

Back then, I knew I could earn more with Bobby than by joining some pseudo, blue-chip outfit straight from the milk round, then slogging it up the corporate ladder for years, before I started making any real money. Plus, I could stay in the north-east and there weren't many jobs going for bright young things here when I came out of my degree course. It's ironic when I think about it now but he was against it and I had to persuade him it was the right move. I often wonder what would have happened to me if he'd just told me to fuck off.'

'There's not a lot of point in dwelling on the "what-ifs",' Palmer advised me, 'we've all got regrets but you can only play the cards you're dealt.'

'True enough,' I agreed. I didn't want Palmer to think I'd come over all weak and sentimental so I snapped myself out of it and said, 'So, are we having a proper drink tonight or what?'

I got monumentally drunk that night. It was the only way I could deal with what I'd been forced to do to Matt Bell. I was going to help his little girl's murderer to evade justice and, if I didn't, I was finished. There was no way I could survive without that five million. Everyone in my crew thought less of me because of it, none of them understood how I could keep an oath sworn to a child killer, but this wasn't some stupid pact that involved my name or honour. Emma was the most precious thing in my world and I had sworn on her life that I wouldn't harm a hair on Baxter's head. There was no way round that, because I wasn't going to risk anything where my daughter was concerned, not even the slim chance that the words of my broken oath might come back to haunt me years from now, that I might somehow be responsible for some unspeci-fied piece of bad luck that I would never forgive myself for. I knew that, if anything happened to my little Emma, my life was as good as over. Without her I'd be a basket case; worse than Matt Bell.

Palmer drank more sparingly than me, so he could stay alert. I drank like prohibition was going to start all over again the next morning. Palmer didn't give me a hard time about Leanne's father. He knew the dilemma I was facing, although I don't think he could even begin to understand it, but then he wasn't a father. I don't remember much of that night but I do recall Palmer helping me to fall into a car driven by one of our lads, because my legs had gone completely. He must have got me home okay, because I woke the next morning in our spare bed, the sunlight burning my brain, which I'd already fried the night before. I woke with a start, just managed to get to the bathroom in time and puked down the toilet.

CHAPTER 26

A couple of days after we told Sharp that Gemma Carlton had slept with Golden Boots and most probably attended his party the next night, when she was killed, the police raided the footballer's house. Dozens of detectives and plain clothes officers descended on the place mob-handed early in the morning and dragged him groggily from his bed. They shoved the warrant in his face and made him sit on one of his big leather sofas while they went through the place, turning it upside down in the process.

'I aint done nothin,' was all Golden Boots could offer as they bagged up everything around him, including small amounts of class A drugs that the Premiership's finest had been too stupid or lazy to find and dispose of when I warned him the police would be coming to see him.

'That ain't mine,' he protested. Then he added, 'I just shagged her. That's not a crime,' but it got him daggers from the two WPCs who were babysitting him.

'This is a waste of my fucking time,' he moaned, when the search had been going on for ten minutes, 'and yours. Where are you going with that?' as they marched past him carrying his personal computer, then informed him all of his cars had been impounded.

Golden Boots started to get angry then, 'Not my wheels! What am I supposed to do without them?'

'Get a bus,' one of the unimpressed WPCs advised him.

'I want to see a lawyer,' he hissed at her through bared teeth, 'now.'

'Could you come this way please?' asked a Detective Inspector politely and Golden Boots just blinked back at him, then finally rose to his feet and followed the detective upstairs and into one of the guest bedrooms. Four other plain-clothes officers were standing there and there was a box on the bed. It was nothing fancy by Golden Boots' standards, just a plain storage box from a wardrobe.

'Is this yours?' asked the Detective Inspector.

'Well it's in my house so, duh,' answered an increasingly irate footballer.

'So it is yours?' the detective persisted.

'Yes.'

'What's it used for?'

'For putting things in,' he said, as if it was obvious.

'What kind of things?'

Golden Boots shrugged, 'Trainers, bits of kit, old DVDs, I don't know. I don't clean up after myself. I have people who do that.'

'So there's nothing in here that you want to tell me about before you take a look?'

'No.'

The Detective Inspector used a gloved hand to raise the lid of the box and Golden Boots leaned forward to peer in. Inside was a purse and a mobile phone.

'I've looked inside the purse. It's Gemma Carlton's and I'd be willing to bet the phone is hers too. So would you mind explaining to me how they ended up in a box, which was covered by a blanket and tucked away in a wardrobe in one of your bedrooms, eh?'

Golden Boots went loopy then.

'You put that there! I didn't put that there! You bastards! You're fitting me up!' Two burly detectives took an arm each and restrained him.

'Do me a favour,' answered the detective, 'you think that two dozen of us got together and decided to plant evidence on you. This isn't 1974 and we don't fit people up. We just want to put the right man inside for Gemma's sake and right now that is looking like you.'

'Fuck you!' screamed Golden Boots, as he struggled against the grip on his arms, but nobody was listening to him anymore.

The little lad was only eleven years old but young Tam already had the street smarts. He'd seen the men walk into the lock-up; five of them had gone in but only four came out. That would normally have been enough to alert the boy to keep his nose out of it and at no point would it have occurred to him to phone the 'Five-O', as the 'Polis' were commonly known on his Edinburgh estate. They could get to fuck. Round here, if a guy goes into a garage and doesn't come out again he either deserved it, because he was a grass or got too greedy, or he was plain unlucky, because he came up against someone stronger. You never got a square go round here and everyone knew it.

But the guy who didn't come out turned out to be a bit special. A few days later, Tam learned that one of Jimmy Law's lads had gone missing and they were supposed to be untouchable, because Jimmy Law ran this patch and everybody knew who he worked for, a fucking Glasgow headcase by the name of Fallon. Tam figured that Jimmy might like to know where his man was and most likely would pay for the news. Young Tam asked around about Jimmy Law and was told he was in the hospital, but Fallon was in town, so he went to Fallon.

Five minutes later, Tam was standing next to the legendary Fallon, flanked by half a dozen members of the big man's crew, staring at a row of dilapidated garages.

'Which one,' asked Fallon and Tam pointed to

the middle one of a block of three. Fallon jerked his head and two huge men prised the lock off and swung the garage doors wide.

'Keep him here.' Fallon ordered, pointing at Tam.

Fallon walked into the lock-up. There was no car, just a jumble of old furniture; some locked, heavy filing cabinets McGlenn used to store some stash away from his flat, in case the Polis ever felt like dropping by unannounced and an old sofa with a table in front of it and two chairs, one on each side, so if McGlenn ever felt the need to conduct some discreet business, away from prying eyes, he could do it in relative comfort. McGlenn was sitting there now in fact, staring serenely out at Fallon who blinked back at him in the darkness. Once his eyes adjusted to the gloom, Fallon could make out the gaping wound across McGlenn's throat and the blood that had poured from it, all down the man's shirt, soaking his trousers and the old couch. Excited flies were spinning around McGlenn's body in tight little circles.

Fallon walked back out of the lock-up.

'Close it up,' he told his men, 'and see to him.' He nodded at the young lad. One of his men peeled off a generous number of notes and little Tam ran off home with the fruits of a grand day's labour in his pocket.

Fallon's men were all looking at him now, waiting

211

for the word, but first he lit a cigarette and took a long drag on it so he could get the sickly smell of blood out of his nostrils then he said, 'Some cunt's gonna burn for this.'

CHAPTER 27

Fallon got the next train from Edinburgh down to Newcastle. It's a beautiful coastal route but he didn't spend any time looking out at the North Sea. He met me in a private room at our hotel on the Quayside where he briefed me about McGlenn. I asked him if he had managed to work out who was behind this outrage.

'Serbians,' he announced with bemusement, like he might just as well have been saying Martians, 'fucking Serbs, over here, on our patch. What the fuck?' The last part was a rhetorical question.

'I don't get it,' I told him, 'we pay Amrein to avoid this kind of shit. Why aren't the local plod all over these Serbs?'

'That's exactly what I have been trying to find out. There's a lot of them, fair dues, but they are led by three brothers who've set themselves up openly in a big old house in Pilton. The fucking cheeky, big, brass balls on these guys.'

'So they're protected?'

'How else can they be doing this?' he asked.

'But who's covering for them?'

'I was hoping you'd be able to tell me.'

'I'll set up a meet with Amrein,' I assured him.

'Good,' he told me, 'because I want to know who I've got to kill to end this.'

'Do these Serb brothers have a name?'

'Stevic,' he told me.

When Golden Boots was taken in for questioning he stuck to the story he'd given Joe Kinane and it wasn't his lengthy interview with the police that finally provided the breakthrough they were looking for. He was released on police bail while forensic tests were carried out.

When the tests came back, the most damning results came from the boot of one of his nine cars; his Aston Martin Vanquish. Fibres taken from the boot of that car proved that Gemma Carlton had been inside it. This must have been the vehicle someone used to take that poor girl down to the woods and dump her there.

Gemma had slept with Golden Boots the night before she died then trashed him twenty-four hours later when he hadn't bothered to spare her the time of day. According to Kevin, several witnesses were sure they'd seen her at his house that night but he denied seeing her at all. Her purse and mobile phone had been found at his house, hidden in a wardrobe, and his car had been used to dump the body. There were also long passages of time where neither he nor his entourage could convincingly account for his whereabouts. He claimed he was in bed with another girl but she either didn't exist or was reluctant to come forward. It didn't help that he hadn't a clue what her name was, so the police couldn't trace her. Golden Boots was charged with Gemma Carlton's murder. The Press loved it.

The evidence linking Golden Boots to Gemma Carlton's death just kept on coming. A lot of the credit for that had to go to Sharp and Kevin Kinane who worked well together, tirelessly going over every lead, tracking down witnesses and questioning them. There were civilians, as we call them, who responded best to the softly-softly approach of the local plod and Sharp went to see them. Then there were the local villains who felt they had to keep their mouths zipped when the police were involved, so it was sensible to send Kevin in to speak to them. They soon thought twice about their vows of silence when Big Kev had a word. These two got the right result; an end to police suspicions that her death was all down to me. According to Sharp, even Carlton came around to the view that Golden Boots must have done it when he was presented with the evidence.

It certainly seemed that Golden Boots had a case to answer, but there was something about this that was really nagging at me. Perhaps I had just seen far too many of those old American private-eye shows when I was a nipper, but the one thing Golden Boots seemed to lack was a motive, or at least a strong one. He'd shagged Gemma Carlton, so she hadn't resisted his advances and, like every girl he ever met, he'd quickly grown bored of her, then dumped her. She hadn't taken too kindly to that but, well, so what? Golden Boots didn't care. He was already onto the next bird. The prosecution was going to try and say he had flown into a jealous rage because she was seen on the arm of another man the next night, or he had taken badly to her implying he had a cock like a marshmallow and the sexual sophistication of a baboon. Again I didn't think he would give a fuck about any of that and it certainly wouldn't put off other gullible young lasses. The CPS might try to claim that during a row in the privacy of his bedroom, he had become so incensed that he lost all control and strangled her but, afterwards, retained the presence of mind to hide all of her stuff and get rid of the body, or persuade someone he trusted to do it for him. A jury might buy that, particularly when the theory was linked to all of the physical evidence, like her handbag and phone being in his house, but I just couldn't see it. They would say he was a spoilt brat, used to getting anything he wanted, that he didn't know when to stop. He was all of that, and more, but why would a lass like Gemma Carlton get under his skin?

Then again, what did I really know about Golden Boots anyway? Maybe he did do it, perhaps he really was that stupid and, frankly, it didn't matter that much now that the police had finally stopped thinking her death was down to me. I even got a 'thank you' from Detective Superintendent Austin.

I met Amrein in Durham city, eighteen miles and a world away from Newcastle. At least it would have felt that way if Henry Baxter hadn't been on remand in Durham nick awaiting his trial. It was a beautiful sunny day, attracting the usual groups of elderly bus-trip tourists and student lovers to the Cathedral square at the top of the hill. We walked through it, then took the steep path down to the river, cloaked by the overhanging trees, where it would be harder for anyone to listen in. Palmer tailed us at a discreet distance, with Amrein's bodyguard walking next to him. Things had calmed down with Amrein since the low point, when I left the severed head of a Glasgow gangster on the windowsill of his summer house, to warn him against ever trying to come up against me again. Neither he nor I ever forgot that at any point in our business relationship it might suit either one of us to have the other killed.

Amrein was a wiry little man in wire framed glasses who looked like a college professor – not the representative of one of the most lethal organisations on the planet. I'd given him a name and now I expected information.

'You want the history lesson?' he asked me.

'Yes.'

'Those Serbian brothers have been around for

a long time. Their names are Dusan, Sreten and Marko Stevic. They started out in one of the hooligan gangs associated with a football team; Red Star in Belgrade. Little more than thugs, with a sideline in drug dealing; very minor but it drew them to the attention of the nationalists and they were recruited into one of the paramilitary units that sprang up during the Bosnian war; extreme right, ultra nationalist, largely uncontrollable. Their unit was linked to atrocities but the numbers involved weren't large, so they were never pursued. It took the authorities years to bring charges against the big guys like Arkan and Milosevic. They gave up trying to catch everyone who'd slaughtered civilians. It was a very messy conflict.'

'And when the war was over they turned to organised crime.'

'What do men of violence always do when the cause they are supposedly fighting for is gone? They fight for money and power instead. The brothers weren't part of a clan but if one of them wished to assassinate its rivals, without leaving a trail back to them, they would hire the Stevic brothers to do it. They worked for the Zemun and Surcin clans plus the Vozdovac, prospering precisely because they had no clear affiliation to any of them.'

'They did other people's dirty work?'

'Yes,' he said, 'and thrived on it.' He stopped speaking until a woman with a baby in a pushchair coming the other way walked past us. When she had gone he continued, 'Then everything changed. Ten years ago, the Serbian mafia assassinated the Prime Minister, Zoran Dindic, and the state finally clamped down on everyone. Operation Sablja resulted in ten thousand arrests, including the country's own Deputy State Prosecutor. The leaders of the main clans were given long sentences, or were killed by police, or they murdered each other. The Serbian mafia has not been destroyed however. New leaders emerged and the Stevic brothers' influence grew.'

'What are they doing over here?'

Amrein hesitated as if he was trying to find the right words. 'They target places for expansion.'

'What's their criteria?'

Amrein took a long time to answer, 'They expand where they see weakness, either from the authorities or . . .'

'Men like me?' I prompted.

'That would be their appraisal, not mine,' he said, 'but Serbian criminals are noted for the brutality of their methods. It is a legacy of the ethnic cleansing from the war, where torture and mutilation of captured soldiers or civilians was so commonplace as to be no longer noteworthy. Understandably, these methods deter business rivals. Fear is a powerful weapon,' he reminded me.

Amrein was right. We both knew the power of fear. Was I scared of these Serbian brothers; the war criminals who would enjoy cutting me into pieces if they got the opportunity? Who wouldn't be?

'How are they getting away with this?'

'It seems they are listed as high-level criminal sources.'

It was one of the oldest tricks in the book, but still one of the most effective and so hard to disprove. If I was a bent copper, being paid to turn a blind eye, I would do exactly the same thing. I'd list the criminal paying me as my grass. Whatever they were involved in, I'd argue, it was far less important than the information they provided. It's often forgotten that a great deal of police intelligence on crooks is provided by other crooks, for a whole variety of reasons. Some are paid and some are looking to get their own crimes overlooked or sentences reduced by cooperating with the authorities. Others just do it to get their own back on former associates or to eliminate the competition. I've said it before and I'll say it again; there is no code.

'So who's protecting them?'

'It goes high. We think an Assistant Chief Constable.'

'Bloody hell. That would explain it. Are you sure?'

'Our people heard they've got something on him. They are most likely paying him as well.'

'The classic combination of bribery and blackmail,' I conceded, 'which ACC is it?'

'Brinklow.'

'What can we do about this?'

'It will be difficult,' he told me, 'with his support

they are untouchable by anyone from inside Lothian and Borders Police and there's a lot of politics. They don't like outside interference.'

'What about SOCA?'

'Won't be interested, unless we can provide conclusive proof Brinklow is on the take.'

'And you don't have that proof?'

'Not yet.'

'Amrein, we pay you a lot of money to fix things like this.'

'I feel sure we can come up with it,' he told me, 'in time. Leave the Serbian brothers to us,' he urged me.

We'd reached the stone footbridge over the River Wear. 'There is one other thing,' he told me, when we crossed to the other side, 'and I suspect you will not like to hear it.'

At this point it was hard to imagine how my day could get any worse, but it did. 'Yaroslav Vasnetsov insists upon a meeting.'

CHAPTER 28

Have you ever wondered what it must be like to have money? I mean real money, not just a few thousand dropped on you by a long-lost uncle you never knew, who dies and leaves it all in his will. If you've ever wondered what it must feel like to have fifty grand tucked away, a hundred maybe or, if you actually have the imagination, to ponder what you'd do with a million quid, then you know just how much it can change your life. No mortgage, a big house, all bought and paid for, the flash car most people only get to see in their rear-view mirror, before it flashes past them in the fast lane. If you want enough to buy anything you could ever want, including high-end, three-grand-a-night hookers, plus mountains of coke and vats full of Cristal, then you're probably already thinking you might need at least a couple of mil, more maybe.

Me, I reckon it would take about four million just to put you in a position where you can actually tell the boss to go fuck himself and his crummy job, to set yourself up so you never need to earn another penny, to be in a position where you can look after yourself and your whole family for the rest of your days.

Now imagine that, instead of four million, you had a hundred or two hundred times that? Serious money. That's your own Lear jet, taking you off to your personal Caribbean island with wall-to-wall Playboy bunnies flown in, until you get bored with them all and send out for more. Let's say you have two hundred and fifty times that four million and now you are a billionaire? You're financing art galleries, museums, Hollywood movies, presidential campaigns.

Now imagine you have twenty times that amount. Twenty billion dollars. What does that make you? It makes you Yaroslav Vasnetsov.

His front lawn was the size of a cricket pitch and the driveway leading up to it from the main gate was so long we were chauffeured down it. The house was enormous; one of those neo-gothic piles with gargoyles that peer down at you from the buttresses. It looked like it had been purchased from the estate of Aleister Crowley; a Hammer House of Horror film-set in the heart of leafy Surrey.

We went through a marbled hallway and I was conscious of how many people were busily going about their business. This wasn't just the man's home, it was the hub of the Vasnetsov empire.

Yaroslav Vasnetsov was not born to wealth, but

into a dirt-poor Georgian family who could barely afford to feed him, or the rest of his siblings. When he was still young, his father moved them all from Georgia to St Petersburg, craving the opportunity a big city could provide. Vasnetsov's first foray into private enterprise was selling toys from a market stall but now, at just forty-five, he had amassed one of the biggest fortunes in the world, estimated at between fifteen and twenty billion dollars, depending on which newspaper's estimate you believed. To fathom how he was able to do this is to understand Russia at the end of the Cold War. When Boris Yeltsin came to power he swept away the Communist old order and plunged his nation into an era of unrivalled corruption. If you bankrolled politicians you got the opportunity to plunder the state's wealth by buying up enormous companies for fractions of their true value. Vasnetsov already understood how to make money by buying political influence and paying off local crime lords, so he merely took this know-how to the next level. His investments were shrewd and the state-owned oil companies and aluminium plants were privatised, modernised and soon began to deliver the billions he now enjoyed.

Of course, the population weren't too happy about a handful of individuals creaming off the nation's wealth and it is said that when President Putin first came to power he made a deal with these oligarchs. Stay out of politics, unless you are on my side, and keep your wealth, or face the consequences. Men like Abramovich toed the line, bought yachts and football clubs and lived happily ever after. Others like Berezovsky and Khodorkovsky didn't and were soon exiled or imprisoned. Perhaps the most outspoken oligarch of them all however, was Yaroslav Vasnetsov, earning him the label of Russia's public enemy number one, but not before he managed to flee the country, taking most of his fortune with him. He set up home in England and soon bought his way into British society, donating entire collections to art galleries, a number of Oxbridge bursaries and even a hospital wing. I mean, how could we deport the man after all that? Vasnetsov's presence in this country has affronted Russia to such an extent that he is now almost personally responsible for a freezing of relationships between the two countries to a near cold-war level. What has all this got to do with me? I had no idea, but assumed I was about to find out.

'Before your meeting with Mr Vasnetsov, there are some documents he would like you to familiarise yourself with.'

The young man in the sharp suit took us into the library and motioned towards a large table with papers laid out on it. Palmer walked over to them while I awaited an explanation. 'I will leave you to examine the information we've provided before Mr Vasnetsov joins you,' was all I got.

Palmer was already looking at the material. I couldn't see what it was, but I could tell from the look on his face that he was taking it seriously.

'What is it?' I asked and when he didn't immediately answer me I walked over and joined him. On the table were a series of folders containing papers but I ignored them and instead scrutinised the dozen ten-by-eight black and white surveillance photos thoughtfully arranged in a line for us to view. They were of an extremely high quality, considering they had been taken without any of us knowing. There was a very clear one of me with the Turk, sitting opposite each other in one of his cafes that we used as a discreet meeting place. The next one showed us leaving the building with Palmer and one of the Turk's bodyguards following behind. The cars we used had been photographed too, but then there was more damning material, including shots of the lorries we used to transport the heroin.

I turned the page and found notes from a surveillance report, listing the makes and registration numbers of some of those trucks and the route they took into the Balkans and beyond. Some were tracked heading west to Amsterdam, where their contents would be off-loaded into freight containers. These were loaded onto ships that crossed the North Sea and were off-loaded at Hull. Others went east, into Russia via a little Ukrainian border post east of Kharkov; a territory Remzi had been ruthlessly fighting his way into for more than a decade.

The next series of photographs included nice close-ups of people who helped us get our drugs out of Turkey and across Europe. Some of our key men were photographed near the lorries and the tankers we used and in incriminating shots with officials we bribed to turn a blind eye. I was in enough of the photos to prove that I had a lot of very dodgy friends indeed. This alone would have been pretty damning, but there was more. I was used to dealing with Amrein's organisation, so I knew how this kind of operation could work but even I was astonished at the level of detail Vasnetsov had amassed on our drug line. He had managed to chart almost every inch of it, presumably by mounting an enormous and highly-sophisticated surveillance operation, the type that the CIA would struggle to fund, on each and every one of us. He had details of our consignments; dates, times, places and estimated yields. I'd say he had us down to almost the last kilo. Palmer and I read this material for a good fifteen minutes and, by the end of it, I realised I was looking at serious prison time. There was enough evidence here to get me a sentence in excess of twenty years in Britain, if this file ever fell into the wrong hands. I was suddenly glad it was Vasnetsov holding it and not the Crown Prosecution Service, but I was worried too, because there could be only one reason for a man like Vasnetsov to invest his time, energy and considerable resources into an operation as thorough as this one. He wanted something from me and that something was going to be big.

'This surveillance . . .' Palmer was shaking his head, 'I don't know how we didn't spot it . . . unless they used an army of bloody good people, but if they did that, the cost would be . . .'

'I don't think you're getting it,' I told him. 'If this surveillance cost him a couple of million dollars he wouldn't notice. He could spend one hundred million dollars on the operation, employ dozens of former agents of the FSB, CIA, Mossad and MI5, and it still wouldn't even put a dent in his fortune. His resources are pretty much inexhaustible and he doesn't have to account for any of it to a government select committee or the US Congress. There are no rules he has to follow. He's unaccountable, beholden to no one, except himself. He does what he likes. Do you get it now?'

We both turned when the door opened. The man who walked into the room was instantly familiar. The phalanx of bodyguards were straight out of central casting, an oligarch's idea of what a minder should look like; absurdly tall, barrel-chested men with shaved heads that proclaimed them as ex-military or FSB, happy to take vast inflations of their state pay to keep the man at their centre breathing.

I recognised two other men from my briefing

with Amrein. Evgeny Gorshkov was Vasnetsov's head of security, a personal bodyguard and rat-catcher who smoked out plots against his boss and dealt with the perpetrators ruthlessly. He was a big man in his forties. The other man I recognised from the photographs Amrein had showed me was Mikhail Datsik, Vasnetsov's personal banker, who shuffled money around the globe at the behest of his boss. Datsik was a small, tubby man of mixed ancestry and dual citizenship, his American mother having married a Russian émigré. It was said that Datsik had managed to double Vasnetsov's vast fortune in just ten years.

Vasnetsov wore a simple, plain white tailored shirt that probably cost more than a working man takes home in a month, black trousers and patent leather shoes that had most likely been custom made in Milan. He wasn't a particularly big man, just average looking; average height, average build, but there was nothing average about his life. He eyed me like I was something trivial that was in his way, and snapped something in Russian to an aide who immediately dipped his head and left the room. He seemed irritated that he had been forced to emerge from the shadows to talk to me.

'You know who I am.'

It wasn't a question.

'Of course.'

'Then you will take what I have to say seriously.'

'Obviously.' The man could buy and sell me,

Amrein and everybody else we'd ever met, in an afternoon. Compared to him we were yachts bobbing on the ocean and he was the QE2.

'Good. Because, if you listen, you will make much money and if you do not . . .' he clicked his fingers, 'all gone.'

He walked up to our table but ignored the surveillance report. Perhaps he felt that it spoke for itself. He put a newspaper down in front of me and tapped it with a finger. 'I am close to a breakthrough and must leave tonight,' then he became quite animated, 'you have heard of my latest business venture?'

'African oil,' there had been a feature on it in the newspaper he was holding and a small piece on the TV news.

He nodded. 'There are five billion barrels of crude oil waiting underground in a small East-African country that will be transformed by my wells.'

'You know this for sure?'

'I have hired many experts; surveyors, geologists, oil company men, it is they that tell me this.'

'The trouble with paying big money for experts is that they often feel obliged to tell you what you want to hear.'

'In Uganda they are already taking one hundred and fifty thousand barrels a day out of the Rift Valley. That's real oil. My wells will be bigger, there will be more of them and I am building the refinery there myself. I will control everything.'

'You think their government will just let you do this?'

'It is taken care of. I have made many rich men already and they will continue to profit by my presence in their country. In one month we start to drill, then the oil and the money will flow.' I had no idea why he was bothering to tell me all of this until he added, 'with this oil I will have five, maybe ten billion dollars a year to put aside to spend on my passion. Do you know what my passion is, Mr Blake?'

'Human Rights?'

He looked irritated for a moment then he brushed my comment aside. 'My country, my homeland, a place to which I can never return. Cowboys and crooks run everything there now. This so-called government everyone deals with, the one even the official EU reports say is no more than a gangster state . . .' and he shook his head in seeming amazement, 'a gangster state? Can you imagine?'

I could, easily.

'When the communists ran everything, when you had to pretend to be on their side, when even a man like me was forced to join the fucking communist party so I could do business of any kind, then it was bad, but now? There is no hope for anyone. The President, the Prime Minister, the FSB, the so-called Red Mafia, they are all just part of the same corruption. The shit has piled so high now you can smell it all the way across the world. I want to bring it all crashing down so there is nothing left. Then we can rebuild it and start again. What we need, Blake, is a new revolution.'

I could hardly believe what I was hearing. The guy might have been worth billions, but he was just one man, and here he was talking about bringing down the government of one of the biggest countries on the planet. It couldn't be done. I was starting to wonder what madness had been festering away all of these years while he was exiled in London, surrounded by flunkies. What did it do to a man if he never heard the word *no*?

'Khodorkovsky already tried that.'

'Khodorkovsky was an idiot. He tried to change Russia from within, by founding schools on political thought and funding opposition parties. He thought he could stay out in the open and give Putin the finger, that he was too rich and famous for the FSB to come after him. Look at him now.'

The FSB is the Russian Federal Security Service, successor to the notorious KGB, which is directly controlled by the President. Less than a decade ago, Mikhail Khodorkovsky had been the richest man in Russia, now he was serving fourteen years in prison for tax evasion and fraud and all because he wouldn't keep quiet and toe the line. Khodorkovsky's trial and conviction has been condemned all over the world as political and rigged but still he rots in jail.

I didn't want to spend any longer hearing a monologue about corrupt politicians in Russia so I just came out with it.

'What exactly do you want from me?'

'Your supply line,' he told me, 'part of it, at least; the part which runs from the eastern ports of the UK to Amsterdam, then through Europe until it reaches Russia. I know about your Russian supply line so please don't bother to deny it. You will waste the time of both of us.'

There didn't seem to be any point in denying anything. He knew everything there was to know about our European operation.

'Why do you need to use our supply line?'

'Men and materials,' he said simply, as if he was discussing a building job.

'What sort of men and what kind of materials?'

'You do not need to know that.'

'Oh, but I do. If you are paying me to use our supply line, I need to know what's going through it.'

He shook his head. 'Let me explain this. I will pay you, sure, but I am not giving you a choice. I will use your supply line to ship men and materials into Russia. If you cooperate with me, you will be generously rewarded, if you do not I will remove you and use the supply line anyway.'

I had already resolved to find any way I could to duck out of this arrangement but not here;

later, when I could get Amrein onside, to help me kick this mad Russian into touch. For now, I went along with it as if it might be a slim possibility.

'I don't need you to explain,' I told him, 'it's not drugs, clearly, that's not your business, so what could you possibly want to ship over a border into Russia that you couldn't just send by air freight with your guys flying in on a passenger jet? You're planning something and you've stated that the men who run your country don't understand democracy, reform or free politics, so what is it? If you are going to blow up the Kremlin using my supply line then you've no chance. They'll go to war on you,' I told him, 'and me.'

'The Russian government declared war on me years ago. They have tried to assassinate me many times. Before I left Russia I tried to follow the political road. I was even the governor of a province. One day I was due to take a helicopter flight with my family, only I had to stay behind and finish a deal, so I let my wife and young son go on ahead. The helicopter was blown out of the sky, shot down by a missile, everyone on board was killed. Nobody could provide a satisfactory explanation for the "tragedy". I have lost my wife and child in this struggle and the authorities in Russia will not rest until I am also dead. I am already at war.'

'That has nothing to do with me.'

'Which is a good reason to use you,' he said, before adding, 'you have no links to me at all. You pay corrupt officials to look the other way while you send heroin and cocaine to the Russian crime syndicates your associate, the Turk, has cultivated. Those same officials will continue to look the other way when my men and materials are delivered by your supply line. The men I wish to send back to my homeland cannot simply fly in on a scheduled flight. They will be picked up as soon as they land. The materials will enable me to bring the war to my enemies.'

'So, you're a terrorist, plain and simple?'

He slammed his hand on the table, hard.

'No!' he shouted. 'I am one side in a war and I must win that war to survive. I am not a terrorist, I am a freedom fighter. I am the agent runner and the men I am recruiting and training are all patriots. My *Joes* are willing to return to Russia to risk their lives fighting injustice and corruption. It is the only way, we have tried everything else.'

'But it's ridiculous,' I said, 'what can one man with a bomb achieve? You can't bring down a government like that.'

'With one man, no, you cannot,' he agreed, 'but with a thousand, two thousand, ten thousand? When the government cannot prevent wave after wave of sabotage and civilian unrest coordinated by my people then it loses all of its authority.'

'You are going to try to send ten thousand

trained men into Russia along my supply line, without anyone noticing? It's madness.'

'Not at first, of course,' he seemed calmer now, more reasonable, 'your route will be for the first men, the vanguard of a new revolution. What they will achieve can change history, believe me, I know.'

'When the first man is ready, I will summon you to me; this could be anywhere in the world but not Britain, never here. I will not jeopardise my good relationship with your government. When you meet the first *Joe*, you will receive a two million dollar fee and leave with him for Amsterdam. Then you will send him down the line.'

'You need to find another route,' I said firmly, 'I can't help you.'

'We have examined many possibilities while devising this strategy,' he informed me, 'yours was the best by far. We will use your route and there is nothing further to discuss. You have some time to think it through, so you can evaluate what it means to say *no* to a man like me. There will be no place for you to go where I cannot find you.'

'You don't fuck about, do you?'

'Are you familiar with the concept of *Krysha*?' I shook my head. 'In English the word means roof. In Russia it means protection. The person who provides *Krysha* enables a man to do business because of their powerful connections, but they expect something in return when they ask for it. You are under my *Krysha*. If you have a problem with your business, I can remove it. Think about that.'

'And if I think it through and still refuse?' I challenged.

There is an old saying in Georgia, Mr Blake. 'If you forgive the fox for stealing your chickens, he will take your sheep,' he told me, 'so I do not forgive. I never forgive.'

CHAPTER 29

'What do you think?' asked Palmer, when we were driving out of the main gate.

'I think he's crazy, out of his fucking mind.' I was angry now. 'He's a Bond villain, sitting in a hollowed-out volcano, stroking a white cat and plotting to blow up the world. He's barking,' I forced myself to calm down, 'but he doesn't know it and there's nobody around him who's brave enough to explain to him that he's gone crazy. He reckons he's at war with a country and, worse than that, he thinks he can actually win.'

'He's got billions,' said Palmer, 'with that kind of money he can cause a whole heap of trouble.'

'Maybe, but that's all he'll ever be able to do. Napoleon and his armies couldn't bring down Russia. Neither could Hitler and his Panzer divisions. Vasnetsov's got no chance and sooner or later they will get him.'

'They've been trying to get him for years and not managed it,' Palmer reminded me.

He was right about that, which left me in an impossible position; trapped between the entire Russian state and a madman.

'What are you going to do?' he asked.

Not for the first time lately, I found myself stuck for an answer, 'call Amrein,' I said, 'tell him to get this crazy Russian off my back.'

When I walked into Susan Fitch's office she was already reading the file she'd asked an intern to prepare for her so she could be up to speed for our meeting. It contained the 'high spots' of Golden Boots' career so far and, as I sat down opposite her, she raised her eyebrows.

'1999,' she said to me, instead of a greeting, 'and he has his first brush with the law, while still a teenager in London, getting into a fight in a night-club and, *allegedly*, smashing a glass into a man's face.' She read further, 'the charges are dropped, when the man who was glassed changes his story and fails to be completely sure who actually did the glassing,' and she looked up at me. 'He was paid off, wasn't he?'

'By the famous old London club Golden Boots played for at the time, so I heard. They didn't want their expensive asset diminished by a spell in prison.' She went back to reading the file, '2001 and he's on the move in the first of a series of transfers.'

'All of them for multi millions.'

'And in the same year a girl slaps him in the face in another nightclub, reason unknown, and he responds by punching her in the face, breaking her nose. Once again the case does not reach court, witnesses are unclear and the girl withdraws her complaint.'

'That cost him forty-five grand,' I said, 'just to pay off the girl.'

'Forty-five grand?' she frowned, 'that's a lot for a nose.'

'It was a week's wages for him, at the time. That was before he *really* made it big. He was on probation back then and she *was* an aspiring model.'

'Obviously,' said Susan Fitch, 'do footballers ever mix with anyone who isn't?'

She fell silent for a time as she read further, then concluded with a shake of her head, 'so there's nothing to worry about here,' she said dryly, 'apart from the alleged racist assault on an Asian cab driver; the numerous domestic violence allegations, including two police cautions for assaults on separate girlfriends, both of whom refused to press charges: half a dozen acts of violence on and off the pitch: convictions for assault and affray with their suspended prison sentences: rehab for drink, rehab for drugs, rehab for sexual addiction: the online porn video of him having full sexual intercourse with an unidentified but widely deemed to be underage girl . . .' She shook her head and sounded gloriously old-fashioned when she said, 'He's an absolute bloody charmer, isn't he?'

'I can't deny that,' I admitted. 'He's vermin, in fact, but he's not the only one, is he? Not all footballers are rotten to the core,' I reminded her, 'just most of them, including at least half of the current England team, if even one-tenth of their reported antics are to be believed. However I'm pretty sure Golden Boots didn't kill this girl,' Susan Fitch was watching me intently. I was choosing my words carefully, 'and we *have* done a little business together.'

'Business of a sensitive nature that he might feel compelled to reveal should he feel unduly threatened by the court proceedings?'

'Indeed.' I shrugged, 'I'm keeping my distance. I just said we'd help him find a lawyer, that's all, so he doesn't feel any ill-will towards us.'

There was a long pause before she concluded, 'Then we must find him a very good barrister. It's a pity Julian Aimes is busy right now.'

The next morning Fallon arrived on an early train from Edinburgh. We met him at the station and, over a fry-up in the platform cafe, he gave us the latest status on his war with the Serbs. 'It's like a goalless fucking draw,' Fallon told us, 'they beat up a couple of our lads, we kick the shit out of one of theirs, but we're not getting anywhere.'

'Why not?'

'Because we can't get near the main men,' he explained, 'not without blowing up their headquarters and starting the kind of war you don't want.'

'My profile is high enough as it is right now without you planting a bomb in a house full of Serbs who are protected by police top brass.'

'So what *do* we do then?'

'We make a deal,' and I had to hold up a hand to stop him from going off on one. 'Hear me out. I'm not talking about splitting the turf or the take. I'm saying we give them a one-off payment to get them to leave. They can go back to Belgrade with their money and let us get on with it.'

'You're fucking joking me!' I had never seen Fallon so furious. A couple of people glanced over at us, but soon looked away again.

'I'll cover it with my cut, not yours.'

'I don't believe this,' he was incredulous. 'They come over here and take the pish and you are going to just pay them off? Well *you* can talk to them then, because I fucking won't!'

'Let me talk to them,' said Palmer.

Palmer was fearless. I've seen him walk right up to buildings full of psychopathic cut-throats without any outward sign of nervousness. I don't know how he does that. He is obviously wired very differently from me. I do feel fear and would never put myself in jeopardy the way he does.

'Okay,' I said, glad of his intervention.

I'd had a long day shovelling a seemingly endless amount of shite. As well as the meeting with

242

Fallon and the briefing with Susan Fitch, some issues came up involving Henry Baxter's impending trial and some short-notice transferring of money from place to place was also required so I could pay my suppliers without a major drama. It was late, I was tired and I had a series of meetings in York the next day. All I wanted was to go to bed.

I returned home to find the kitchen in darkness, but Sarah was sitting there, all alone at the table, with only the light from the moon outside to illuminate her. In the half-light I could make out the half full bottle of wine in front of her and the half empty glass standing next to it.

'What's the matter?' I asked her.

'You know,' she was slurring, 'you know what's the matter. I want you to talk to me.'

'About what?' We both knew I was stalling.

'About dad. I want you to talk to me about dad. I want to know what happened to him.' Sarah was speaking slowly and deliberately, as if she was worried she might mess up her sentences. It was only then I realised there was a second empty wine bottle on the kitchen counter.

'And I don't want to talk about it. Not now,' I told her, 'I was there, remember.'

'Of course I remember!'

'Then you should know why I don't want to relive it. Do I ask you what happened with that Russian guy?'

'You did ask,' she reminded me, 'and I told you. He tried to rape me and I killed him.'

When I'd returned to collect Sarah from her old man's house after I'd killed Bobby, I'd gone into her bedroom to find her sitting on the floor in shock. She was staring at the dead body of a Russian goon who she'd stabbed in the neck with her father's lock knife.

'He was my dad. I have a right to know.'

'And I told you, I don't want to talk about it.'

I turned to walk away and she called out, 'That's what he said you would say.'

I stopped and turned back to face her then, watching as she reached for the wine bottle and topped her glass right up to the brim.

'Who?' I asked.

At first she ignored me. Instead she reached for the wine and took a huge gulp, then turned to face me with the bravery of a drunk, 'The policeman.'

'What policeman?' I demanded.

'The one who came to see me,' she said, 'the detective.'

I couldn't believe what I was hearing. 'A policeman came to talk to you and you didn't tell me? Why the fuck did you not tell me?'

'You were away,' she said, which we both knew was a bullshit reason, 'and he didn't come to talk about you. He came to talk to me about my dad.'

'Even so, Sarah, you should have told me. Who was he and what did he want?'

'His name was Carlton,' she told me, 'DI Carlton. And he wanted to warn me.'

'Warn you? About what?'

'About you,' she told me, then she repeated it slowly and deliberately, 'he wanted . . . to warn me . . . about you. He reckoned you had something to do with dad's disappearance.'

'That's bollocks and you know it.'

'I do know it,' then she corrected herself, 'I *did* know it but since you came back from your last trip you haven't been able to look me in the eye and you won't tell me what happened. That has got me thinking; it has got me worrying.'

'What about?'

'Something he said before he left.'

'Which was?'

Sarah deliberately avoided my eye when she uttered the words that changed everything between us.

'Ask yourself this question, Miss Mahoney, who stood to gain the most from your father's death? Who stood to gain?'

It took what seemed like an age for me to find the words to reply. I kept looking at her, trying to work out if she was completely off her face and rambling or if she actually believed I'd killed her father just so I could take over his firm.

'And what did you say to that?' I hissed the words at her.

'I told him to fuck off,' she said, finally looking me in the eye, 'and he did, but he made it clear he was after you,' she took another swig of wine, 'and then a funny thing happened.'

'Oh yeah?' I was trying to contain my anger with the woman I loved, 'What funny thing? Go on Sarah, you've got something to say to me, so finish it.'

'A few days after, I picked up the newspaper and he was in it,' she said, 'because someone had murdered his daughter.' Then she took another sip of wine before remarking, 'I wonder who stood to gain from that.'

I drove back into the city and took a room at our hotel but went straight to the bar and got the barman to pour me a large one. He kept them coming. All I could think about was Sarah and what she had said to me. Where the hell could we possibly go from there?

This wasn't the first time I'd walked out on her, but I knew that it might be the last. And it wasn't just Sarah who was occupying my thoughts. I couldn't bear the idea of losing my little Emma. Every time the notion went through my mind I drank a little more.

It was midday by the time I got my act together, called Peter Kinane and left the hotel. He picked me up and we headed south. I was glad when he didn't comment on my appearance. I knew I must have looked like shit. I could really have done without this trip to York but the meeting with the architect had already been postponed once.

At least it gave me an excuse not to go home. I didn't want to face Sarah in this state. I didn't want to think about Sarah at all in fact.

CHAPTER 30

That afternoon Palmer parked a car two streets from the Serbs' makeshift headquarters in Edinburgh. They'd set themselves up in a crumbling old house in Pilton; not the best part of the city, but it was a good way to avoid casual police scrutiny. Palmer walked slowly up the road, hands deep in his pockets, not looking directly at the building he was checking out. Instead he used his peripheral vision to take in the number and make of cars parked in the street and whether any men stood back from the Serbian brothers' house, watching.

The main security was provided by two burly bodyguards; one on the gate and one on the front door. Palmer had to assume they were both armed. He was patted down three times before they let him near the brothers; both men at the front of the house searching him in turn, in case one of them missed anything. Next he was ushered up a staircase and a new man was waiting for him at the top. This guy was huge and Palmer guessed he was one of the brothers' main enforcers. He wore a black leather jacket and, when he raised his hands to indicate to Palmer he should do the same, for the inevitable pat-down, his gun was clearly visible in a shoulder holster that hung low and loose inside his jacket.

The room had a reinforced steel-plated door, which would have taken a long time to break down, giving anyone behind it ample time to ready themselves or call for help. When the man had finished searching Palmer he called through the door in Serbian. He must have indicated his satisfaction because a moment later there was a buzz from inside the locked door and it came free automatically, opening slightly. The big man ushered Palmer through it.

Palmer placed his hand on the door, opened it completely and stepped into the large room that served as the brothers' headquarters. There were three men waiting for him and, from the resemblance, Palmer took them to be the Stevic brothers. No one else had been admitted to the inner sanctum so it appeared they kept the big decisions within the family. The brothers even dressed alike, in jeans and T-shirts and were sporting the same heavy gold chains around their necks like a badge of office.

Palmer noticed a machine gun propped up against a wall, within easy reach, and two shotguns. Two of the brothers had handguns in shoulder holsters they didn't even bother to cover with jackets. These guys were beyond blatant, but they were protected, so maybe they thought they could leave shotguns and machine guns lying around without worrying about a raid.

'Skorpion vz61,' was the first thing Palmer said to them.

'What?' asked the brother who looked like the oldest. Palmer took this to be Dusan.

'Haven't seen too many Skorpions,' added Palmer indicating the machine gun, 'not lately. Czech-made but there's not been a new one in thirty years. Where'd you get it?'

'Took it from the dead hand of a Muslim bastard in Kosovo,' said Dusan proudly, 'he didn't need it any more. It still works,' he assured Palmer.

'I'll bet it does, they were built to last. Eight hundred and fifty rounds a minute.'

The brother who appeared to be the youngest reacted angrily, 'You are not here to talk about guns.'

'No,' confirmed Palmer, 'I'm here to talk about you leaving Edinburgh,' he said it quietly, 'and the terms we will agree with you for your return to Belgrade.'

The middle brother, Sreten, spoke then as if he too was determined to say his piece, 'You don't make terms with us. We make terms with you and the terms are nothing. That's how much we will give you to leave the city to us. We are already driving your men out.'

'And we've given some of your boys a battering too,' countered Palmer, 'there's no end to the number we can put on the streets. Can you say the same?'

Dusan Stevic had been listening calmly, but he

intervened then. 'I could summon a hundred men tomorrow and you should know they would arrive with no problems from your police.'

'Having bent law in this country isn't always enough. You can't buy everyone. Believe me, it's been tried. Even in your own home you failed to do that.'

'What is it you are offering for us to leave this city? I ask out of mere curiosity.'

'Half a million Euros,' Palmer let the amount sink in, 'plus whatever you've made here already. That's a hefty profit for a few weeks in a foreign land.'

'Then what?'

'You set up somewhere else; Marseille, Hamburg, Riga?' Palmer shrugged as if it was of no consequence to him.

'And if we don't leave?'

'Then you will never leave.'

The youngest brother, Marko, took exception to that and pulled his gun. Dusan barked something at him in Serbian and Marko's face flushed, then he put the gun away reluctantly.

'You come here to threaten us, it makes Marko angry. If it was his choice we would take you from here and cut you to pieces for that insult.'

'Perhaps all three of you could do that,' admitted Palmer, 'but not all of you would live.'

Dusan's eyes widened in disbelief, 'Fucking balls on this guy,' and he laughed without amusement. 'I'll tell you what will happen. I will let you keep those balls and you leave here. Return to Blake, yes I know who your boss is, and tell him what I smell when I hear his offer; weakness and fear. If he thought he could make us leave he would try, but no, he wants to pay us and he offers what he thinks it is worth to him. If he can afford to pay this, it cannot be enough for us to go. Tell him the city is ours. Now leave, before I let Marko and Sreten do what they want to do.'

I don't usually travel alone. I normally take a bodyguard with me and I've grown used to that. It comes with the turf for men like me and the inconvenience factor is far outweighed by the flip-side of being lifted or killed by a rival or wannabe gangster. Usually it's Palmer, but if he isn't with me I'll use Joe, or one of his sons. That day it was Peter Kinane and I was comfortable enough with it. All of Joe's sons know their shit. It's part genetic and part training from their dad and Palmer.

It was late when we finally called for coffee at a shabby Service Station on the way back from York. The place was virtually deserted at that hour. The newsagent was closed and shuttered and we were the last visitors to trouble the coffee bar, before the guy upended chairs onto the other tables, then fucked off home and left us to it. I couldn't see anyone else around, apart from two old blokes in overalls, absent-mindedly swishing mops back and forth across a grey, tiled floor that shone for a few moments each night when no one was around, until it dried and settled back to its usual dull, scuffed appearance. A yellow plastic sign next to them reminded us that stepping on their handiwork was likely to prove dangerous; a cartoon of a man, his feet thrown high into the air, warned us to give them a wide berth. We drained the dregs of our coffee and walked to the main door but Peter was looking uncomfortable.

'What's the matter with you?' I asked him.

'Actually,' he said, 'I could do with a slash.'

'Well go then. I'm not stopping you.'

'I know you want to get going like.'

'You taking a wazz isn't going to delay me that much, Peter, and it's preferable to you fidgeting all the way back up the A1,' I said, 'I'll see you at the car.'

I walked out into a crisp night. The air was fresh and cold and there was no one around. Most people would be in bed by now. I looked over at the lorry park and there were maybe a dozen huge artics lined up with makeshift covers over their windscreens to blot out the light. The drivers would be getting their heads down for a few hours before waking early, then pegging it miles down empty motorways before most normal people had brushed their teeth. I was still looking at the lorries when I heard a heavily-accented voice close by me.

'Come with me now,' it told me, 'or I will kill you here.'

CHAPTER 31

I turned slowly around to face the man who had threatened me. He had a young face but his eyes were cold and showed a determination that made me take him seriously. That, and the gun in his hand.

'Come with me,' he said again and he motioned with the gun for me to follow him. It looked like one of those Russian-made Makarovs that had flooded the streets a while back because they were so cheap. I guessed this guy was about twenty, he was heavy set and wore a white sweatshirt under a black leather jacket. There was a thick gold chain around his neck, 'Come now,' he ordered, his accent of east European origin.

I glanced back towards the Services, but there was no sign of Peter, or anyone else. The guy had chosen his moment perfectly. I wondered if our every move was being captured on CCTV somewhere, or if he had been thorough enough to check beforehand. Either way, it wasn't going to help me if he was eventually convicted of my murder.

'Where are you taking me?' I asked, stalling for

time and praying Peter would finish his piss before I was driven away.

The young guy didn't answer me. Instead he took a few swift steps towards me then smashed the end of the barrel hard into my guts, doubling me up and winding me in the process. The pain was intense and before I could recover from it, he was dragging me towards a car he'd parked just yards from ours. Predictably it was a big silver BMW with blacked-out windows. The doors had been left unlocked. He opened the driver's door, then bundled me inside.

'You drive,' he told me. The keys were in the ignition and I briefly contemplated starting the car and gunning it away from there, possibly straight through the plate glass doors of the Services, to attract as much attention as possible, but he warned me, 'Don't start the car till I am inside or I shoot you here. If you try to run, also I shoot you.'

You have to let your mind go as cold as possible when a man like that points a gun at you. You have to try to forget the fact that, if you make the wrong decision, if you make your move too early or leave it too late, then you are a dead man, because that will make you nervous and jumpy and the chances are you'll fuck up and wind up dead. You have to try not to think about the people in your life; Emma and Sarah, even though it is natural to want to. You have to stay focused on every little detail. Right now, as I was buckling my seat belt, I was thinking that there was no way I could start the car and drive away without him shooting me. As he went round the back of the car to get in, I finally spotted Peter. He was emerging from the Services and looking down because he'd only just realised his flies weren't done up. I watched him tug at them instead of looking for me and I took a calculated risk because I needed him.

I opened the door and shouted, 'Peter! Peter! I'm here!'

That was as far as I got before I felt a searing pain in the side of my head from the pistol-whipping the young bastard gave me. He'd climbed into the passenger seat of the car, smacked me round the side of the head with his gun and leaned past me to tug the door of the BMW closed.

'Start the car,' he ordered, because we could both see Peter Kinane running towards us across the empty car park. He levelled the gun at me. 'Drive!' he shouted and I knew from his tone that he wouldn't be asking again. I did what I was told, started the engine and drove away. Peter was still a few yards from our car and I could only pray he would give chase and somehow catch up with us. As the car picked up speed, the young Serb did up his seat belt, putting one idea I'd had, of crashing the car into something at speed and hoping he came off worse, right out of my mind.

'Faster,' he ordered and I accelerated as I came down the slip road and out into the empty A-road.

He kept urging me to go faster but I was stalling, glancing in the rear-view mirror until finally I saw him. Peter Kinane had taken our Mercedes out of the Services at a rate of knots and he was coming after us like both our lives depended on it.

'You fucked up,' I told the Serb, hoping to undermine the fragile confidence of youth with a bit of honest-to-goodness sledging, 'should have done the tyres in our car first, a schoolboy would have known that. Now my guy is after you and he's going to kill you.'

'Shut up!' he ordered, but I could tell I'd planted some uncertainty. He should have done our car. 'Keep driving,' he told me, then looked back behind us through the gap in the seats where he could see Peter swiftly gaining on us.

'Go faster,' he ordered and I stepped on the throttle.

'Where do you think you are taking me?'

'Edinburgh,' and the word came out as a mangled eastern European version because he couldn't pronounce the name of the city his bosses were trying to take over, 'I am taking you to Dusan Stevic.'

'That's not going to happen,' I said, pressing the accelerator down further, 'I won't let you take me there to be sliced up by that fucking animal. No way.'

'Then you will die now,' he told me confidently.

'So will you at this speed,' I informed him, 'that

was your second mistake; letting me drive. You can blow my brains out now if you like but at ninety-five miles an hour I wouldn't give much for your chances of walking away from the wreckage and, even if you did, my guy will be waiting for you. He'll make you wish you hadn't lived.'

'Shut up and drive,' he hissed, but I could tell he was seriously rattled now.

'You should have had a partner,' I informed him, 'that's how you are supposed to do this kind of thing. It's a two-man job; one to drive and the other to hold the gun on the guy you are lifting. Not done this before, have you? I can tell. Shame it's not the kind of work where you get to learn from your mistakes.'

'You just drive,' he said and all the while he was watching Peter's progress as the Merc gained ground on our Beemer and was inching closer and closer.

'Faster!' he ordered and I did as I was told, edging the car up above a hundred miles an hour. I had to be a bit careful as the road has two lanes and the slow lane attracts late-night casual drivers and lorries.

'I've just realised,' I told the young Serb, 'he doesn't know you're here does he? Dusan Stevic doesn't know you're doing this. He's not going to agree to a one-man op with an inexperienced guy like you? So that's means you're doing this on your own, to make a name for yourself, but there's an expression over here, son, "don't walk before you can run". I'm sure you understand its meaning.'

I'd obviously got to him because I got another smack in the side of the head which knocked me off balance and I couldn't see for a moment. The car lurched to the left, crossing into the slow lane before I could wrestle it back. I could barely see, but when my vision cleared, I heard the Serb swear and I became aware of something big and black up ahead – the arse-end of a huge lorry. The Serb swore again and I wrenched the wheel to the right. The front end of our car missed the lorry by millimetres. Somehow I managed to straighten the car and continue when, out of the corner of my eye, I saw Peter in the Merc. He'd taken advantage of our near miss and managed to accelerate forward till he drew up alongside us in the slow lane. I could see him snarling and mouthing obscenities at the Serb, whose reaction was to wind down the window and produce the gun. Just as he was about to fire at Peter from point-blank range, my bodyguard braked and we shot past him, the bullet harmlessly hitting the bushes.

Peter eased the car back until he was behind us, then moved right up close. The young Serb twisted in his seat and aimed his gun back at him through the rear window. I accelerated some more and jiggled the steering wheel just as he fired. He cursed in his native language as the back window disintegrated in a shower of glass, but the bullets missed their target. Peter was still behind us.

The Serb was ranting now; at Peter, at me, at his inability to hit the target and I knew I wouldn't get away with another manoeuvre like that last one. I was haring down the road at a hundred and ten miles an hour with Peter in mad pursuit, desperately trying to think of a way out of this and then I had a moment of clarity; a realisation that everything I'd said was true. This guy *was* a lone gun who was trying to make a reputation and he'd fucked it up. He couldn't shoot me because he'd die seconds later. There was no way we were going to have a protracted car chase with a shoot-out on an A-road in England, no matter how quiet it was. The police would soon hear what was going on and they'd be after us, but I still couldn't rely on a good outcome if that happened. All of a sudden I got angry. Who did this little fuck think he was to come after me on his own?

I floored the car, taking it up to a hundred and twenty miles an hour. There were no other vehicles on this stretch of road. I waited until he fired again, sending a round into the Merc which forced Peter to slam the anchors on and pull back. The young Serb was turned around in his seat, holding his gun in both hands and levelling it again for what he must have dearly hoped would be the final shot, when I reached out with my left hand and pressed the red button by the side of his seat. He didn't hear it over the din of the roaring engine, but he sensed something had changed and he turned to look at me as his seat belt loosened and slid away from him. I slammed on the brakes with all my force and the car juddered like it had suddenly hit a brick wall. The Serb didn't even have time to let out a cry. Instead he was flung forwards, his back striking the dashboard with great force, but it wasn't enough to break his forward momentum and he went straight through the windscreen, head first.

Cars aren't designed to make an emergency stop at a hundred and twenty miles an hour and this one was no exception. It went into a slide, then a spin and turned a whole three-sixty degrees, while I tried to ignore the searing pain across my chest from my seat belt, the whiplash I was already feeling in my neck and back and the shock of the driver's airbag exploding in my face. All I could do was hold on tight like this was a fairground ride that would eventually stop. Then I crashed hard into the metal barrier of the central reservation.

Peter dragged me out of the wreckage. The car had done its bit by crumpling in all of the right places and I was pulled free, feeling like every piece of me had been punched hard, but I was alive. It was the only thing that mattered; that and the fact that the young Serb was lying motionless in the middle of the road way back behind me, his body twisted unnaturally. I'm certain he was already dead when he bounced off the road but

Peter's car going over him at speed removed any lingering doubt.

As Peter got me out of the car, he retained the presence of mind to wipe the steering wheel, gear stick, handbrake and door handles, to remove any of my prints. He carried me to the car and we drove out of there fast, before anyone could come along and link me to the tragic accident, which saw a poor young man somehow lose control of his vehicle, before crashing through his windscreen and drawing his final breath against the cold tarmac of the A-road.

CHAPTER 32

When we got back I called Palmer and he told me there was no deal with the Stevic brothers. We were using pay-as-you-go mobiles so I took a risk and told him about the young Serb's attempt to lift me and take me to Dusan. He heard me out and agreed it was probably an unsanctioned operation. 'They don't need to kill you,' he said, 'they're bedding in, taking over the territory, inch by inch.'

I was in a fair bit of pain from the crash, but pretty sure nothing was broken, and I could arrange to be seen by a friendly doctor in the morning. In the interim, I could dull the pain with booze. I crashed at our hotel again. The next morning I drove home, parked up and took my bruised and battered body inside. Every step was an effort. Sarah and Joanne were sitting in the living room together while Emma played with her toys on the floor. I walked over, picked up my little girl and gave her a kiss. Sarah just looked at me, not mentioning my bruised face, waiting for me to say something.

'Do you want to do this now?' I asked her simply.

Joanne looked down and Sarah got slowly to her feet.

'Can you keep an eye on her?' she asked her old friend.

'Course,' said Joanne, and she smiled over at Emma. 'Come on chicken. Let's go to Auntie Jo's and we'll bake some cakes.'

I put Emma down and she took Joanne's hand. They left without another word. I sat down opposite Sarah.

'Are you sure you want to do this?' I asked her firmly, 'you really want to know everything?'

She seemed to hesitate for a moment then said, 'Yes.'

'Some of it you know,' I told her, 'and some you don't. Your dad controlled a lot of what went on in this city, some of it legal, but not all.'

'I know he was no saint, Davey, but nor are you. I'm not that naïve.'

Maybe it was her tone that irritated me, or perhaps I had been through too much lately to really spare her feelings, so I went on. 'Protection money; security, by which I mean muscle on the doors of nightclubs; prostitution; drugs; armed robbery; money laundering – and he would hurt people, when it was required.'

I could tell by the look on her face that she had known about this all along but it was still a shock to hear it finally confirmed by me. 'Where do you think all of the money came from? Your father controlled a city, which made him a powerful man, but it also made him enemies. One day Alan Gladwell came down from Glasgow and tried to take it all away from him. Men died as a result and one of them was your father. I had to take the city back from Alan Gladwell. You don't need to know the details of how that happened.'

'I hope you killed the bastard slowly Davey,' she said. I had done, but I wasn't about to confirm that, even to her.

'Before I took back the city, Gladwell and his Russian henchmen took your dad and Finney away.'

'I was there, remember?'

'I remember,' I confirmed, 'they took them both to a lock up, a disused factory on the outskirts of the city. They brought me there too. By the time I arrived Finney was already dead. They strapped him to a chair, tortured him, then garrotted him with wire. They took Northam, our accountant, there too. They got the information they needed from him, then they shot him in the head. When I got there your father was the only one left alive. They wanted me to see him. Gladwell wanted everyone to know that your dad was finished.'

'Did they torture him too,' she asked me, 'did they hurt him before they . . .' She couldn't complete the sentence. Tears formed in her eyes.

'They beat him,' I said, 'pretty badly, but your dad was the toughest old bugger I ever met. It wasn't the first time he'd taken a few punches. He could handle that.'

'What did they do then Davey?' she asked me, 'tell me. I have to know.'

'Your dad was tied to a chair and they made me watch while a man called Vitaly drew a gun and pointed it straight at your father. Gladwell then said he was going to kill him and I assumed he would kill me too. He gave your dad ten seconds, I think he wanted your father to beg for his life, but he didn't, quite the opposite in fact, he told Gladwell to go and fuck himself. Gladwell counted down the ten seconds.' I hesitated before telling her.

'What happened when he finished counting?' she urged me.

'Vitaly shot your father in the head.'

The tears were falling from her eyes now, tracks forming on her cheeks. She nodded silently and after she had absorbed that she said, 'But how did you get away, Davey? How come they let you go? When you'd seen them kill my father, you were a witness, so why would they let you just walk away?'

'They weren't scared of me,' I explained, 'they didn't think I was a threat. They thought I was just a suit and I couldn't possibly harm them. Everyone who could do that was already dead; Jerry Lemon, Finney, Geordie Cartwright, your dad, they were all gone by then. They thought I was the only one left, but they didn't know about Palmer, Danny or Kinane. I still don't know why they let me live but I think they needed someone who could tell the world that Bobby Mahoney was really gone. Your father was a legend in this city. Nobody would have believed a man like Alan Gladwell could have brought him down without me to corroborate his story.'

I couldn't tell her that they had film of me shooting Bobby for them, which meant I was in their power by then and could be conveniently put in the frame for his killing if the heat became too much. 'The truth is they could have killed me if they'd wanted to, it made no difference to them whether I lived or died. In the end they put me on a train to London, told me not to come back, that there was nothing in Newcastle for me anymore, but they didn't know how I felt about you, Sarah. I came back for you.'

She could barely speak now because of the tears. 'I know,' she sniffed, 'and I'm so sorry. I've just been so messed up about dad, not knowing what really happened to him and then that detective came round, and more or less said you were involved, and I got confused, and then his daughter was killed . . .' The words came out in a rush.

'That had nothing to do with me.'

'I know that now. I should have always known it. I'm so sorry,' and she took a deep breath then to try to quell the sobbing. 'Did he say anything?' She was in floods of tears now, 'Before he died, did my daddy say anything?'

'Yes,' I answered, 'he told me to get away from there. "Find Sarah," he said, "take care of her" and that's what I did. That's what I've been doing ever since.'

'Oh Davey,' she collapsed into my arms, sobbing, 'I'm so sorry . . . I'm so, so sorry . . . I'm so ashamed I doubted you.'

'That's alright,' I told her, 'it doesn't matter now.'

I didn't want to talk about it anymore because her shame was nothing compared to mine.

CHAPTER 33

Everyone knew my link to Henry Baxter, so it didn't matter that I was in the public gallery. Opposite me, Matt Bell listened intently to the court proceedings, taking copious notes. Things didn't get properly interesting until the third day of the trial, when our barrister took centre stage.

Detective Chief Inspector Argyle, who headed up the original case into the murder of Leanne Bell, took the witness stand. Argyle couldn't have been far from retirement age. He stood in the dock in his crumpled grey suit and M&S tie and, when our barrister cross-examined him, he stared out at the court like a rabbit caught between headlights.

'Detective Chief Inspector, the investigation into the murder of Leanne Bell was a large and extensively-resourced one,' Julian Aimes reminded him, 'involving more than thirty detectives, all of whom reported to you.'

'That is correct,' he answered, in a strong Bristolian burr.

'During the course of this investigation, your

team interviewed a large number of people, did you not?'

'We did.'

'How many?'

'I can't recall the exact number, but it was significant.'

'One hundred and seventeen.' Aimes prompted him.

'If you say so.'

'Whether I say so or not, that is the number, according to the documentation provided by the prosecution. Are you now telling me this is inaccurate?'

'Of course not. I'm just saying I couldn't remember, but it sounds about right to me. If that number has come from the prosecution, I have no reason to doubt it.'

'Nor have I. One hundred and seventeen people spoken to in the course of your lengthy investigation into Leanne's murder,' Aimes told the jury. 'I have the names of each and every one of them detailed here, but there is one name missing from the list, isn't there Detective Chief Inspector?'

'Is there?'

'Yes there is,' Aimes assured him, 'Henry Baxter's name is not on the list. Why not?'

'Well,' the Detective Chief Inspector looked uncomfortable, 'we didn't consider him to be a suspect . . . at that time.'

'Why was that, I wonder? Sounds like a bit of an oversight to me. Here is a man who lived within a couple of miles of the girl and he is not even interviewed by you, despite having a link to Leanne and her friends due to the piano lessons that have already been mentioned in court. Yet you did not even bother to interview him. That's little more than police incompetence, isn't it?'

'Not at all. We never received a complaint from any parent whose child had piano lessons with Henry Baxter. It's only in hindsight that they seemed suspicious. We weren't aware that he was giving free lessons and other incentives to young girls who visited him. There was no evidence to suggest the man might have been responsible for her death.'

'Really? No evidence. None whatsoever? I find that very hard to believe.'

'There was none. Nothing that would lead us to believe he was Leanne's killer.'

'Ladies and gentleman of the jury, you just heard it from the lips of the chief investigating officer; there was no evidence to link Henry Baxter to the murder of Leanne Bell.'

'At that time,' countered the DCI, realising too late that he had been baited into a trap while trying to defend a charge of incompetence.

'And there is still none,' said Aimes, firmly.

'There is DNA evidence,' replied the police officer.

'Yes, well, we shall demonstrate how the DNA evidence is very far from reliable and, since it is the cornerstone of the prosecution case against

Mr Baxter, I expect him to be acquitted. I put it to you, for the time being at least, that *aside* from the DNA sample, there is absolutely no other evidence against Henry Baxter. Is there?'

'Well no,' admitted the DCI, 'but the DNA evidence is enough.'

'Is it?' asked our lawyer, 'the jury shall be the judge of that.'

After the break for lunch our lawyer went for the DCI once more.

'You have arrested and charged Henry Baxter with the murder of Leanne Bell and wish us to believe that you did not carry out this arrest lightly.'

'No. I mean yes, of course we did not do it lightly. The police are not in the habit of arresting people on serious charges for the fun of it.'

'In other words, an arrest in a murder case isn't something the police do without considerable thought. You would expect us to read into the fact that Mr Baxter has been arrested for the murder, that he is your chief, your only, in fact, suspect in this case.'

'Absolutely.'

'But he is not the first man to be arrested for the murder of Leanne, is he?'

There was a long pause before the DCI answered, 'No, not the first, no,' he muttered.

'How many people have been arrested for this poor little girl's murder, prior to the arrest of Henry Baxter?'

The DCI took a long while to answer. You could

almost hear the cogs whirring in his brain as he struggled to find the form of words that would be least damning. In the end he settled on a single word, uttered quietly, 'Four'.

We all heard him say it, just, but our lawyer went for maximum impact, 'Could you speak up, please, so that the members of the jury can hear your answer?'

'Four.' He said it loud and clearly now, but no less reluctantly.

'Four?' the barrister's tone was incredulous, 'but I thought you did not arrest members of the public for murder lightly and yet, on your own admission, Henry Baxter is the fifth person to be arrested for this murder. How can that be?'

'Well, there was evidence at that time . . . sufficient evidence to warrant . . . look, it's not a simple matter of . . . you have to weigh up the evidence and sometimes you arrest a suspect in a case when you don't yet have the full picture but, in the course of an interrogation, more facts become clear. That can lead to a charge of murder and, in the fullness of time, a conviction, but it could just as likely lead to a situation where no further action is taken.'

'Mmmm,' Aimes paused, as if ruminating on that last statement, 'would you please reveal to the court the identity of the first man arrested for the murder of Leanne Bell.'

DCI Argyle looked as if he would rather have had a tooth pulled from his mouth than the name he was about to offer up. Eventually he said, 'Matthew Bell.'

'And please explain what relationship Matthew Bell had to the dead girl.'

'Father.'

'He is Leanne's father?'

'Yes.'

'So what was the evidence which led you to believe that Matthew Bell could possibly have killed his only daughter?'

The delay in replying spoke several volumes, 'There were statements to the effect that the relationship between Leanne and her father had been strained.'

'Statements from whom?'

'Neighbours.'

'How many neighbours?'

'More than one.'

'So, two then?'

Through gritted teeth, 'Yes.'

'Can you be more specific regarding these statements? What was it exactly that the neighbours reported seeing or hearing that gave you cause for suspicion?'

'Arguments, raised voices, the father shouting and the girl shouting back. That kind of thing.'

'Rows, in other words?'

'Yes, rows.'

'So a teenage girl and her father are heard having an argument, several arguments possibly, and you arrest the father on suspicion of his daughter's murder. Inspector, are you aware of a home in this country containing a father and teenage daughter where there have not occasionally been harsh words exchanged? What evidence did this provide?'

'It showed the father had a temper and he *had* served in the armed forces previously in a highly stressful environment.'

'Northern Ireland?'

'Correct.'

'So Mr Bell occasionally shouted at his daughter and she shouted back at him, plus he had served his country loyally as a member of Her Majesty's Armed Forces in a hostile environment, therefore he must have murdered her.'

'I never said he must have murdered her. It made him a possible suspect, that's all.'

'Not in my view, and I suspect not in the view of anyone in this courtroom today. Inspector, can you imagine the anguish you must have caused Mr Bell; the man who, as we have heard in his own words earlier, during a highly-moving testimony to this court, has had his life destroyed by the death of his only child,' our barrister raised an eyebrow, 'and, at the very height of his grief, you arrested him and accused him, during several hours of interrogation, of being his own daughter's murderer. Why ever would you do that?'

'Obviously I very much regret that now, but at the time we were all under a lot of pressure and . . .'

'Pressure to find Leanne's killer, you mean?'

'Yes.'

'That pressure has never really gone away has it?'

'The case has remained open until now, which was a cause of concern to us all, but we were absolutely committed to finding her killer one day.'

'So you readily admit that you remain desperate to resolve the case.'

'Yes,' he replied, 'I wouldn't use the word desperate though, committed was what I said.'

'Bit embarrassing though, don't you think? It must have been. Arresting four different people for the same murder, with the Press baying for your blood and ridiculing your every move as, one after another, you were forced to release them.'

'I don't recall the Press baying for our blood. On the whole they were supportive, sharing a common aim of finding Leanne's killer.'

'Really?' asked our lawyer, in the manner of an unimpressed Jeremy Paxman on *Newsnight*.

'Yes, really.'

Aimes picked up a piece of A4 paper and read from his notes.

'I'm quoting from a well-known broadsheet now, "The Police have clutched at suspects in the manner of a drowning man clutching at straws."'

'That was sensationalist nonsense.'

'So you weren't clutching at straws?'

'Absolutely not.'

'Mmm,' Aimes paused, as if considering that last

statement, 'would you be kind enough to tell the court the name of the second man who was arrested and questioned over the murder of Leanne Bell?'

DCI Argyle looked quite nauseous at that point. Eventually he said, 'Darren Bell.'

'And what relationship does Darren Bell have to the dead girl?'

'Uncle.'

'He was Leanne's uncle?'

'Yes.'

'Oh dear, Chief Inspector.' The tone was pitying and our lawyer shook his head slowly, 'Oh dear . . . oh dear . . . oh dear. Tell me, is there a family member you didn't arrest for her murder?'

'Objection!' pleaded the prosecution lawyer.

'I withdraw the question, Your Honour,' conceded our barrister, but it was already out there and the jury heard it loud and clear.

By the time Detective Chief Inspector Argyle stepped down from the witness stand, he looked like he had been repeatedly slapped in the face.

CHAPTER 34

Julian Aimes took just minutes to discredit the prosecution's two star witnesses; a couple of young women who claimed they had known Henry Baxter a decade before, when both were in their early teens. They each claimed to have been indecently assaulted by him while he gave them those notorious free piano lessons.

Aimes got the first girl to talk about her life as a teenager and by the time she had described her home life, negligent parents and succession of foster families, the run-ins with the law and the absconding from a care home, he'd managed to make her sound like a prostitute. She left the witness stand in tears.

The second girl was undone by Aimes' assertion she was only testifying against Henry Baxter for money and, when she denied this, he asked her if she would be willing to sign away any future civil claim against him right now, should he be found guilty. The prosecution objected strongly, but the girl hesitated for so long that when she finally answered, she made herself sound like a lying gold digger.

Next up was Professor Raymond Harris, the prosecution's expert witness and a man who clearly thought he was the most intelligent person in the room and was just about to prove it.

'Professor, could you begin by telling me how much DNA is common to every individual?' asked Aimes.

The portly professor spoke with the confidence of a courtroom veteran. 'Well, I could, but that wouldn't be relevant to the technique of DNA fingerprinting, which focuses on the percentage that is unique to each individual.'

Aimes regarded the professor as if he might have something to hide. 'Humour me,' he demanded, before remembering that he was in front of a jury and adding the word, 'please.'

'Alright,' conceded the professor, 'it's around ninety-nine percent.'

'It *is* ninety-nine percent or it is in excess of ninety-nine percent? Could you be more precise? If you recall the question, it is how much DNA is shared by every human being on the planet?'

The professor looked a little flushed already, his plump face was reddening and he had only been asked one question. 'I recall the question, it's ninety-nine point nine percent.'

'Ninety-nine point nine percent. Imagine that?' Aimes was speaking rhetorically but I could see the jurors were taking a lot of notice. 'So the element of DNA you use in genetic fingerprinting must be just nought point one percent. Am I correct?'

'You are.'

'Such a tiny percentage,' mused our lawyer, as if to himself.

'But entirely sufficient to distinguish one person from another.'

'So you maintain,' Aimes' voice was a low whisper, but he pitched it perfectly. All of the jurors were listening intently. One or two even leaned forward to hear more clearly, as he presumably intended them to.

'Would you mind explaining to the members of the jury and myself how the DNA fingerprinting process works in practice?'

'Well, we use variable number tandem repeats and short tandem repeats.'

'Really,' Aimes sounded almost bored now, 'how fascinating.'

The professor attempted to continue, 'Variable number loci are so unique that it would be highly unlikely for two people to have the same variable number tandem repeats.'

'But it's not impossible?'

'The odds are millions to one.'

'But . . . it . . . is . . . not . . . impossible,' affirmed Aimes. 'What is the population of the United Kingdom, Professor?'

The professor sighed. 'I gather it is approximately sixty-five million people, according to the last census.'

Our barrister shrugged, 'That's millions,' he asserted facetiously, 'isn't it?'

'Oh come on,' replied the professor, 'I can see what you are trying to do but this is a hackneyed argument.'

'Is it?' replied Aimes reasonably. 'In that case I shall ask a different question entirely.' He paced the courtroom for a few moments, as if only now thinking of that question. 'How did you come to analyse the DNA of my client?'

'From a buccal swab taken following his arrest for drink driving.'

'For *alleged* drink driving. The case has not been heard, so your comments could be deemed highly prejudicial, Professor. I'm afraid I must remind you that it is not down to you to decide upon a man's guilt, in this case or any other. That is the preserve of the members of the jury.'

'Then I apologise,' replied the professor, 'I understand the drink-driving hearing was postponed because your client is facing the rather more serious charges of raping and murdering a young girl.'

'Everyone in this room is aware of the charges, Professor. What must be decided upon is his guilt or innocence,' replied Aimes. 'So, a buccal swab taken from the mouth of my client by the police and stored where exactly?'

'It was taken to a laboratory in sealed conditions.'

'To the Forensic Science Service lab?' He asked the question lightly.

'Well no,' countered the professor, 'the Forensic

Science Service no longer exists. I'm surprised you weren't aware of that. These days the analysis of DNA samples is conducted by private firms.'

'Yes, of course, I apologise,' answered Aimes, 'how silly of me to forget that the government chose to save money by closing down the world-renowned, state-funded body that for many years conducted ground-breaking study and analysis into the DNA left at crime scenes, choosing instead to farm it out to little known, private companies whose main motivation is profit. Companies like DeoxyNuc Forensics, for example, whose much-criticised laboratory is in Birmingham. Now then, Professor, to which laboratory was the accused's DNA sample sent?'

There was a pause long enough for the professor to realise he had been duped, then he answered flatly, 'DeoxyNuc Forensics.'

'In Birmingham?'

'In Birmingham,' confirmed the professor.

'I see, and would this be the same DeoxyNuc Forensics, let us refer to them as DNF for the sake of brevity, who processed the DNA sample in the case of Andrew Cox.'

'I believe they did process the sample in that case, yes.'

'I'm not surprised you recall the case. It was thrown out wasn't it?'

'Yes.'

'Andrew Cox had been accused of raping a fourteen-year-old girl in Glasgow on the basis of a DNA sample you said proved that he must have done it, because you were the expert witness on that case, weren't you Professor?'

'I was, yes, but I gave my testimony based on the information that was available to me at the time. All of the evidence indicated he was the man who raped that poor young girl.'

'All of the evidence? You mean the DNA sample?'

'Yes.'

Aimes paced up and down some more, making it appear he was thinking, but really he was building up the suspense levels. Even the jury seemed to sense he was going to hit Professor Harris right between the eyes at any minute.

'But he *wasn't* guilty, was he, Professor?'

'No, it would appear not.'

'Despite the DNA sample and your sworn evidence that he was? Professor, please explain to me why the case against Andrew Cox was eventually thrown out.'

'It turned out that the DNA sample had been compromised.'

'The DNA sample had been compromised? What does that actually *mean*?'

'It appeared that the tray used to analyse the DNA sample had been used before.'

'Can that really be possible? A used tray was not disposed of, nor was it clearly marked as having been used, so when the DNA swab from the unfortunate rape victim was placed in the tray it was allowed to mingle with the residue from an earlier sample, in this case the DNA taken from Andrew Cox, following his arrest on suspicion of drink driving, which I need hardly add is an obvious parallel with the case here today. It's all tragically similar; the same circumstances leading to the surrender of a DNA sample, the same incompetent company analysing that sample, and the exact same expert witness standing before us, confidently stating that it would be tantamount to an impossibility for the accused to be innocent. But Andrew Cox *was* innocent, wasn't he, Professor, and so is Henry Baxter.'

The professor did not reply, so Aimes continued, 'Professor, how many cases have been thrown out because of poor handling by DNF?'

'I really have no . . .'

'Twelve,' interrupted Aimes, 'it's twelve; a dozen citizens of the United Kingdom who could have found themselves undergoing the terrible ordeal of a lengthy sentence behind bars because the practices at DNF are clinically unsafe.'

'Yes, perhaps, but they were old cases, historic ones.'

'Twelve errors,' Aimes reminded him gravely, 'twelve miscarriages of justice due to shoddy clinical practice. How can any of us honestly state, hand on heart, that Henry Baxter would not make it thirteen?'

'But processes have been tightened up since then. The possibility of any kind of miscarriage of justice has been virtually eliminated now that there are a series of proper checks and balances in place at DNF.'

'So you are certain of Henry Baxter's guilt?'

'Yes, yes. I would say it is virtually assured.'

Aimes smiled then and there was nothing fake or contrived about his pleasure. 'You said that before, Professor.'

'I said what before?'

'That the accused's guilt is virtually assured.'

'What? No . . . I don't think . . . I'm sure . . .'

'Yes, yes you did, believe me.'

'When?'

'Two years ago when you were involved in the prosecution case against Andrew Cox. I've read the transcripts you see, every word of your testimony, and the phrase stuck in my mind. You said, "I would say the guilt of this man is virtually assured,"' Aimes quoted, 'but it wasn't, was it Professor?'

CHAPTER 35

Aimes had the good sense to keep Henry Baxter off the witness stand for all but a short denial of wrongdoing and a deep desire to clear his name. He had no idea why the police had arrested him, he said, but it was surely a mistake that would all soon be cleared up. Of course the prosecution tried to tear him apart, but a combination of Baxter's own self-confidence coupled with a comprehensive briefing from Aimes on how to handle every question meant they rarely drew blood.

Julian Aimes summed it all up neatly at the end of the trial. The two girls were untrustworthy, the police incompetent and desperate for a conviction, and the prosecution's expert witness had been wrong before.

'The DNA evidence in this case is entirely unreliable,' said Aimes, 'it could have been caused by cross-contamination in the police station or a carelessly discarded tray, previously used to analyse the DNA of an entirely different person, as it was in a dozen other cases, all of which were potentially serious miscarriages of justice involving DeoxyNuc

Forensics. If your faith in that company remains entirely undimmed then you might want to consider a guilty verdict in this case. If, like me, you feel slightly nervous at the prospect of entrusting a man's life to a company that cannot even be bothered to rinse their trays out, then you should find my client innocent of any and all wrongdoing.'

The jury deliberated for less than a day before returning their verdict.

Not guilty.

Leanne's father left the courtroom immediately.

Henry Baxter couldn't help himself. As soon as he was released from custody he did exactly what I told him not to do. He strode right out of the front door and stood on the court steps, so he could address the Press – and how they loved it. 'I stand here before you as a vindicated man but I have been through a terrible ordeal, made worse by the refusal of both the police and Crown Prosecution Service to consider any possibility of my innocence. However, I never lost faith in the British justice system, which is the finest in the world. I have been tried before a jury of my peers and found wholly innocent of the heinous charges levelled at me. I now leave the court without a stain on my character and wish to be left alone. I intend to take a long holiday and simply request you respect my right to privacy. As to the culpability of the senior police officers and CPS officials, who brought this travesty of a case to court at considerable cost to the taxpayer, I leave that for others to consider. Thank you.'

Then he flounced away, exiting stage left, while the photographers snapped away at him as if he was a movie star. Baxter walked with his chin up and his head held high. Anybody with a shred of decency would have avoided making that speech, but child killers don't have decency. Men like Baxter think laws don't apply to them and they can do whatever they like. Thanks to our barrister it seemed that he was right.

Palmer tailed Baxter halfway across the city to make sure nobody else was watching him. He was clean, as you would expect. The police were already embarrassed enough at his acquittal. They weren't going to compound that by following the guy who'd just made them look so stupid in front of the media. Baxter was on his own when he walked into a hotel on the Quayside and checked in. He went to his room and surveyed it to see if it was to his satisfaction, but he didn't hang about. Instead he left the room and walked down the rear staircase. We'd chosen the hotel carefully, so he could slip quietly out the back unnoticed by the girls manning the reception desk. Palmer was waiting with a car. Baxter climbed in and Palmer sped off.

The lock-up we'd chosen was well outside the city. We used the warehouse to store all sorts of stuff we needed to keep from prying eyes but it was as good a place as any to keep Baxter out of sight while he freed up my money.

Baxter seemed calm when he walked into the room with Palmer. He obviously thought I'd keep my end of the bargain and he was right. I might be a cold, hard, over-logical fucker but I'm not going to break the terms of an agreement I've sworn on my only child's life. The important thing now was to make sure I got our five million back.

Baxter looked at me as if we were old friends who'd had a row and now he wanted to patch things up with me. 'Thank you,' he said, 'I mean it. That lawyer you hired . . .'

'Shut up Baxter,' I told him, 'I don't want to hear it. All I care about is the money. You keep your end of the bargain and I'll keep mine.'

'Haven't you forgotten something?' he asked.

I reached into my pocket and handed him the flight ticket I'd bought him, and his boarding pass. He scrutinised them for a moment, to check they were genuine, then went to put them in his pocket, but I snatched them from him. 'Not yet Baxter. Not till I get my money back.' I put the tickets on a table set against the wall.

Palmer steered Baxter towards a chair in the centre of the room then he handcuffed both of Baxter's wrists to the arms of the chair.

'Oh come on,' protested Baxter, 'is this strictly necessary?'

'Yes,' I told him, 'it is. I don't want you trying to do a runner.'

Kinane was scowling at Baxter from a corner, but I had given him strict instructions not to intervene. There are a whole bunch of unwritten rules in the criminal world but the biggest by far is that you do not rape or murder children. I knew Kinane wanted very badly to kill Baxter and take a long time doing it.

'Shall we get on with it then?' asked Baxter waspishly. 'I have a plane to catch in the morning.'

Robbie wrote down every word, as Baxter outlined how we could access the funds he had buried in that Cayman Islands bank. When Robbie was finished recording everything Baxter told him, he left the room so he could get word to Vince, our man out in the Caymans to handle the transaction. Then we waited. And waited. Baxter should have had the sense to shut up, but he couldn't help himself.

'First thing I'm going to do when I get out of here is take a long, hot bath.'

Kinane looked like a dog being held back by an invisible leash; a leash that I was holding.

'You're not going anywhere until I'm convinced we can access that money,' I reminded him.

'That's just a formality,' he reminded me. 'I have no intention of cheating you out of your millions,' and he smiled slightly, 'don't think I'd sleep too well if that were to happen. Would I, Joe?'

This was too much for Kinane and he climbed to his feet and stepped towards Baxter. He bent low so he could look right into Baxter's face.

'Let me do him anyway,' he implored me, without taking his eyes away from Baxter's, 'even if he gives up the money. We'll give him the same chance he gave that little girl. That would be fair, don't you think?'

Beads of sweat were forming on Baxter's face and I took my time before replying. I was enjoying watching him shit himself like this. In the end though, I was forced to say, 'No Joe. I gave him my word on Emma's life, you know that.'

'That was *your* word,' Kinane protested, 'not mine.'

'And I'm the boss,' I reminded him, 'I swore that no one who worked for me would harm him.'

'Jesus Christ!' shouted Kinane and he slammed his fist down hard on the table in front of Baxter. Then he added, 'Maybe not today, but one day. One day, Baxter. It will be you, me and a dark alley somewhere and then you'll be sorry for everything.'

'I wouldn't say another word if I were you Baxter,' I warned him and he finally saw sense, staying silent for more than an hour while we waited.

Eventually, and not before time, we got the call from Robbie confirming that we could access the money and would be able to transfer it whenever we wished. I tried not to show how relieved I was, but we were so close to running out of operating cash I doubt we'd have gone another month without a serious intervention from someone.

'It's done,' I told Baxter.

'Then you can let me go,' he told me acerbically, 'I fulfilled my side of the bargain, now you can keep yours.' Then he added, 'Oh, and don't forget the money.'

'It's in the car,' I told him. 'Keep an eye on him you two,' I told Kinane and Palmer, 'but make sure he doesn't trip and hurt himself while I'm away.' Palmer accepted this but Kinane shot me an evil look.

I walked out of the room and back to the car. I took out the holdall that contained the generous sum of money Baxter had extorted from me, in return for the repatriation of my five million, then I nodded at the guys standing outside the warehouse so they knew we were done. One of them followed me to the warehouse door and stepped inside with me. He walked quietly behind me all the way to the inner office, but waited outside. I stepped in and placed the holdall on the table next to his airline tickets and Baxter's piggy little eyes lit up.

'My end of the bargain,' I told him, 'it's all in there. I promised you that and I promised that neither I nor anyone who worked for me would ever lay a hand on you, as long as you delivered our money.'

Baxter nodded, 'I'm grateful, I really am,' he said, then he glanced at the handcuffs, 'now if you could just let me go?'

'Not yet,' I told him. 'The deal was I have to let you go on the same day,' I looked at my watch, 'there's still five hours to go before I have to uncuff you.'

'Oh come on, you are joking aren't you?' asked Baxter. 'I can't believe you are going to be so petty. Are you really going to leave me here for five hours until you take these cuffs off me? Seriously?'

'Yes,' I said, 'seriously, but don't worry, one of the boys will come back and uncuff you before the day is over.'

'Christ,' he said in extreme irritation, then he seemed to compose himself, 'very well, play your little games if you must. Just make sure you take these two out of my sight and make sure someone you trust comes back to let me go. Remember your oath.'

'I remember it alright,' I said, 'every word. Come on boys,' and I walked away from Baxter. Palmer and Kinane followed reluctantly.

When we reached the door, I looked back at Baxter who seemed little more than irritated by this inconvenience. 'There's one last thing Baxter,' I told him.

'What?' he asked sourly.

'There's someone outside I'd like you to meet.'

He looked confused then, so I opened the door and gestured for the man who had been waiting outside to come in. I relished the moment when Baxter realised who he was and his eyes went wide with terror.

'This is Matt Bell,' I told Baxter, 'the father of the little girl you raped and murdered, but then I think you know that. He *was* in the courtroom.'

'What's he doing here?' Baxter croaked and he instinctively tugged at the handcuffs on both wrists but they held firm.

'He'd like a word with you,' I said, 'in private.'

Matt Bell took a step further into the room and stared fixedly at Baxter. Baxter's gaze moved lower until he noticed what Bell was carrying; a large, heavy, metal tool box. Bell set the box down on the table and started to remove items from it one at a time; a hacksaw, a claw hammer, a cordless drill, some nails, a small sledge hammer. Baxter's eyes widened in terror as Bell carefully placed each item on the table next to him. Finally he took out a roll of gaffer tape.

'You swore to me!' Baxter pleaded, 'You swore an oath on the life of your child! You can't let him touch me!'

'I swore I wouldn't harm or kill you Baxter,' I reminded him, 'I swore none of my men or anyone hired by me would harm or kill you. Mr Bell doesn't work for me and I haven't hired him to do anything. I merely agreed to his request to give him a little alone-time with you, one on one, just the two of you.' All the while I was speaking Matt Bell was removing items from the tool box and setting them down. Baxter was struggling hard against the cuffs, but he couldn't free himself. 'I think a man deserves that, don't you? He deserves the chance to look his daughter's killer in the eye and make him suffer. That's what I call justice.'

Bell turned to me and I told him, 'You have five hours. Whatever is left after that my boys will dispose of but don't take a minute more.'

'Nooo!' Baxter was shouting. 'Pleeease no!'

Bell ignored him. 'I won't, and thank you.'

'Nobody will ever find him,' I told Leanne's father, 'they won't even look, but we'll make sure there's nothing left to find.' I meant that we would take Baxter's body off to the pig farm. Baxter knew that too and his eyes widened even further. Sweat was plastered all over his forehead.

'Don't do this!' squealed Baxter. I could tell by the smell in that warm room that he'd already soiled himself, but Bell didn't care. He was past caring about anything now except the time he was about to spend alone with the man who'd killed his daughter.

I walked over to the table and picked up the airline ticket. 'You won't be needing this,' I told Baxter, then I turned to Matt Bell.

'When it's over, take Baxter's money and go abroad somewhere. Stay away for a while.' He nodded like he understood but I knew he just wanted me to leave. I could tell he was eager to get started.

Baxter was swearing and pleading, almost

frothing at the mouth now as he rocked from side to side, desperately trying to break free. 'I think it's time to shut you up, Baxter,' I said and Bell reached for the gaffer tape. I watched as Baxter struggled but he couldn't prevent it from being wrapped tightly round his mouth to stifle his screams. Not that anyone would have heard him out here in any case.

Kinane, Palmer and I watched as Bell slowly walked back to the table and selected the claw hammer. I got the impression he had given this day a great deal of thought. Baxter's terrified eyes widened even further as Bell stepped towards him once more, raised the claw hammer and brought it down fast and hard, striking a sickening blow to Henry Baxter's kneecap. His loud but muffled screams were almost too much, even for me.

'You deserve this, Baxter,' I told him, 'remember that, all the while it's happening to you and, by the way, the tool box was my idea, but castrating you before you die was his. Goodbye, Baxter.'

I turned away and walked through the door with Kinane and Palmer. We heard the muffled screams of the child killer all the way back across the warehouse floor. They grew more and more desperate and were only finally stifled when the huge outer door was pulled shut behind us.

'Why didn't you tell me you were going to let that little girl's old man at Baxter?' asked Kinane when we were back in the car on the road to the city.

'Because I needed Baxter to see you angry and resentful,' I told him, 'otherwise he would have been deeply suspicious and would never have released the five million. This way everyone wins.'

'Except Baxter,' added Palmer, 'and that's the way it should be.'

Amrein had arranged for someone who looked remarkably like Henry Baxter to meet us in Newcastle and take the airline ticket and Baxter's passport, which we had quietly lifted from his apartment. The next day he flew from Newcastle to Luton, then took a train into London and the Underground to Heathrow. From there he caught a flight to Bangkok. With Baxter's passport, he sailed through Customs. When he touched down in the Thai capital he checked into a hotel for a few nights and ate in several restaurants, leaving a paper trail for anyone curious enough about him to enquire, then he checked out one morning and vanished. Henry Baxter disappeared forever. No one ever saw him again and nobody cared. He was just another dubious westerner lost in the fleshpots of Bangkok.

The death of Leanne Bell became another unsolved cold case, destined to lie on file for decades. It was the best solution for everyone and, with Baxter seemingly exiled abroad, no one could point the finger of suspicion at Leanne's old man when he also went missing for a while. One of our lads cleaned up the mess and got rid of the body.

He was a veteran of the firm and he didn't say too much about it but he did confirm one thing; what he found there proved to him without doubt that every minute of the last five hours of Henry Baxter's pathetic life was spent in unendurable agony.

CHAPTER 36

We'd barely seen the back of one murder trial before we were embroiled in another, but this time I suspected the accused might not be guilty. I didn't like Golden Boots, not many people did, but I didn't have any great desire to see him banged up for life for a crime he hadn't committed; having said that, I far preferred it to be him than me.

His barrister seemed to be struggling to combat the CPS case.

'The prosecution is big on circumstantial evidence and the accused's character, or lack of it,' Susan Fitch had observed, 'but they are weak on motive. He has to concentrate on that. As far as I can see they have yet to conclusively establish any kind of motive for the killing of Gemma Carlton and if they can show he had no reason to murder the girl then they are halfway there'.

She was right about one thing; when the trial started, the Prosecution tore straight into Golden Boots' character.

'Do you watch pornography on the internet?' asked their barrister.

Golden Boots, wearing a suit and tie for possibly the first time in his life, shrugged, 'Doesn't everybody?'

'But you watch a lot of it, don't you?'

The footballer sniffed, 'Not as much as you probably.'

That earned him a ticking off from the judge before the lawyer continued.

'The police did a check on your internet history. They found a great deal of pornography. In fact I don't think it is an exaggeration to say that was pretty much all they found.'

'I like to play Angry Birds too,' he smirked, 'unless they got confused and thought *that* was a porn site.' He laughed at his own weak joke, but nobody else did. The lawyer ignored him.

'I appreciate that in these more liberal times it is not entirely uncommon for young, adult males to view porn online.'

'You're telling me,' answered the footballer.

'But not many would view the sites you look at for recreational purposes.'

'How do you mean?'

'Girls being punished, adolescent girls being punished, schoolgirls being punished,' the lawyer recited.

'Oh, well yeah, but that's bollocks isn't it, they aren't real schoolgirls and it's all an act isn't it? It's just a bit of caning and naughty stuff before they get down to the real thing but it's all basically harmless, you know, fake and that.'

The lawyer continued unabated, dispassionately rhyming off a list of extremely hardcore porn sites, 'MILFs being punished, ex-girlfriends degraded, embarrassed girls stripped in public, real women groped in the street. Are they all basically harmless too?'

Golden Balls took a while to stammer an answer to that one. 'Look,' he said, 'you don't always know what you are going to get when you land on those sites do you? And if you use porn, which I do, a lot, as you said, you get a bit desensitised to the vanilla stuff.' I could see at least two members of the jury squinting their incomprehension at that phrase. 'So, you know, you try a bit more specialist material.'

'Yes, I see, and your specialist stuff all seems to revolve around the theme of women being tied up, punished and degraded doesn't it? You don't like women very much do you?'

'Course I do. I've had loads of them.' His joke was greeted with a stony silence in the courtroom.

'Indeed,' said the lawyer and something about the way he was taking his time made me realise he was saving the best bit till last. He didn't disappoint. 'And what about the rape videos?'

'Eh?' was all Golden Boots could respond with.

'The rape videos,' repeated the lawyer and you could have heard the proverbial pin drop at that point, 'the ones you used a search engine to find – the nasty videos that aren't on the more conventional pornographic sites. I have viewed one of those videos, one of the ones you downloaded for your personal pleasure and I have to say it was completely sickening. But I will allow you to answer me, so we can hear your side of things. You can tell us why you downloaded a video which contained fifteen minutes of a woman screaming and sobbing while she was stripped and raped by two men in her own home, while a third man videoed the whole thing.'

'I saw that by accident,' protested the Premiership's finest.

'You went on that site by accident?'

'Yes!'

'Seventeen times?'

'Look, I don't think it was real or anything. I reckon she was just acting. I reckon they was all acting in all of them videos.'

'Really,' the lawyer went on, 'so you like to watch video footage of men pretending to rape women? Why ever would you do that?'

When Golden Boots finally answered he did so in a very small voice indeed, 'It was just a laugh, that's all. I never meant nothing by it.'

'It was just a laugh?' repeated the lawyer, 'no further questions.'

Susan Fitch told me that Golden Boots had no real motive for killing Gemma Carlton. She'd said it was the big flaw in the Prosecution case, but their barrister never even bothered to counter that. He didn't just admit there was little motive. The way he portrayed it, motive was meaningless when dealing with someone as disturbed as Golden Boots. 'We may never reach an understanding of the motive of this spoilt footballer for this violent act,' he told the jury. 'Was he slighted in some way by the young girl he had slept with, then discarded, as if she was little more than a piece of meat? Had she flirted with a teammate and made him jealous, did she gossip about his bedroom performance, leaving him open to scorn or ridicule, did she fail to comply with some degraded sexual request? We may never know but it is enough for us to realise that here is a man who has been denied nothing since the day he first signed professional terms as a footballer. He thinks he can have anything he wants, whenever he wants it. It is the Prosecution case that Gemma Carlton, in some way, however slight, managed to annoy, offend or irritate a man with a long history of casual violence, often against women, to such a degree that she became the victim of an assault that led to her death. He even managed to retain the presence of mind to don gloves before carrying out this heinous act of strangulation on his innocent victim, driving her out into the woods and dumping her body as if it were refuse.'

After that little speech, I sensed that Golden Boots was irretrievably fucked.

CHAPTER 37

I was as certain as I could be that Golden Boots was going to be convicted of the murder of Gemma Carlton. Everything stacked up; the evidence all pointed to him as the killer; he'd slept with her, she'd been rebuffed and slagged him off, he'd argued with her, she was seen at his party that night and the DNA proved she'd been driven out to the woods in one of his cars, either by him or someone who was protecting him. The presence of her purse and mobile phone in his house was the final piece of evidence in the Prosecution's favour but, every time I thought about it, I kept feeling the whole thing was just a bit too easy.

I know I shouldn't have cared. I was off the hook, but I was thinking like Austin now. I didn't want the man who had done this to be walking around the streets of our city while the wrong guy did time for Gemma's murder. I thought about it all for a while and suddenly remembered the CCTV footage of Gemma in Cachet with that other girl before they met Golden Boots. We'd never had a satisfactory explanation from Gemma's best friend for her absence from the party on the

304

night her flatmate died. Louise Green had said fuck all to the DC who'd interviewed her, according to Sharp, and wasn't very forthcoming when Kevin went to see her either, but I wondered if he had been asking her the right questions.

There was no particular reason why I found this whole thing unsatisfactory. I certainly had enough on my plate already but, like it or not, I was involved in Gemma Carlton's case, which was probably why I found myself instinctively turning my car into the small street of terraced properties that housed the student digs Gemma had shared with Louise Green.

The girl who answered the door was not unattractive, but clearly thought she was. You could tell by the baggy sweater she wore, which did its best to disguise whatever curves she had. The leggings were shapeless too, like pyjama bottoms. She wasn't much older than eighteen, but she looked like she'd given up already. Maybe it was the effect of sharing a flat with two very attractive girls like Gemma Carlton and Louise Green. She was telling the world she wasn't interested in being pretty and girly, so there. She looked like the kind of lass who wrote long heart-felt poems late at night when she was alone but never showed them to anyone.

'I'm here for a quick word with Louise,' I told her and she turned away from me without a word, called her flatmate's name up the stairs then left me standing on the doorstep.

Louise Green eventually padded down the stairs to greet me, a look of trepidation on her face. 'What is it?' she asked, before she stepped down off the bottom step.

'I'd like a word if I may, about Gemma,' I explained.

'But I've already been through it all,' she said, folding her arms across her chest defensively. She was dressed in jeans and a sweatshirt but was still wearing full make-up, and her hair had been straightened. 'Are you with the police?'

I didn't confirm or deny it, I just said, in an authoritative voice, 'I've been in the court all week. I just have some questions for you about the night Gemma died. Is it okay if I come in?' and I crossed the threshold before she could reply.

'Alright,' she said doubtfully, 'we can talk in my room.' I guessed she didn't want the mousy friend listening in, so I followed her up the stairs. She led me into a tiny room with a bed, a desk and a wardrobe, but not much else. There were piles of clothes on the bed, but little evidence of study.

'I'll make us a brew,' she suggested, 'tea or coffee?'

'Tea's fine, thanks; milk, no sugar.'

While she was gone I looked around the room, but there was nothing of any note. I walked over to the window and stared out at the rooftops. It was a grey day with ominous-looking clouds hovering. A moment later I heard the back door open and watched as Louise Green came out in a hurry. I noticed she had her coat on and she didn't look as if she was putting the rubbish out. She dashed out through the back gate and was gone.

'Fucking bitch,' I said aloud and I turned to go after her, only to find the slight, mousy-looking girl waiting for me on the landing. She gazed at me intently.

'You the police?' she asked me, 'or some sort of private eye?'

'Private,' I said. I should have knocked her out of the way and shot down the stairs after Louise Green but there was something about the way this girl was looking at me, with a combination of interest and nervous hesitancy, that made me wonder if I might actually get more out of her. She looked like she had something to say.

'I'm David, by the way. My mates call me Davey,' and I held out my hand to her. She shook it limply.

'Theresa,' she told me.

I smiled at her, 'I popped round to ask your mate there a few questions but she went to put the kettle on and . . . well it looks like she isn't coming back.'

'I'll make the tea,' she said and I followed her down the stairs. 'You won't get anything out of Louise,' Mousy told me, 'she's too scared.'

'Scared of what?'

'Taking the blame.'

'What for?'

'Everything she's been up to with Gem,' she

looked like she couldn't wait to twist the knife into the girl who ran out on me.

'You mean the drugs?' I offered.

She didn't want to put it into words. 'All of it; being out every night, not bothering with essays or studying, going to the clubs where the footballers hang out all the time, not coming home after, all of that.'

When we reached the cramped kitchen she took two clean mugs from a cupboard and made tea. We sat at a small table opposite one another.

'Must have been lonely for you if they were never around.'

'I didn't care.' And I realised I had the chance to exploit this girl's loneliness and isolation.

'So it was Louise leading Gemma astray then? Not the other way round, like some people are saying?'

'Who's been saying that? Gemma was really nice,' she took a reflective sip of her tea, before adding, 'at first.'

'Until all Louise wanted to do was party.'

'She just wants to get drunk and be with boys the whole time. I didn't. I came here to get a degree. Gemma was the same to begin with but she only really moved out of her parents' house because they were strict with her. They didn't like her going out, always wanted her home early, you know.' It sounded like the classic case of a girl who hadn't been allowed to do much suddenly finding herself off the leash and not knowing when to stop. 'And Louise can be so . . .'

'Persuasive?'

'Yeah,' agreed Theresa, 'we all went out a few times but she has to get really hammered and I don't like that.'

'That's understandable,' I said, 'particularly if you have lectures in the morning.'

'Louise doesn't *do* lectures.'

'So Louise went out every night and persuaded Gemma to do the same thing.'

Theresa started mimicking Louise's voice, 'You're only young once Gemma, don't be so boring, live a little, life's too short,' and for a second she looked like she might cry, 'that's a laugh isn't it? Life's too short.'

'Did they always go to the same spot?'

'Pretty much,' she said, 'some club where they could get free drinks because Louise knew all the footballers. By *know* I mean *shagged*, obviously. She met them when she worked up at the football ground, handing out drinks to stupid businessmen in suits in corporate hospitality.'

I asked her if they went to parties at Golden Boots' house and she confirmed they had done on several occasions.

'They were bragging about it. "Trees", she calls me *Trees*, I hate it. "Trees you should have been there, it was awesome, they drink champagne like it's tap water," but they all sounded like wankers to me.'

'Did you tell the police that Louise was the one persuading Gemma to be out partying every night?'

'No.'

'Why not?'

'They never asked me. They didn't ask me anything.'

'They didn't speak to you about your flatmate's murder?' I found this pretty hard to believe.

'The morning after the night Gemma was killed, I took a train home for the week to see mum and dad. I just assumed Gem had spent the night with her footballer. I didn't even know she'd been killed because I wasn't here. I read about it in the papers days later. If the police came round to speak to Louise while I was gone, she probably didn't tell them about me. She wouldn't want me talking to them.'

The DC who'd questioned Louise was a numpty. He should have realised there was a third girl in the house and gone back to talk to her but Theresa was probably correct, Louise had thrown him a curveball to avoid any inconvenient facts from coming out.

'But you saw Gemma and Louise before you went home? That weekend I mean? You saw them going out on the town?'

'Yes. They both went clubbing together on the Friday night but Gem went out on her own on Saturday. She wanted to go to that footballer's party again but she didn't want to take Louise.'

'Why not?'

'They had a row.'

'What about?'

'Some bloke, obviously. It's always a bloke with Louise. Some famous guy was after Gem, the one who killed her I suppose. Louise got jealous so they had an argument. Gem wanted to see this guy again the next night but she didn't want Louise to know about it. I caught her creeping out late at night.'

'You saw her go?'

'I was up late, planning an all-nighter. We've got exams,' she sounded defensive, like she didn't want me to think she'd been snooping on her flatmates. 'I went down to the kitchen to make some tea and she was just going out.'

'And she told you what she was up to?'

'She told me not to make a noise in case Louise heard she was going out again. She was all dressed up.'

'But she wasn't going to the club? She was going straight to his house?'

She nodded, 'She was excited about it. She said he must really like her because he was sending a driver.'

'Yeah, they do that.'

'When they want a girl?'

I nodded.

'But it doesn't mean anything, does it?' she asked me, 'not what Gemma thought anyway?'

'No, it doesn't.'

'He just wanted to use her and dump her, but she must have had a row with him and now she's dead.' She did start crying then, dabbing her eyes with a scrunched-up tissue.

I didn't want to get into a discussion about the guilt or innocence of Golden Boots so instead I asked, 'Did you see him? The guy who came to pick her up?'

'No, he was waiting around the corner in his car. She asked him to do that so Louise wouldn't see.'

That was bad news. If we knew who the guy was, if we had a description even, we could have found him and made him tell us what really happened when she got to the house. 'So you didn't see him at all?'

'No,' she admitted, 'but I know who it was.'

'You do?'

'Yes.'

'How could you know who he was, if you didn't see him?'

'Gem told me who was picking her up. She joked about him, because he was a bit weird looking. He was a regular at those parties, so he didn't mind taking her.'

'Do you know his name?'

'No,' she admitted, 'but Gemma used to call him "Jaws".'

'Jaws? Like the shark?'

She shook her head, 'Like those old James Bond

films they put on the telly. There was a man in one with funny teeth.'

'Oh yeah, I remember. He was a big guy.'

'Yes,' she said.

'This fella was big too, I s'pose?'

She nodded, 'I saw him once through the window when he called to pick the girls up.'

'You saw him.'

'Yes,' she said.

'And he was a big guy?'

She nodded. 'Could you describe him a bit more, do you think?' I was trying to sound like it wasn't that big a deal, hoping I could coax it out of her.

'He was really big and he had the funny teeth, like that Jaws guy?'

'He had metal teeth?'

'No,' she scoffed, 'just funny teeth.'

'How do you mean?'

'His front teeth were missing.'

She brought her finger up till it was right in the middle of the top row of her front teeth and pressed it against them, 'Just there. He had a gap where his teeth should have been and it was just there.'

CHAPTER 38

I could tell Kevin Kinane was pleased I'd sent for him. He looked relaxed when he walked into the Cauldron with his father. He'd done a good job investigating the death of Gemma Carlton; I'd already told him that, and he was expecting the reward that was coming to him.

'Did you ever do any history at school, Kevin?' I asked him, when he was seated opposite me with a drink in his hand. His father was to one side of him, nursing a good whisky while we talked. I made sure Palmer was in the room with us.

'I didn't do much school at all, if I'm honest,' and he smiled self-consciously at that.

'He was always out on the rob or twocking cars with his mates,' said Joe Kinane.

'I've read a bit of history,' I continued, 'there was a king once who fell out with his archbishop, who happened to be an old friend of his but, in a rage, he demanded of his courtiers "Who will rid me of this turbulent priest?" Two knights got the wrong idea about that so they went round to see this archbishop and they cut him to pieces, thinking they were doing the king's bidding. Of

314

course when the king found out he was devastated. He couldn't believe that a casual remark had led to a man's death. Worse than that, everybody thought he'd ordered the killing, so his reputation was destroyed in an instant. It didn't matter what he said or did, everybody just assumed he was a murdering bastard.'

'Tough break,' acknowledged Kevin Kinane and he sipped his whisky a little too casually.

'It was,' I said and I stayed silent for a while to see what he would do. When he said nothing in reply I asked, 'Is that what you did Kevin, heard me say something about what a pain in the arse Carlton was, then went away and thought how can I really fuck up this copper's mind and throw him off the scent, without actually killing him? I know, I'll murder his daughter.'

'What the fuck are you talking about?' demanded Joe Kinane.

There hadn't been a reaction from Kevin at all, not even a glimmer, so I continued, 'A senior policeman once told me that he didn't like my organisation but he couldn't believe I was stupid enough or so far beyond redemption that I would arrange to have a young girl murdered to further my own ends. You are though Kevin, aren't you?'

'What did you just say?' asked Joe Kinane sharply and he was leaning forwards in his seat now like he was about to launch himself at me. I could sense Palmer tensing in readiness.

'It was him Joe, your son. He killed Gemma

Carlton. Your eldest here heard me ranting about DI Carlton getting in our way. There I was, wishing this annoying copper would just pack up and fuck off out of it, because his obsession with bringing me down was getting to me, so he decided to solve the problem, though he had a funny way of doing it. I can understand your shock Joe, but Kevin has to account for it.'

'Don't be bloody stupid,' Kinane told me, 'you've got this all wrong . . .'

'Kevin hangs out at Cachet all the time, meets loads of girls there, always chatting to them, so who's gonna remember one more, eh? And the CCTV doesn't cover the VIP bar, only the lift, so he could meet anyone he liked up there. One day he hears about Gemma Carlton. Maybe she'd mentioned to someone that her dad was a copper so Kevin took an interest, then he realised who she was. He figured getting rid of her would knock the stuffing out of her old man, and he was right about that. So he got to know her, just a little bit, enough to slip her a VIP pass on the QT and give her a lift home. He was seen doing that. Did you get her to introduce herself to Golden Boots too Kevin, or just encourage Louise to do that for you? I reckon so. She was his type wasn't she; young, pretty and a bit naïve, the way he likes them. When he shagged her you had the perfect patsy; a suspect that surprised nobody.'

'I'm warning you,' Joe Kinane told me and he

got to his feet. Palmer took a step towards him and they eyed each other.

'Hear me out Joe, you'd be wise to. We've been looking for the driver, the one who took Gemma Carlton from that party out into the woods but I found him. I've had Kevin looking for the guy and it was him all along. That's why he volunteered to work with Sharp to hunt for the killer. It was him and he didn't even take her to the party. He didn't have to. Kevin arranged to pick her up at her student house, drove her somewhere and killed her in the car. That's why nobody really remembers her being there. Not because they were all off their tits on drugs but because she really wasn't there. Kevin told everyone she'd been seen there that night but she couldn't have been. She was already dead.'

'You're out of your fucking mind,' Joe Kinane told me. He looked at his son, but Kevin was saying nowt. Instead he was listening intently so he could learn what I had against him before he tried to deny it.

'Kevin stuck her body in the boot of a car he'd lifted from Golden Boots' place, leaving traces of her hair and fibres from her clothes all over it. His too, probably, but then nobody was looking for him and he could just say he'd driven it before, loads of people had. The important thing was leaving traces of Gemma for the police to find, so they could build a case against Golden Boots.

'Kevin drove her out to the woods and dumped

her body. It looked like someone had panicked and ditched her there but Kevin wanted her to be found. The bit he thought was really clever was taking her phone and handbag and planting them at Golden Boots' house later. That, and the DNA in the boot of the car, is doing the work of the Prosecution for them.

'Gemma's dad was out of the picture and we had a fall guy he knew the police would love to put away. Trouble was, DI Carlton immediately thought it was me who'd killed his daughter. You see he thought she was a blushing virgin, tucked up in bed at night with her school books and a hot-water bottle for company. He knew nowt about Golden Boots and his parties, so obviously he thought I was responsible for her death and he was right, wasn't he Kevin? I was, indirectly.'

'Why are you saying all this?' Joe Kinane's tone had changed to one of pleading. It was hard to tell what was upsetting him more, me talking or his son staying silent.

'Because we have a witness, Joe. More than one, in fact. A girl in Gemma's street, for one, who saw the man who took Gemma Carlton away in a car that night. He's a distinctive-looking lad, your Kevin. Not a face you'd easily forget,' then I looked Kevin right in the eye, 'you should have had your teeth fixed Kevin. If you'd done that I might never have known.'

Kevin Kinane looked sick. I'd deliberately worded the bit about the witness so he wouldn't know who it was or how many people had seen him that night. I didn't want him charging down to Theresa's house and trying to shut her up. The way I'd told it, he was screwed.

Eventually I said, 'Your dad is waiting for you to deny it, Kevin, but I know that you won't. I just want to know why. What the fuck got into your stupid, sick head that made you think killing a copper's daughter was a good idea?'

Kevin Kinane stared back at me, then he turned to his father. Joe Kinane looked as if he was finally really seeing his son for the first time.

'It isn't true,' said Joe, 'tell him it isn't true Kevin, please. Tell me and him that he's got it wrong. No son of mine could . . .' and his words tailed away.

'We killed a girl before, remember?' Kevin told his dad. 'She was innocent too, or have you forgotten about her?'

'Jesus, that wasn't . . . that was an accident,' Joe Kinane protested, 'and no, I have not forgotten about her. I think about her every day. Not a single night goes by when I don't wish I could turn the clock back and find a way to see off Braddock that doesn't involve killing that poor lass. All this time it's been eating me up inside,' and I believed him, 'And you? What do you do? You don't lie awake at night thinking about her. You go off and do something far worse. How the hell could you do this Kevin? How can you live with it?'

Kevin Kinane wouldn't, or couldn't, answer that one.

'You once told me that when we finally found the lowlife who'd killed this young girl we should kill him,' I reminded Joe, 'you told me that was what he deserved. I said no, that we needed to hand him over to the police to clear my name and when he got a life sentence *that* would be justice of sorts. Well, now you know it's Kevin, so what are you going to do, kill him or send him down for life? You tell me Joe, because I have run out of answers.'

I had never seen Joe Kinane knocked down by anyone before but those words, and the knowledge that came with them, floored the big man. He took a step backwards and his legs seemed to give way, as he dropped back onto the couch, brought his huge hands up to his face and buried his head in them.

CHAPTER 39

It took the jury eleven hours to reach its verdict. It was a big day for the Premier League. They finally had their first convicted murderer.

Afterwards the Press had a field day, going into moral overdrive, reminding us that Golden Boots was a beast of our own making, while conveniently forgetting their role in the feeding of that monstrous ego. It was our misplaced adulation, our distorted sense of the importance of celebrity that had really killed Gemma Carlton, or so they told us. By indulging Golden Boots throughout the whole of his pampered life, by never saying no to him, always finding excuses for his behaviour, giving him more second, third and final chances, than any human being should reasonably be allowed, we were all of us complicit in her death. They told us it was only ever going to be a matter of time before a footballer had such an overblown sense of the importance of his own life that he thought nothing of robbing a young girl of hers.

Of course, like much of what passes for journalism in this day and age, it was bollocks. Golden Boots didn't kill Gemma Carlton at all. I knew that, but I wouldn't have been able to save his worthless hide even if I'd wanted to.

He wept in the dock when he heard the verdict. The next day he was sentenced and he sobbed again, as if getting life, the only permissible sentence for murder, was a surprise. Perhaps even now, at the very end, he still believed there was one rule for him and another for the rest of us mere mortals.

The judge was particularly critical of his complete lack of remorse and failure to admit guilt, even when the evidence against him was overwhelming, further compounding the misery of Gemma's family by putting them through the agony of a trial. His final words were reserved for the sickening manner in which he had blackened the good name of a policeman's daughter by indicating she had been a promiscuous drug-user. The judge hinted that this alone might be enough to deny him his first shot at parole and, since Golden Boots would be at least forty by the time he was released, his football career was effectively over. The club wasted no time in cancelling his contract, so they could stop paying out any more of his eye-watering wages. A civil suit from Gemma's parents was expected to wipe out the rest of what remained of his fortune

After sentencing, Golden Boots was sent down and placed in a holding cell. He was told someone would be along soon to offer him a sedative, to alleviate some of the shock he was feeling. I'm reliably informed he sat there, intermittently weeping and staring off into space. When the sedative finally arrived it came with a message from the officer who delivered it.

'A little tip when you are on the inside, Mister Billy Big Bollocks; there's time and there's hard time. You keep your mouth shut about some of the people you've been doing business with and you'll find you're less likely to be stabbed in the exercise yard or raped in the showers, you hear me?' Golden Boots looked up into our tame guard's eyes in disbelief. 'If you're sensible, there'll be a little protection for you but if you're not, if you get to thinking you can get a bit shaved off your sentence, by spinning the police a bunch of lies about gangsters you knew on the outside, well, that's when the really hard time will start. You think you're tough, but the proper hard men are queuing up to make you their bitch. You got that?'

Golden Boots started nodding vigorously to show he had got the message.

'Good lad,' said our guard, then he put out a hand and patted him on the cheek, 'take care now and you watch yourself, you hear, because we sure as hell will be.'

I suppose there is an irony here. Henry Baxter was judged to be innocent of a crime he actually committed, whereas Golden Boots was starting a life sentence for a murder he had nothing to do with. It could convincingly be argued that real justice was eventually served in the case of Henry Baxter. No one in my crew thought he got anything less than the fate he richly deserved. It could also be argued that Golden Boots merited a few years jail time, for all of his collective misdemeanours put together, and I wouldn't argue too strongly against that, but he was inside now for one reason, and one reason alone. I had to keep my main enforcer's son away from a life sentence because, if Kevin Kinane went down, there would be no knowing what Joe might do. This way he stayed by my side and now he owed me big style. Like I've said before, loyalty is everything in our game.

Kevin Kinane had to be punished though. We all knew that, even Joe, especially Joe. I gave Kevin seven days to get his life in order, before making him leave the city he had known all of his life.

There was no opposition from Joe. His disgust at what his son had done was very clear to me. He didn't even see him off at the station. We left that job to Peter and Chris Kinane who, early one bright morning, put their older brother on the first train out of Newcastle Central Station to London, with one suitcase, then reported that he was gone for good. I could tell they were as shocked by what he had done as their dad. Aside from the obvious evil of murdering a young girl who had done nothing to offend us, which was a bad enough sin on its own, he had brought a huge amount of heat down on our organisation, putting all our lives and livelihoods in jeopardy in the process. That was indefensible and there was no future for him with us anymore. I had no idea what he was going to do with the rest of his life and I didn't care. For such a big man, he went like a lamb.

CHAPTER 40

With two murder trials behind us and the police off my back, I was keen to be rid of the rest of my problems. Only one man could help me do that.

Amrein was taking afternoon tea in his hotel on the Quayside when I arrived. He was sitting on his own at one table, with two burly bodyguards occupying another, watching over him.

'Amrein, I keep telling you, I need you to persuade this crazy Russian you set me up with that I don't want to climb into bed with him, no matter how much he is offering. I need you to scare him, buy him, kill him if you have to, do whatever it takes, but I want him off my back permanently. Have I made myself incredibly clear about that?'

'Yes you have . . . it's just . . .'

'It's just what?'

'Okay, you pay us for this kind of thing, usually, I understand that and so do the people I work for. They are highly sympathetic to your plight but we have a major problem here that we are thinking is beyond our capability.'

'I don't believe this.'

'We anticipated you would be reluctant to do this kind of business with him, for obvious reasons, but the man is not known for accepting a refusal of any kind.'

'I gathered that.'

'And now you know a little of his plans, he will be even more reluctant to allow you to carry on outside of his *Krysha*, as he calls it.'

'Are you telling me he is not scared of your organisation? Not in the slightest?'

'The FSB and the GRU have been trying to get Vasnetsov for a decade. You think he is frightened of us?'

As well as attracting the ire of the FSB, Vasnetsov had to contend with the GRU, the Russian Foreign Military Intelligence service. He had made some powerful enemies.

'Then kill the fucker.'

'This is exactly what the Russians have been trying to do. They've had agents penetrate his organisation with the sole purpose of assassinating the man.'

'And?'

'They were exposed by his men and killed. He has some very clever people working for him and he pays them crazy money.'

'What about a tribute of some kind; a pay-off, to make him look in another direction for his supply line.' I was getting desperate now and I knew it, just as I knew Amrein's answer before he gave it.

'The man is worth twenty billion dollars. His fortune will increase massively if he can get this African oil project off the ground. What use does he have for your money or ours?'

'And you can't protect me from him?'

'We could,' he assured me, 'if you were willing to live your life in something resembling a witness protection programme; change your name, your appearance, move to another country, never see any of your friends and family again then, yes, we could save you from this man, but that would be expensive, and how long could you continue to pay for this service if you are running your company from a desert island?'

'Not long,' I admitted, 'this business doesn't exactly take kindly to sleeping partners. You'd soon be dealing with someone else in Newcastle and then I'd just be an expensive house guest.'

'Regrettably so,' he told me, with characteristic honesty.

'So then, in summary, I'm fucked.'

Amrein said nothing. It was the first time he hadn't contradicted me, which told me everything I needed to know.

'Let me ask you something Amrein, what would make the Stevic brothers come all the way from Belgrade to take me on?' He opened his mouth as if to answer but I cut him off, 'and don't give me that bullshit about them thinking we're weak.'

'That is usually the way they operate.'

'Since when has taking over Newcastle, Glasgow and Edinburgh been a sign of weakness?'

'What then?'

'It's Vasnetsov,' I told him. 'He's the man behind them. He's got to be. I wasn't certain until I offered them money to walk away.'

'Money you had no intention of paying?'

'I needed to be sure.'

'It would explain why they turned you down,' he admitted, 'if they already have his money.'

'Remember what he told me about *Krysha*? If ever I have a problem I could come to him and he would make it disappear.'

'And the Serbs would return to Belgrade and you would think it was because of him.'

'And it would be,' I said, 'he'd send them home because he was the one who ordered them over here in the first place. How else could they get something on an Assistant Chief Constable? He set that up.'

Amrein thought for a moment, 'I think you may be right, but what can you do about it?'

'I can show him I don't need his help to get rid of the Stevic brothers.'

As soon as I concluded my meeting with Amrein I took Palmer to one side. 'I need you to use your skills and contacts,' I explained, 'the guys you knew from your time in the intelligence services.'

He was immediately evasive, 'I was only ever seconded to those guys for short periods . . .'

I interrupted him, 'Can we cut the crap, Palmer, because I haven't got time for it? How long have I known you? I've seen what you can do. You weren't seconded to anyone. You were the real deal, so can you afford me the courtesy of stopping with the denials?'

Palmer thought for a moment then said, 'Sure. What is it you want?'

'I need you to go off the grid for a while. Can you do that?'

'Of course.'

'There's something important I need you to do for me.'

As DI Sharp walked into the station he immediately realised something was wrong. The whole atmosphere seemed different and he soon learned why. The top brass were here. He could see them at the far end of the room, across a sea of desks, but they hadn't spotted him yet. They were standing outside his boss' office, deep in conversation. He could tell they were waiting for something or someone and his first impulse was to turn around and march straight from the room. He'd go back down to the car park, climb into his car and drive away as fast as he could. He knew he'd not get far, but Sharp would take his chances that way rather than be arrested here in front of everybody he'd worked alongside for years. *Ten years minimum*, he thought and felt sick.

To the left and right of him, desks were occupied by fellow officers but nobody acknowledged him. They all knew. He'd witnessed this kind of thing before. An unsuspecting detective would walk in one day to find a reception committee waiting for him; senior brass, his boss, a couple of hand-picked fellow officers, chosen for their bulk and ability to quietly contain him without a fuss being made. Everyone would know in advance, no one would blink as he was arrested on suspicion of corruption, then escorted from the building.

Sharp was about to turn on his heel when his boss DCI White spotted him and shouted across the room, 'Sharp!' he called, just loud enough. Sharp couldn't possibly claim he hadn't heard.

'Boss,' replied Sharp, with a strained smile, but he could already feel his cheeks burning with shame.

DCI White nodded towards his vacant office, 'We'd like a word.'

I was at home when the call came through. He didn't say who it was but I didn't need him to. The sound of those deep, rasping breaths was enough.

'I didn't tell you everything,' he wheezed, 'there's something you want to know, but I'm wanting another five grand for the information.'

'Really?' I replied, astounded at the cheek of this guy, because I seriously doubted he had anything new to tell me, 'and what would that be?'

'The name of the man who killed your fatha.'

Like most pubs, the Newcastle Arms is busy at the weekend, particularly on a match day, but quiet during the week. I met my asthmatic informant in a near-empty bar.

He was already there waiting for me. I bought my pint and sat down. 'Well,' I said, 'this had better be good.'

He gave me a grim smile, 'Why? Will you kill us if it isn't like?' He had another coughing fit from the effort involved in asking me that. 'Well, you'll have to be quick. I've got three months, so they say.' From the look on his face, he wasn't bluffing.

'Is that why you wanted to see me? To unburden yourself?'

'For the money,' he told me, 'I've got nowt, man,' and he shook his head bitterly. 'I want five grand for me daughter and her kiddie. That's loose change in your pocket. If you give it me, I'll let you have the name of the man who saw to your fatha.'

'And how would you know that,' I challenged him, 'if you were on the outside looking in?'

'Aye, well, I lied about that? I did more for Bobby Mahoney than I care to admit.' He didn't look like he was lying this time, so I let it go.

'Then why didn't you give me this name before?'

'Because the bloke's still alive,' he explained, 'and he's an evil bastard.'

'And you were scared he'd come after you?'

He shrugged, 'Doesn't matter now, does it?'

'How would I know it's him?' I asked. 'You're desperate. You could be spinning me any old yarn.'

'Go and see him,' he suggested, 'judge for yourself, persuade him to tell you the truth. I bet you could, an' all.'

'Maybe.'

'If you're convinced, you can give me my money.'

'You're a trusting soul, all of a sudden.'

'Aye, well, you'll either give us it or you won't but, like I said, it's loose change to you and I've heard you don't welch.'

'You'll get it,' I assured him, 'if the information you give me is correct. Out with it then.'

He leaned in close. 'Have you heard of Mickey Crowe?' he asked me.

'No.'

'No reason you should have,' he admitted, 'he found God,' and he let out a little snort of derision, because clearly he hadn't. 'Jacked it all in when he was born again, turned his back on a life of crime and went off to save the souls of bad people instead,' he smiled at that, 'he must be a busy lad in Newcastle.'

'Jacked what in exactly?'

'Killing people for money.'

CHAPTER 41

I don't know what I was expecting from the church of the Tyneside Bible Fellowship, but I wasn't expecting this. The place was huge and looked more like a corporate headquarters than a church. I wondered how much the congregation had been fleeced to pay for it. I guessed they didn't mind. After all, they'd been 'saved'.

There was a sign on the lawn at the front of the church that proclaimed, 'The Bible is inspired by God and is the final authority on all matters.' Not much room for debate there then. I could never understand how quoting lines from a book, written by men, decades after the death of Jesus Christ, could prove anything to anyone about the existence of a god.

There was nobody in the church at this hour, so we ignored the big glass doors at the front and walked around the back. We found a door that was unlocked. Joe Kinane and I walked inside. We followed the corridor until we reached a small kitchen. There, sitting all alone at the table, drinking his tea, was the Reverend Michael Crowe.

I recognised the man from his picture on the church's website.

'Who are you?' he asked, clearly disconcerted by our presence. 'What do you want?'

'That's not a very Christian welcome, Reverend Crowe. You know Joe Kinane from your old life,' I reminded him, 'it doesn't matter who I am. Kinane works for me now. That's all you need to know.'

The reverend looked nervous, but was he scared of Joe Kinane or of having his past life exposed to his congregation? Maybe it was both.

'Is this what you really do now Crowe?' asked Kinane.

'Since I was saved, yes,' he answered, with the glassy-eyed conviction of the brain-washed.

'Saved?' asked Kinane, 'you're fucking joking, aren't you?'

'I was saved and anointed by God to spread his word,' Crowe told us firmly.

'Anointed by God personally?' asked Kinane. 'Nice of him to take time out of his day, like that. He must be hellishly busy, poor bastard.'

Kinane went over to the kettle then. He picked it up and filled it from the tap in the kitchen sink. The sound of the water pouring into the kettle made Crowe turn his head and watch my enforcer. Kinane put it back on its stand and switched it on. Crowe continued to watch him as Kinane went to the oven and turned on all of the gas rings. There was a hiss and a click, click,

click until each ring fired and flames shot up from them.

'Good screw is it?' I asked, 'making a canny living are you, from your flock I mean? Or is that not what it's called in your church?'

'You can mock me all you wish,' Crowe told me, 'but the time is fulfilled and the kingdom of God is at hand' he said; 'repent ye and believe the gospel; Mark, Chapter one, Verse fifteen.'

'Shut the fuck up and listen or Kinane will break both of your arms. That's David; Chapter one, Verse one.'

Kinane opened a drawer and selected some large kitchen knives. He checked that Crowe was looking at him as he placed the knives blade first into the flame of one of the gas rings, then he took a saucepan and filled it with water and put that on a ring too. Finally he took a frying pan and poured a load of oil in it until it made a deep pool and he placed this on one of the rings. I said nothing while he did this and Crowe watched him intently the whole time. 'This is quite a change of lifestyle, I must say,' I said, 'was it gradual or did it happen overnight? I mean one day you are killing people and the next saving them. That's what it says on your website anyhow; the bit about saving them, I mean. You don't mention the killing. Funny that.'

'Salvation is a miracle, only through the goodness of God can we be led to repentance,' he recited.

'So you repent all of your sins do you?'

'I have made my peace with God, yes.'

'But you were never punished, were you? For those crimes you committed, for the men you killed. You just stopped, changed your life and got off scot-free. No prison term, no nothing in fact, just renounce evil one day and set yourself up preaching the word of the Lord to the gullible the next. Does it not feel strange telling fairy stories to nut jobs while fleecing them out of their money? I suppose it's undemanding work.'

'I feel sorry for you,' he told me, 'it's obvious to me you are in great pain but it isn't too late, it's never too late to renounce evil and hear the word of Christ. He is your salvation, believe me.'

'I am in great pain,' I admitted, 'I've got this terrible pain in the arse right now listening to you banging on about your imaginary friends Jesus and the Lord.'

'There shall be false teachers among you, who shall bring in damnable heresies,' he was quoting at me again.

I ignored this. 'Kinane didn't bring his tool box but he doesn't need it here, not with boiling water, red hot knives and scalding oil. Kitchens are very dangerous places for men who don't provide answers to my questions.'

'What questions?'

'How many men did you kill for Bobby Mahoney?'

'I told you, I have made my peace with God.'

'But not with me and I'm the one that's in the room right now asking you. God can't protect you

337

from me, Crowe. If you really think he can, you'd better call on him now and ask him to smite me down, before I get Joe to put one of your hands in that pan of hot oil. Are you taking me seriously? I hope so. How many was it? Some say a dozen, there are others who claim it was more.' He went silent on me then.

'Perhaps when we are done here,' I admitted, 'we'll just call the police and give them the information they need on all of those cold cases they've got on file from the seventies. They've got retired coppers working on them part-time and they love it because, no matter how old the case, they've always got a good chance of linking a suspect to a corpse due to the DNA. Must be your worst nightmare that Crowe? I mean, when you were killing folk nobody had heard of DNA. Bit sneaky of them to change the rules like that, eh? Not very sporting. I reckon we'll start with the four people I know you killed for Bobby. I've been asking around you see. Should we tell them about James Connor? Or Martin Pearce?' There was recognition in his eye at those names. 'Maybe Patrick Donnelly will ring a bell with them or Susan Carter; poor lady was strangled in her bed one night because she knew the names of a gang who'd carried out a bunch of armed robberies and she was going to give up the lot of them. Bet the police kept her night clothes and bed sheets all these years.'

'Bound to have,' confirmed Kinane.

'I killed six men for Bobby Mahoney and one woman,' Crowe admitted suddenly, snapping out of his bible-speak. 'I think about them every day and pray to God to earn his forgiveness.'

'He might forgive you but Northumbria Constabulary most definitely will not,' I reminded him.

'What do you want from me?'

'I want you to tell me about another man you killed, Alan Blake.'

'What do you want to know?' he asked, 'and why do you want to know it?'

'I want you to admit that you killed him. I know it already, but I want to hear it from you.' I was bluffing the man. Armstrong sounded convincing but I didn't know if he was right about Crowe's role in my father's disappearance. 'Then I want to know why he was killed and where he is buried.'

'Why?'

'I have my reasons. They're not your concern.'

'And if I tell you, you'll leave me to continue my work here?' he asked me.

'Yes,' I said.

It took the Reverend Michael Crowe a long time to summon up the nerve to talk about it. He wasn't the only one who was nervous. I had to hide the way I was feeling inside. I was so close to finally understanding what had happened to my father after all of those years of wondering. I had to resist the urge to shout at Crowe to come out with it.

Finally he said, 'I was a different person then.'

He was explaining or rather justifying himself, 'Godless, lost, in great pain. I drank and took drugs and I did terrible things for money. Bobby Mahoney ordered me to kill Alan Blake because Blake had stolen from him. The man I was then never thought to question that.'

'Alan Blake stole the Stuart & Brown payroll and tried to keep it all for himself?' I prompted.

'Yes,' Crowe seemed relieved I knew a little of it already.

'How did he do that?'

'Bobby's lads were trying something new. Instead of them all disappearing with the money after a job and lying low, they reckoned it would look better if they handed it straight to someone else and were seen in public shortly after. There were two getaway cars that day; one for the men and one for the money. That way the lads could be seen sitting in a pub in the city-centre minutes after they'd pulled the job, which put the police on the wrong track.'

'Not a bad idea, but why was Alan Blake trusted with the money?'

'I doubt he was anybody's first choice but someone will have vouched for him. Usually no one was foolish enough to steal from Bobby Mahoney.'

'But he was, and he got away with it to begin with. Why did he come back?'

'How do you mean?' he answered.

I realised there was no point asking the Reverend

why my father had blown his cover and returned to the north-east years after stealing from Bobby. Crowe might have been anointed by God, but he wasn't a mind reader.

'Where did you find him?' I asked instead.

'He was hiding out in a friend's flat in Scotswood. The friend was away in Northern Ireland with the army. We were told where he was staying and I went down there.'

'How did you kill him?'

'With a knife.'

'And what did you do with the body?'

'Got it out of there and buried it where Bobby told me.'

'Which was?'

'On a building site. There was a trench already dug, part of the foundations of the new supermarket they were building. His body is under the car park.'

'Thanks for the information.' I told him, and he just couldn't help himself. He had to ask me.

'Why ask about Alan Blake now, after so many years? What was he to you?'

'I'm David Blake,' I told him, 'Alan Blake was my father.'

'Jesus Christ.'

'Won't help you,' I said, 'I told you that already.'

CHAPTER 42

The Reverend Michael Crowe must have given up a longer than usual prayer to his God when we left him sitting in the kitchen unharmed. I couldn't see the point in killing the man. He might have admitted to the murder of my father, but he didn't order it. The man who did that was already dead, killed by me years later, an irony I'd been wholly unaware of until now. When I left that church I walked up to the car and before I climbed in I leant against it and took a few deep breaths. I felt like something invisible was crushing me all of a sudden, robbing me of breath. I'd been getting feelings like this more and more lately. I didn't need a doctor to work out they were some sort of stress-related panic attacks, but there was fuck all I could do about them. Who wouldn't have panic attacks in my world?

'You alright?' asked Kinane.

'Hunky fucking dory,' I told him and climbed into the car.

'This would have been a big deal once,' I told Joe Kinane. We were looking down on the red brick, flat-roofed so-called supermarket, closed down now and awaiting redevelopment; which was code for ripping it all down and starting again from scratch. This building would have been the pride and joy of the supermarket chain's family once, these days it was the embarrassing uncle. It had probably been opened by a local celebrity back in the seventies; a TV presenter or 'comic', now it waited for the bulldozers.

'There's a Tesco near us five times the size of this,' said Kinane, confirming why it would soon be consigned to memory.

We walked across the car park and I couldn't help wondering if we really were walking on my father's grave. There was no real reason for Crowe to lie about that. When we reached the front door of the supermarket we stopped, because it was boarded up and we could go no further. I was wondering why I had even bothered to come down here. Myself, I didn't want a gravestone or a shrine of any kind for Emma to feel guilty about if she didn't come to visit me every week. They could burn me and scatter the ashes on the pitch at St James' Park when nobody was looking. As I stood on my father's final resting place, I felt nothing at all. Kinane looked troubled though.

'What's the matter with you?' I asked.

Kinane looked at me, then he glanced back at the front of the supermarket. There, on the wall, was a faded wooden plaque with a metal plate on it. There was an inscription and I took a step forward so I could read it. I was right. The place had been opened by a northern comic but that wasn't the bit that made my blood boil. There, under the comic's name, was the date the place had been opened and it was four years before my father had finally disappeared.

'Get back round to that lying bastard,' I told Kinane, 'and get Peter and Chris to go with you. I want you to give that Reverend a proper going over. The kind even his precious God would flinch to look at.'

I knew Kinane could handle the job of beating the truth from Michael Crowe without me and I didn't want to waste any more time on this fool's errand involving the fate of my father. There were things I had to put in order before the mad Russian oligarch realised I was going to be of no use to him. I wasn't exactly drafting my last will and testament here but it certainly felt like it.

I caught up with Joanne in the park. Emma was in her pushchair chomping on a bright red ice lolly. I gave my little girl a kiss and she smiled but went back to slurping on her lolly. I asked Joanne to walk with me.

'I've got something for you,' I said. Joanne had her rough edges, but she'd always been straight with me, a friend to Sarah and great with Emma. I reached into my inside jacket pocket, took out an envelope and handed it to her. She stopped pushing the buggy. She looked shocked.

'What's this?'

'It's not your P45, if that's what you're thinking. You've been terrific with Emma and a big help to Sarah. This is just . . .' I'd rehearsed this conversation in my mind but now I was a bit stuck for words. Joanne wasn't a member of the firm, she was practically family . . . 'look upon it as an insurance policy . . . in case our circumstances alter. If Sarah or me . . . and Emma obviously . . . if anything were to change. Say we had to move away or something like that.'

'And you couldn't take me with you?'

'Precisely,' I said. 'Obviously we would want to but if we couldn't.' I was glad she was thinking in terms of moving house or country and not the very real prospect that her employer could wind up dead at any point. 'I want you to have some security and it's my way of saying thank you for helping Sarah when she's not been feeling too great, you know.'

She nodded, 'So what is it, like? A season ticket to the Wonga-Dome?'

'The deeds to your flat.'

'What?'

'The apartment is yours, legally, you own it. It's fully paid up. From now on you can decide if you want to keep it, sell it, move a bloke in with you, whatever.'

'But I can't . . .'

'Yes you can,' I told her and when she tried to give the envelope back to me, I took both her hands in mine and repeated, 'yes . . . you . . . can . . . and I want you to. You'll be doing me a favour.

This is one less thing for me to worry about and, believe me, right now I need that.'

'I don't know what to say.'

'Good.' I kissed her on the cheek, waved to my daughter and said, 'I'll see you both at tea time. I've got a meeting.' And I left Joanne standing there clutching her brown envelope.

Sharp was late for our meeting, very late, but I wanted him to be there, so I made everybody wait. When Joe Kinane walked in I took him away from the rest of the guys and into my office so I could speak to him privately.

'We gave Crowe a proper beating like you told me,' he explained, 'he was loudly renouncing his God when we left him. I kid you not.'

'And?'

'He stuck to his story, never deviated from it once, told us over and over again that Alan Blake had stolen the proceeds from the wages robbery. Bobby had realised he was stalling on handing it over and he got suspicious. He thought Alan Blake might be planning to leave the country. Apparently he bought a car from Hunter and that was the final straw. Bobby sent Crowe round to retrieve the money and kill him. The Reverend reckons he knifed the man in his bed while he slept, then took his body down to the supermarket site and dug a hole in the foundations and dropped him in. We used to do that sort of thing back in the day, before we got the pig farm.'

'And you are sure he wasn't lying?'

'About as sure as I can be,' he told me.

'But that doesn't make any sense. My mother was in touch with him for years after . . .' and I stopped then, because it suddenly hit me in a flash. I was an idiot, a complete fool and I needed to stop acting like one in front of Kinane. I could feel my face burning with the embarrassment of it and I had a sick feeling deep in my stomach. 'Fuck him anyway,' I said, in as dismissive a manner as I could manage, 'it doesn't matter. It was years ago and we'll never know the real truth, so what do I care.'

'Right,' he replied and when I said no more he finally left me to it.

'When Kinane had gone I sat down in my desk chair and stared out of the window. Considering I always prided myself on being the clever one, the guy who worked things out before anyone else, it had taken me a very long time to finally see what had been blindingly obvious for years. Reverend Crowe had been telling the truth; Alan Blake never left Newcastle for a job down south. He was killed back in 1972 and buried under that supermarket car park, which meant my mother had lied to me all of my life because, whoever Alan Blake was, he could never have been my father.

There was laughter coming from the big office next to mine and I forced myself to get to my feet and join them all. Sharp had finally arrived and was holding court.

'I was absolutely shitting it,' he explained to a captive audience, consisting of Palmer, Kinane, Vince and Robbie. 'My DCI called me into his office, introduced me to the brass, sat me down and said, "we've been watching you, DI Sharp. We've been watching you very closely in fact."'

'I didn't know what to say, so I just said "oh right".'

'And he looked at me some more, and I'm sitting there expecting at any moment for him to say, "Detective Inspector Sharp, you're under arrest". Instead he said "Safe pair of hands" and I was still none the wiser, so he finally adds "that's what I think, that's what your colleagues say about you, so that's what the Chief Constable is thinking. It might not be glamorous but it's exactly what we need right now".'

'Well, at this point I'm looking at him like he's been drinking or something but I just say, "Thanks very much," and finally the Chief Super chips in and says, "So you'll do it for us, Sharp? You'll be our safe pair of hands?"'

'And I say, "Of course, sir," because I'm so bloody relieved not to be in handcuffs, but I still have no idea what he's banging on about. Then he stands up, so I stand up and he says, "congratulations, Acting Detective Chief Inspector Sharp," and he shakes my hand. I almost fell back down in my chair again. When I walked in there you could have cut the atmosphere with a knife. I thought they were all giving me the silent treatment,' he said, 'turns out they were all just really busy.'

'I have to say *that* is fucking priceless.' I told him.

'That's not the best bit,' said Sharp.

'Tell him the best bit,' said Palmer.

'What's the best bit, Sharp?' I asked.

'I have been given a special brief,' he said, 'to combat organised crime and bring down the local gangsters. And guess who is top of his wish list?'

'Me,' I said.

'You,' he confirmed.

'I think this deserves a drink,' I told them and we poured one for everybody. When we were holding them, I raised mine and the others followed suit.

'A toast,' I said, 'to Acting Detective Chief Inspector Sharp . . . *acting* being the operative word. May his quest to bring down the notorious gangster David Blake be a long and fruitless one.'

'I'll drink to that,' Sharp told me with a grin, 'and I strongly suspect it will be,' and we clinked our glasses together.

It was a nice moment and I needed one. This was one less thing for me to worry about, but my troubles were a very long way from over.

This wasn't just any old meeting. This was me getting everyone together to talk about Armageddon; a new scenario, which would see the business ticking along somehow without me. I even included Amrein and he showed up a few minutes later, because everyone needed to know how to work together if I was no longer around. We went through everything, starting with the Drop and the political connections Amrein had worked to our mutual advantage. Then Amrein left us and we covered every other aspect of our business and how I wanted it to be run if I went somewhere and never came back. At the end, when we had discussed the bits of our business too sensitive for the ears of our solicitor, I invited Susan Fitch to join us and we signed a bunch of papers that gave trusted members of my crew access to funds, property and corners of our business that up till now had been my sole preserve. I answered a lot of questions that day, but the toughest was explaining just why I had called them in to talk about all of this now. I told them we were at war with the Stevic brothers and I didn't want them to be left high and dry if something should happen to me. Nobody seemed to suspect there was more to it than that.

The only question I couldn't answer was the one that was bothering me the most; exactly what I was going to say to Yaroslav Vasnetsov when I was face to face with him once again and he asked me to take his first *Joe* into Russia.

CHAPTER 43

I wanted to be on my own so I went for a drive. It was late and I should have been home, trying to catch up on sleep, but that wasn't going to happen. I kept churning it over and over in my head. If my dad wasn't my dad, who the fuck was? My mother wasn't like that, she never had a boyfriend or a bit on the side the whole time I could remember, so who the hell could have got that close to her? Who did she have an uncharacteristic soft spot for? She didn't know anyone except the men who came into the club and the members of Bobby's crew.

Mum never really spoke about the lads in the firm. She thought they were all over-grown boys who couldn't take care of themselves, let alone a woman. I can recall her moaning that none of them had a clue how to treat a lady and they were all such scruffy buggers but she never really talked about them that much, except to bad-mouth them. She had a grudging respect for Bobby, he employed her after all, even though she knew how he earned his money, but she would have never got herself mixed up with him. She had no way of knowing he had murdered her husband but Bobby Mahoney was married at the time and my ma wasn't the sort to let herself end up as a gangster's mistress. So I didn't have to drive out the idea that I might have inadvertently murdered my father and was shacked up with my sister. My life was fucked up, but it wasn't that bad. No, I knew Bobby wasn't the one, but who was?

She did talk about Jinky Smith though and he was always dressed smart back then and, judging by his success rate, he certainly knew how to talk to a lady. Could she have fallen for his chat, I wondered? Had he given her a glass of wine, laid on the patter and somehow talked her into his bed? It was possible. She must have been bloody lonely without any male company. In fact, now I thought about it, she did mention Jinky more than the others in Bobby's crew. But no, that was stupid, she never had a good word to say about the man, all she ever did was do him down. She was always calling him 'god's gift to women' in that snide sarcastic . . . and *hurt* way all the time. She sounded hurt. All of a sudden I got a prickly feeling all over my skin, which came with a sudden memory, but not one that involved my mother. It was meeting Michelle again at Privado that night I walked in unexpectedly and how did she greet me, even though I knew she had always had a massive crush on me? Like I was some kind of tosser, that's how. '*Look what the cat dragged in*'.

It was the hurt that comes from rejection, from

knowing that no matter how much you like a guy, he isn't into you, even though you've given him your body and tried to give him your heart. That was what I heard in Michelle's voice and it was why I went easy on her. I now finally realised I was hearing the exact same thing in my mother's words all those years ago. Every time I told her I'd seen Jinky, or he'd given me a couple of quid to run an errand for him, she'd roll her eyes and say 'Huh, Jinky Smith thinks he's god's gift he does,' and she'd do him down some more. I never understood why at the time but I did now. It sounds daft but that's all it took to finally solve the mystery; a feeling deep in my gut, nothing more. All of a sudden, I just knew. I was so sure I'd have been willing to bet thousands on it. Jinky Smith was my father. I just never knew it, and neither did he.

Here I was, working with gangsters and spies all this time but it was my mother who came up with a cover story even I couldn't crack for nearly forty years. All that bullshit about dad moving away, working down south, saving up so he could send for us. She invented it all. There were no letters. There were no phone calls and there could never have been a tearful reunion during that special week when Aunty Vi looked after Danny and I was conceived. God knows where she went but, if it really was London, it wasn't to visit dad. He'd been dead for years and even she didn't know it. She probably thought he'd just got tired of her and run off, leaving her with a bairn to bring up on her own. I wondered how many nights she'd lain awake wondering what happened to Alan Blake and where he ended up; the Merchant Navy, the Foreign Legion or just some bartending job in the smoke; not knowing he was buried under a supermarket car park just a couple of miles from where we lived.

Of course there was one guy who knew all along what had happened to the man I have always called dad and I wasn't thinking of Michael Crowe. Bobby Mahoney knew, because he had Alan Blake killed. The answer to the question why my law-abiding mother ended up working in Bobby Mahoney's clubs all those years was finally answered. He employed her because he felt guilty for robbing the woman of her livelihood when he put her old man in the ground. The gangster in Bobby Mahoney reasoned he had no choice but to kill the bloke who'd stolen from him, the senti-mental patriarch in him felt the only decent thing to do for his wife was to give her a job.

When mum invented that bullshit story about going off to London to meet up with dad, Bobby must have wondered what the fuck she was playing at. When she started to show signs of being preg-nant he would have worked it out right enough. I wondered if he tagged who the father was? Probably, knowing Bobby. I doubt if Jinky gave it a second thought. Bobby wouldn't have broadcast the fact that he'd had Alan Blake killed, so if Tina

Blake was getting back with her husband, that was none of Jinky's business. He would have moved on to the next girl by then.

'If it wasn't for other men's wives, I'd still be a virgin,' he'd told me. He was probably only nice to me because he liked my mum, not because he suspected he was my real father.

'I've managed to get you a place,' I told Jinky, and he stared back at me uncomprehendingly. 'I know some people from a housing association that specialises in ex-cons. It's called the Second Chances centre. They provide jobs for the young ones and, in special cases, housing for the older ones.'

'Special cases?' he asked, presumably wondering how he could qualify for any form of special treatment after the life he had led.

'Well you're clearly not one, are you, Jinky?' I agreed, 'but it's a system like any other and we both know that a system can be played.' There was a glimmer of recognition there. 'Wheels can be oiled, favours called in, so that's what I did.'

'Right,' he said, eyes sparkling.

'Anyhow, they've found you a flat and it's way better than this one,' Jinky looked a little surprised at that. He seemed to suddenly take in the squalor of his flat as if he was noticing it for the first time. 'It's in a good area too, with no druggies hanging around outside your front door. All you have to do is meet the guy who runs the scheme and make a reasonable impression.' His face dropped at that and he looked down self-consciously at the clothes he was wearing. 'Don't worry about that,' I told him, 'I'll sort you out with some new threads and we'll get you a haircut. As long as you turn up sober and looking smart, the apartment's yours.'

'But what about the rent?' he asked me. 'I haven't got a pot to piss in, man.'

'It's all taken care of. The Second Chances scheme is legacy funded,' he frowned again, 'it means everything's paid for by rich people who die and leave some of their money to the centre.'

'Nice of them,' he observed disbelievingly.

'You could say that,' I said, 'I reckon most of them are trying to buy their way into heaven.' I didn't want him to know that the real, sole bene-factor of the Second Chances centre was me.

I turned down his offer of a cup of tea because I didn't want to die of botulism, then I ushered him out of the door and drove him into town. I took him to a Marks and Sparks and bought him some shirts, trousers, socks and underwear.

'Are you sure this is alright like?' he asked me.

'Of course,' I said, 'you're one of Bobby's old boys. We do this these days. We're all minted and there's plenty for everyone,' he shook his head in disbelief.

'There'll be money too, later.' I said. I meant I wasn't going to trust the guy with cash yet, because I figured he'd be straight down the pub, then the bookies. 'Haircut first though.'

I made sure I gave a generous tip to the poor lass who had to wash Jinky's hair before the hairdresser got to work. I watched as she snipped away at Jinky's locks, removing several inches from the long straggly strands and using all of her skills to make the man look respectable. She was nearly done when Malcolm arrived. I introduced him.

'Malcolm's from Second Chances and he's going to get you ready for your appointment later.'

I meant that he was going to take him away and make sure he took a bath before he put the clean clothes on. I'd given instructions for the old clothes to be binned. The hairdresser was already sweeping up the strands of hair with a brush and pan. Jinky didn't notice when she took a clump of his hair and put it into a little plastic packet with a zip top.

I took out my wallet and paid the girl. The money I gave her was way more than the cost of the haircut. I took the remainder of the cash from my wallet and counted it. I was going to give some of it to Jinky. I looked up to see his expectant face staring at the money in my hand. In the end I handed the whole lot to Malcolm. 'That's for you Jinky,' I told him, '*after* your meeting, not before.' He nodded gratefully like he understood my reasons. 'Just relax and answer the man's questions, tell him the truth about your . . .,' I struggled to find the right word and finally settled on '. . . background. Don't bullshit him and try not to fuck this up, eh?'

'I won't Davey,' he assured me, 'I'm real grateful to you like, honest I am.'

'That's okay man,' I told him. I wanted him to think the interview with our Second Chances manager mattered. It didn't. The flat was already sorted but I wanted Jinky to believe that he had to earn it. That way he might not go too far off the rails if he thought it could ever be taken away from him.

'There'll be more money on a regular basis, provided you keep your nose clean. Someone will tidy the flat and there'll be groceries delivered every week.'

He opened his mouth to say something, but suddenly stopped and seemed to be pursing his lips, like he was making an effort to say the words, then I realised that what he was really doing was trying to keep something in. I could see the tears forming in his eyes.

I put my hand on his shoulder. 'Just forget about it Jinky,' I said, 'it's no bother like. It's your share. You earned it man.' Then I walked out of there as quickly as I could.

I got the DNA test back in record time. The sample they got from Jinky's hair was clear enough and proved it beyond all doubt. He was definitely my father.

CHAPTER 44

Be careful what you wish for. That's what they say, isn't it? My life is a fucking Greek tragedy. I wanted to find out all about my father, so I could tell my little girl something about him, but what was I going to tell her now? The man I thought was my dad didn't really walk out on me when I was small. He died two years before I was born, killed by the man I later called boss, until I in turn killed him. If Alan Blake had been my true father there would at least have been some fucked-up sense of justice at play when I shot Bobby Mahoney but no, my real father was a washed-up gangster; a con man and hustler, a part-time armed robber who couldn't even do that right, a jail bird who spent years inside and came out with a torn heart and lungs as black as tar. Now he's old and broke and sitting in God's waiting room but he's all I've got left, apart from a half-brother who's stuck in a wheelchair. At least I can take care of him.

Thank God for my little Emma. If it wasn't for her I don't know what I'd do. The whole fucked-up, shitty mess I've managed to get myself in wouldn't be worth jack-all if it wasn't for her. That night, I looked down on her while she was sleeping in her little bed and she looked so beautiful, sweet and peaceful that I wondered how anything so precious could ever have come from me.

Obviously I confronted Our young'un.

'You knew, didn't you?' We'd been arguing about it for a while now and he didn't want to go over the details again but I wanted him to admit it. 'Why didn't you tell me?' I asked him for what felt like the umpteenth time and he finally gave in.

He gave an exasperated sigh, 'Because she didn't want you to know, man. At the end, she made me swear not to tell you. What was I supposed to do? Break a promise I'd made to my dying ma?' Then he turned from exasperation to anger, 'I told you not to. I said that nowt good would come of it! Didn't I?'

We were alone in Cachet so nobody could hear us. 'Yeah,' I said, 'you did!' In some dark recess of my brain that was still logical, I could understand why he hadn't told me but I was hurting and too angry for that. 'You still could have told me. You owed me that. I always took care of you Danny, always!'

'And a lot of good it did me!' he roared at me. 'You taking care of me put me in this chair!' and he gripped the sides of his wheelchair in frustration and shook it.

Somehow I managed to retain the sense not to push it any further because there was still a lot of unspoken shit between us about that and neither of us would profit from any of it coming out now. Danny had been a fuck-up for most of his adult life and I made it my job to save him. I was well intentioned but now he was paralysed because of his involvement with the firm and he thought that was my fault. If we said all that out loud there'd be no going back for either of us. Instead, I stormed out of that room.

I drove around for so long I lost track of time. When I finally got home Sarah was cooking a late dinner in the kitchen. Emma was asleep upstairs. I walked up behind Sarah and wrapped my arms around her.

'I've always solved our problems haven't I?' I asked her, 'whatever's been thrown at us, I've always tried to protect you?'

'Of course,' she answered, 'but I don't need as much taking care of as you think. I'm a bit tougher than that Davey,' and she turned to look at me and gave me a humourless smile, 'it must be genetic.'

'I know and I'm sorry if you've felt trapped with me sometimes, it's just that I promised your dad and . . .'

'What is it?' she looked concerned then and I realised that, for once, I had failed to mask my feelings. They must have been written all over my face. I knew the stress of dealing with so many problems all at the same time was beginning to get to me. Sarah put her arms around me then, 'What is it, Davey?' she repeated.

I was reluctant to tell her, but knew I had to. 'I think I have a problem that I can't solve. I think there is something that's beyond my control.'

'Tell me,' she urged, and there was a fire in her eyes that I found strangely comforting, 'there's nothing we can't solve together. You always keep me on the outside, you don't tell me things . . . I know why you do it, to protect me, but this time I want you to tell me. Do you think I don't know when something is wrong? I can see it in your face every time you step out the door. I'm not stupid Davey. I love you. Let me help.'

'I love you too,' I told her, 'you and Emma mean everything to me. I know there are times when I haven't shown that and I'm sorry. I know you are strong Sarah but there's no way you can help with this.'

I told her everything then. How I was trapped between a powerful man who would kill me if I didn't do his bidding and a vengeful superpower that would never tolerate me helping him.

'There must be something we can do,' she said.

'There isn't,' I told her, 'and you and Emma won't ever be safe while I'm still breathing.' And I drew her tightly to me then so she couldn't see the look on my face.

When I arrived at Cachet, Danny was talking to the DJ and a couple of our dancers. I hung back and let him see me but didn't approach him. He seemed to take a bloody long while to say his piece to them, so I guessed he was keeping me waiting to punish me or he was stalling because he didn't know what to say to me. Finally he was done and they walked away. He turned his chair towards me and came over. He was wearing his 'What the fuck do you want?' face.

'We okay for tonight?' I asked, meaning the club, something I never normally asked him about.

'Yeah,' he said, but that was all he said.

'And the gala dinner,' I reminded him, 'do you need anything?'

'No,' he shook his head.

'Okay,' I said, 'I'll leave you to it then,' and before I could say what was on my mind he started to back his chair away so he could turn it in an arc from me. 'About yesterday,' I said and he stopped, 'I didn't mean any of it. You of all people know that. I was upset so I took it out on you. I was a cunt.' I was apologising in a manner that I thought Danny might understand.

'It's nae bother,' he lied, 'we were both upset and we were both talking shite man. Forget it.' That last bit was an order. Danny meant he understood and accepted my apology and this was his way of saying sorry too. You just had to know Danny really well to understand that.

'Got time for a pint?' I asked.

'Always,' he said quietly.

'I worked it out man,' he told me when we were in a quiet corner with our drinks, 'not at first like. I was still only a bairn when you came along. She told me she'd been away and seen me dad. He had a job down south but he couldn't get back 'cos it was too far away but maybe one day he might come home for good. She said we'd have to be patient for a bit longer and see how things worked out. Then, later on, she told me I was going to have a little brother or sister. I was only young but I didn't believe her about dad coming back, even then. I mean, it was shite, wasn't it?'

'When did you start to suspect?'

'When I was a bit older. I can't remember what was said but I overheard one of the nosey old bints in the street making some comment about me ma being "no better than she ought to be" or some such crap. I didn't say anything about it but it got me thinking about why she might have said it.'

'So you asked her about it?'

'Not then, no. It was later,' he admitted, 'much later, when I got back.' He meant from the Falklands. I guessed, after what he had seen there, it put our mother's extra-marital affair into perspective. 'Anyhow, it didn't go well. She got very upset. I told her it didn't matter to me but she was ashamed, I mean she was *well* embarrassed by it and she made me swear not to tell you. I think she thought you'd have been really upset.'

'And she didn't tell you who the father was?'

'No bro, she didn't. She wouldn't let on to me, honest.'

'And you had no idea?'

'No, not really. I mean there were always men around but that was down to her job. She worked in Bobby Mahoney's clubs and pubs, so I'd see her chatting away to the regulars and the guys in his crew but she never brought one home. Sometimes she'd get a lift off one of them but they wouldn't come in.'

'She got lifts off Jinky?'

'I can't remember,' he said, but I guessed he was just being evasive, 'maybe, yes, I reckon so, a couple of times, but like I said he never came in. Our ma wouldn't allow that, you know what she was like, bit of an old prude really when it came down to it.'

Our young'un laughed. 'Guess she wasn't quite as big a prude as we thought.'

'You and me though,' I reminded him, 'we look alike. I mean obviously I'm the young, handsome one and you're the old, clapped-out version but there is a resemblance.'

He nodded, 'We both look like ma though.'

'I s'pose so.'

'There is one way you take after Jinky though.'

'How do you mean?'

'The lasses,' he told me, 'I don't know if it's what you say to them, or the way you say it, but you've always had more than your fair share, just like him.'

'And look how he ended up,' I reminded Our young'un.

I hired a young lass to do the singing and she was ace; classically trained, with gold albums, the works. She'd sung for royalty, appeared at the Royal Albert Hall and belted out *Abide with Me* at the Cup Final to a crowd of ninety thousand. She had a voice like a bloody angel, plus she was as fit as fuck, so the mostly male audience loved her. I paid her well and asked her to sing some patriotic numbers because I knew the guys on these tables would lap it up and part with more of their cash for *Help the Heroes*, our chosen charity. She did *Jerusalem* and *I Vow to Thee My Country* and the applause was loud and warm. They were stuffing notes in envelopes and making credit card donations like they had money to burn.

It was a bit over the top but I got her to sing *Land of Hope and Glory* at the end and they all waved the little Union Jack flags we'd placed on the tables. I think the booze helped with that. They actually got to their feet and gave her a standing ovation afterwards. I walked on stage, gave her a kiss on the cheek and presented her with a big bouquet, while she smiled like she was having the time of her life, bless her.

She placed the bouquet carefully to one side and moved her microphone out to the front of the stage, so it was right by the top table. The band put down their instruments and let her get on with it.

'I've one last song before I finish,' she told the audience, 'two actually, because I want to start with this one,' and she then looked straight at Danny, who up to that point had been completely oblivious, and softly started to sing 'Ha-ppy Birth-day to you, Ha-ppy Birth-day to you,' at which point Danny's eyes almost fell out of their sockets. I stayed poker faced as she finished, and the crowd all cheered and applauded.

Our young'un smiled self-consciously and gave them all a wave, then he mouthed 'thank you' at her, but she wasn't finished yet. She waited till the crowd stopped applauding and held the microphone close to her lips and gave Danny a look like he was the only man there. Then she started to sing something everybody in the room recognised, 'Oh Danny Boy . . . the pipes, the pipes are calling . . .'

Our young'un was transfixed. I don't think he could quite believe that she was singing this for everyone in the room and only for him, all at the same time. He was staring goggle eyed at her, hanging on every word. Then, about half way through, as if he suddenly remembered me, he looked over and I winked at him. He looked away quickly.

When she reached the chorus of *Danny Boy* he started pulling some strange faces and it took me a while to realise that, like Jinky Smith, he was desperately trying not to blub. In the end he had to put his hand up to his eyes to stop the tears, so I was saved the spectacle of seeing two grown men crying in the same week. The funny thing was, I had to turn away too and fake like I was trying to stifle a cough. Because, when she sang that bloody, corny old Irish song to my older brother and he almost wept, well it got to me too. I told myself not to be such a soppy fucker, took a deep breath and just about managed to hold it together.

CHAPTER 45

It was the drive-by that sparked Fallon's latest visit to the Cauldron.

'The guy'd been with me for years,' he told us, 'they shotgunned him as he stepped out of the pub for a fag. They drove off before anyone could do anything, left him bleeding to death in the gutter. We can't let this one go,' he told me, and he meant that I wouldn't be allowed to let it go, not if I wanted to retain any credibility with Fallon and his men.

'There is a way to sort this,' Palmer told us before I was able to answer Fallon, 'but you've got to let me do it on my own. If we try to go in there mob handed with Fallon's lads it'll be like the gunfight at the OK Corral and the police will be all over us in minutes.'

'What do you have in mind?'

'Let me go and see them. I'll have another word,' answered Palmer. 'I'll send them away,' he said simply. He was deliberately cagey and I knew why. He didn't want anyone to know the details of his plan. The more people who knew, the more likely it was that someone would leak it to the police, maybe even sell details to the Serbs. It wouldn't have been the first time we'd been betrayed, so I didn't ask again.

'What do you need?'

He took a while to answer then said, 'I need Robbie to take out any CCTV in their street and a few streets either side, so they can't link my arrival to the scene.'

'Okay,' I said, 'what else?'

He shook his head, 'Nothing. Just leave me to it.'

'Fair enough,' I said, 'when?'

'Might as well be tomorrow. No point fucking about, eh?'

'I'll drive you,' Kinane said.

'No,' Palmer answered quickly and Joe Kinane looked a little put out.

'He's right Joe,' I told him, 'you're known. You'd stand out a mile in that street,' and I turned back to Palmer, 'take someone else, somebody who isn't known to them.'

'I'll do it,' said Peter Kinane and we all turned to look at him, including his dad. What we saw was a man who looked so damned determined to prove he wasn't like his older brother that I didn't hesitate.

'Okay,' I said and Joe Kinane stayed silent.

Palmer checked his watch and let the final seconds tick away, then he glanced at Peter Kinane. He climbed out of the car, closed the door behind him and commenced a leisurely walk along the street.

Peter Kinane was unlikely to be seen from his position. He'd parked far enough away from the house on a corner. From here he could clearly make out the property, the huge, bald, Serbian enforcer guarding the doorway and the comparably slight figure of Palmer as he walked unhurriedly towards it.

The Serb heavy was expecting Palmer and watched him all the way. When he reached the man he said, 'I have a message for Dusan Stevic from David Blake. He wants to talk. He has a new offer, to end this.'

'Wait,' he was told and a second heavy manning the door left his post and went in to announce Palmer's arrival. Palmer waited, the first guard watching him intently the whole time, huge arms folded across his tree-trunk chest.

The second heavy eventually returned and said something in Serb to his colleague. He stood aside and Palmer was allowed to walk up the steps. As soon as he reached the front door they patted him down thoroughly to ensure he wasn't carrying. When they were satisfied, there were more words in Serbian between them and Palmer was waved on into the house and up the stairs. One of the men called 'Zoran!' to alert the man standing outside the brothers' secure room.

As before, Zoran wore his long black coat open and Palmer could see the handle of the gun protruding from the shoulder holster. Zoran went about the rigmarole of searching Palmer all over again but Palmer was unarmed. He knew he could never get a weapon past these guys. When he was satisfied that Palmer was clean, Zoran called through the locked door and one of the brothers answered him, Zoran spoke again and there was a pause. The enforcer surveyed Palmer intently as he waited and Palmer stared straight back at him, saying nothing.

There was a buzz from inside the secure room and the door clicked open. Zoran stepped to one side to enable Palmer to walk up to it and open the door. Palmer advanced towards the door but, at the last moment, as he reached out with his gloved left hand to push it inwards, he turned his open palm into a fist then moved so quickly Zoran had no time to react. Palmer's left fist became a blur that flew sideways and landed hard on Zoran's throat, crushing it. Zoran's eyes bulged and he began a panicked battle to breathe now that his windpipe and throat had been crushed. As the big man swayed, Palmer pushed him backwards against the wall and forced his other hand into Zoran's jacket. It came out holding the silenced pistol and in virtually the same movement Palmer wedged the end of the barrel up beneath Zoran's chin and fired. The round tore through him, taking the top of his head off and splashing blood all over the ceiling. As the big man's body slumped to the ground, Palmer kicked in the door.

The Stevic brothers were already moving, the sound of Zoran's choked breathing, the suppressed gunshot and the tell-tale splash of blood, some of which had spattered through the door, alerted them. Palmer strode into the room with his gun held out. He shot the nearest brother, Sreten, in the face as he tried to get up out of his armchair and the body slumped back down into a seated position, eyes still open in shock. The second brother Marko had already reached a shotgun and was turning to aim it straight at Palmer when he was shot twice in the chest in quick succession. He fell backwards, upending the table, dislodging glasses and papers and making a din that alerted the men on the ground floor. They began to run up the stairs, shouting.

Dusan was the last brother left alive – he managed to pull out a gun and dive behind the upturned table. He reached his hand out over the top of the table and fired blind three times, missing Palmer by inches. Palmer returned fire, pinning the guy down. Dusan's hand went back behind the table, as bullets hit the solid wood but failed to penetrate it. Palmer could hear the two big Serbs crashing up the stairs. They would reach him in seconds and he'd be caught in a fatal crossfire between them and Dusan. It would all be over for him if he couldn't kill the last brother quickly.

Palmer made a decision then and dropped his gun. He took a step forwards and scrambled for the shotgun Marko had dropped. As Dusan raised his gun hand to fire once more, Palmer turned the shotgun on him and returned fire. The first round went into the table and there was a scream from the other side as the pellets did some damage and Dusan let the gun fall from his injured hand. Palmer ran towards the upturned table, put one foot on the edge and peered over at him. Palmer pointed the gun downwards just as the wounded Dusan rolled onto his back and looked up into the barrel.

His terrified scream of 'No!' was stifled by a shotgun blast in the face.

Palmer threw himself over the upturned table and hit the ground just as the two big Serbs burst into the room, still shouting. He rose to his feet again with Dusan's handgun and took out the first enforcer before he had time to take in the scene of carnage before him; two bullets into the chest putting him down. The second Serb swore and brought round his own gun but, in his panic, he was too quick to fire. His bullet cannoned into the wall behind Palmer who took more care with his shot. The first round hit the big Serb in the shoulder but, amazingly, he stayed on his feet. Instead of falling, he tottered backwards, cursed loudly, and tried to raise his weapon once more. Palmer took a step forwards, aimed carefully and put three more bullets into him. The man went backwards and fell onto his colleague who was still moving, desperately trying to drag himself to his feet, despite the bullets inside him and the dead weight on top of him. Palmer put a bullet in the back of his head on his way out of the room.

Palmer went down the stairs like they weren't there and was out into the street. He had entered the building unarmed and left six men lying dead behind him.

CHAPTER 46

The day after Palmer killed the Stevic brothers, Vasnetsov finally lost patience with me and a file arrived at my house. In it were photographs of my daughter out for walks in the park with Joanne and a bodyguard. The message was clear. Cooperate or Emma would face the consequences.

Later that same day, I took a call from one of Vasnetsov's men. He gave me a date, a time and a flight number. I had been summoned to meet Vasnetsov's first *Joe* and my destination was Helsinki.

Detective Sergeant Nigel Kelly was wading through the files on Dusan Stevic's computer, as part of the Lothian and Borders Police investigation into the killing of six Serbian gangsters who'd set themselves up in the city. It made for interesting reading. Some of the files were encrypted but others weren't. It seemed the Stevic brothers were not as careful as they might have been, exhibiting an arrogance that, according to some, had been fostered by a belief that they were somehow untouchable by the authorities. Well, they might all be dead now but the information they left behind could be priceless, enabling a thorough investigation into their criminal network, which would undoubtedly lead to further arrests. There were even spreadsheets detailing payments received and those made, along with the names of the recipients.

Kelly was about to take a break when he stumbled upon a Real Player flash video with a Serbian title. On a whim he clicked on the file and waited while it opened. He wasn't expecting such a stark image.

The girl was bent over with her face virtually pressed into the camera. She was naked and her large breasts dangled beneath her, swaying from side to side, as the older man took her from behind. From the look on her face, she was enduring the sex, not enjoying it. From the look on his, he had no idea they were being secretly recorded.

'Wahey!' shouted Detective Constable Russell when he looked over and noticed the film playing on Kelly's computer, 'Kelly's watching porn!' and he wandered over to get a better look. The first thing he noticed was the naked girl being taken from behind by an old, fat bloke. His eyes zeroed in on the distinctive tattoo on the girl's arm, then he clocked her face.

'Bloody hell, that's her,' he said, 'that's the girl we've got downstairs. She's one of those trafficked Ukrainian lassies the Serbs brought in. We picked her up a couple of hours ago. I didn't recognise her with her clothes on but she's got that big fuck off tattoo on her arm. It's definitely her alright,' but Detective Sergeant Kelly didn't answer him. He had not been so easily distracted by the naked girl and her tattoo, instead he simply whispered the same word three times. 'Fuck . . . fuck . . . fuck.'

It was then that Russell tore his gaze away from the girl and finally took a closer look at the man who was screwing her. He was podgy and balding, with a thin wisp of combed-over ginger hair, his face was red, sweat poured from his forehead and he was grunting like a pig, as he thrust into the unfortunate girl over and over again.

'Bloody hell,' said Russell, when he finally recognised the man, 'Jesus Christ.'

'No,' answered Kelly, 'but it might as well be.'

Colleagues heard the muttered curses of the two detectives and wandered over to see what had distracted them. Others followed and soon there was a small cluster of men and women who'd abandoned their desks to view the film of the fat man and the girl. He was putting his back into it alright. From his face, it was hard to tell whether he was having an orgasm or a heart attack. The finale was greeted in near silence by the posse of detectives.

It was DC Heather Shaw who finally put it into words, 'Is that . . .' but she couldn't quite bring herself to finish the sentence.

'Assistant Chief Constable Brinklow,' confirmed DS Kelly, who'd at least had a little time to get used to the idea, 'it only bloody is!'

News travels fast, particularly when that news involves the arrest of an Assistant Chief Constable on charges of corruption. We watched it on the TV at the Cauldron.

'They reckon Brinklow will get at least fifteen years,' explained Sharp, 'five years for what he did, five for his rank,' then he added, 'and five years extra for that bloody video.'

Brinklow's unwitting porn video was already the stuff of police legend. It was probably true that the footage of Brinklow raping that trafficked Ukrainian girl would be the difference between ten years, out in six and fifteen years, out in ten, if the parole board didn't actually think he should go right to the end of his full term because the abuse of power had been so great.

I took a long while to say my goodbyes to Sarah and Emma. I didn't want to go but knew I had to, for their sakes. Picking up my daughter and holding her to me so I could kiss her goodbye was the hardest thing I have ever done. Sarah stood in the doorway with Emma in her arms as I drove away.

I couldn't take Palmer or Kinane with me on this journey so I left on my own. Before I drove to the airport, I took a drive through Newcastle, so I could have one last look at the streets I had known all my life, because I knew I wouldn't be coming back.

There was no private jet to transport me to Vasnetsov's property near Helsinki. Instead, I was instructed to take a scheduled flight from Heathrow to Vantaa airport in the Finnish capital. I was met there by one of Vasnetsov's men, a tall, corporate type in a suit who recognised me but did not bother to introduce himself. He walked me to a large Audi and gave me the keys.

'Use the sat nav,' he ordered, 'it's programmed to take you to a house in Anjalankoski Kouvola.'

This meant nothing to me, but when I climbed into the car the display told me I had a hundred and thirty kilometres to go. Vasnetsov's man tapped on the window and I wound it down. 'Don't stop,' he warned me, 'or we will know.' And I had no reason to doubt that.

The sat nav guided me away from Vantaa and down a wide, tree-lined road that took me past apartment blocks, then houses, until we reached the suburbs which were lightly dusted with snow. Finally I joined the main highway and made steady progress – the traffic was light compared to the UK. I found myself subconsciously slowing down, as if I was trying to delay the inevitable. I felt like a condemned man being dragged to the gallows.

I passed mile after mile of woodland, huge conifers either side of me, with nothing to break the tree lines apart from a succession of bridges that spanned the road I was on. It was getting dark when I finally left the main highway and took a minor road with no destination sign or lighting. I had to rely on the sat nav to ensure I was headed the right way and my headlights to guide me, along a road which seemed to be narrowing progressively as I neared my final destination. I was glad of the snow, because it reflected the beams and helped to light my way. I'd gone nearly two miles down this winding excuse for a road when I turned a corner and the house came into view. It wasn't quite the gothic monstrosity of his English home but the faded, white-stone mansion had clearly been here for a very long time before Vasnetsov added it to his portfolio.

A reception committee of half a dozen guards awaited me. They carried weapons openly; pistols in holsters, submachine guns slung over their shoulders. Lights burned in the house and there was a tense atmosphere.

Evgeny Gorshkov came out of the house to meet me, just as one of his men had finished patting me down.

'He is clean,' the man said.

'Of course he is,' answered Vasnetsov's head of security, 'he is not so stupid as to bring a weapon, a wire or a tracker to a meeting with us. Blake knows that, if he did, we would bury him out here,' and he glanced towards the forests.

Evgeny took me inside. We went into a large

room at the front of the building that had a huge open fireplace with logs burning ferociously in the grate. Vasnetsov was sitting there with Mikhail Datsik, his banker, along with another three bodyguards.

'I am glad you did not miss your flight,' said Vasnetsov dryly by way of greeting, 'so much easier this way.'

'I'm here,' I admitted, 'but I still don't see how I can help you.'

Vasnetsov frowned at me. 'You will help me by carrying out my instructions. Soon you will meet my *Joe*. He has been in training for two years and you will provide his route in to my homeland. That much I have already explained,' and he shook his head. 'You should be happy, Blake. When you leave here in the morning you will take my *Joe* and your fee. I promised you two million US dollars and it's yours.'

'So I get to stay the night here?' I asked.

'Your flight to Amsterdam leaves in the morning. Tonight you eat and sleep. In the morning you leave here a wealthier man,' and he shrugged as if it couldn't be easier. 'Once you arrive in Amsterdam you send my agent down the line. It really is very simple.'

'And if I refuse?'

His face hardened, 'I already told you that I do not forgive.'

'You did,' I conceded, 'so tonight I will eat and sleep and tomorrow . . .' I shrugged, as if I would likely go along with his plan but I was stalling, buying myself some precious time before I made him my enemy with a refusal.

'Good,' he said but abruptly the lights in the house went out and we were plunged into darkness. I could only dimly make out shapes in the room. There was some shouting in Russian, a panicked question and an authoritative reply, then people began moving in and out of the building.

Vasnetsov barked something in Russian and waved an arm. I was willing to bet it was something like, 'Get out there, find out what's happening!'

Someone activated a hand-held flare. One of the bodyguards held it and three of them started towards the main door. They didn't get very far. The weapons must have had suppressors because I never even heard the shots. All three bodyguards were dropped in the hallway with ruthless efficiency. I instinctively threw myself to the floor.

'Evgeny!' Vasnetsov had panic in his voice as he called for his personal bodyguard who drew a pistol, dropped to one knee and aimed his weapon at the window, then at the door, then back at the window again, as if unsure where the attack would come from. I could hear shouting and the sound of boots running along wooden floors. The sound of gunfire that followed was deafening. Vasnetsov's bodyguards were determined not just to combat the threat outside but to obliterate it.

After the initial bursts of machinegun fire there was a brief pause and I heard orders being shouted in Russian. I could also hear the screams of dying men then further gunfire but the bursts were more focussed now, as if they were trying to pick out individual targets. Evgeny was chattering away into a tiny hand-held radio, trying to work out what was going on. I didn't speak a word of Russian but I knew panic when I heard it. The men he was communicating with were trying to brief him, while at the same time fighting for their lives. I lay on the wooden floor praying they had bigger problems to worry about right now than me.

This pattern was repeated for a while; short bursts of gunfire from Vasnetsov's bodyguards, then return fire that held an eerie quality because it was silent, but we knew about it because bullets were hitting the front of the house, shattering windows and thudding into the brickwork. It sounded like there was a whole bloody army out there. The shouting continued, but it was getting less and less regular. Evgeny was still calling out his list of names, 'Lev! . . . Ivan! . . . Oleg! . . . Pyotr!' and I could see by the light from the flickering flames of the fire that he was sweating. I realised they were losing.

I didn't know how long the firing lasted but it seemed like hours. Eventually, as abruptly as it started, the shooting ceased and there was an incredibly tense silence. There were only Vasnetsov, Evgeny, Mikhail and me left in the room and we all held our breath as we waited for something to happen. I was looking at them and they were staring at the door.

Just as I turned my head it happened, the window exploded, the glass bursting inwards and showering us, then there was an enormous bang and a cloud of smoke and my ears began to ring from the stun grenade. I was dimly aware of figures somehow swinging themselves through the shattered window and bursting into the room.

The four men who came through the window all wore black uniforms, black helmets and night-vision goggles and carried submachine guns. I knew they could make us out through the smoke and darkness and I was thankful for that, because they were less likely to gun me down if they could see I was lying harmlessly on the ground, my hands outstretched, palms down against the carpet, looking as much like a non-combatant as possible. One of them zeroed his weapon in on me and levelled it like he was about to fire. I thought 'This is it, he's going to kill me, just to remove any witnesses,' then he hefted the weight slightly so that it sat more easily in his hands and kept it trained on me. 'I'm not moving,' I told him, 'I'm not moving.' I was hoping that hearing me speak in English might make him hesitate to kill me. Perhaps he would be fearful of some sort of international incident and in any case they were clearly not after me.

I managed to turn my eyes slightly towards Vasnetsov and I could see that his bodyguard had given up. He had placed his weapon on the ground and very slowly put his hands up. He looked entirely helpless. 'Evgeny!' hissed his boss, as if he expected the unarmed man to do something, even though the presence in the room of four armed men indicated he was the only one of Vasnetsov's private army still breathing. Evgeny was pleading with his eyes. He was trying to tell the commandos he was prepared to go quietly. One of the attackers took a step towards him, carefully aimed his semi-automatic and shot him anyway, putting three, perhaps four rounds through his chest. Evgeny fell backwards and his lifeless body hit the ground.

That was when Vasnetsov made a break for it, a desperate, stumbling run. He didn't get far. They moved quicker than he ever could and soon caught up with him. He was cursing, kicking and screaming but they sat him down in an armchair and one of them gave him a hefty slap around the face to silence him. A second later, the lights came back on.

I put my face down because the bright light was hurting my eyes and the smoke made them sting. I was blinking furiously, trying to focus, when a man marched purposefully into the room. He was dressed in black combat trousers, a black army-issue sweatshirt and combat boots and his face had been blacked out by camouflage paint, but his only weapon was the pistol he wore on his belt. He glanced over at me, then at the half-American banker and finally Vasnetsov and when

he spoke it was in English, so we could all understand him.

'Yaroslav Vasnetsov, I am Major Uri Nikulin of
the GRU. You are under arrest; charged with
treason and acts of terrorism, along with many
other crimes against the state.'

'No,' Vasnetsov's voice cracked.

I could hear the sound of a helicopter's rotors,
perhaps more than one, and they were getting
closer.

'You will return to Russia where you will stand
trial.' Vasnetsov was pressing himself back against
the chair, as if he could somehow disappear into
it. 'You will go to prison for the rest of your life.
This has already been decided,' then he said, 'one
last thing, my president says hello.'

'I will give you twenty . . . thirty million dollars
. . .' Vasnetsov's panicked eyes were darting round
the room, looking for signs of weakness, seeking
out corrupt men who, like everybody else he had
ever done business with, would be willing to take
his money, 'Each . . . every one of you . . . thirty
million dollars!' He was pleading now. Nobody
moved, nobody even flinched.

'You!' he shouted at the man who had his gun
trained on me, 'Kill your Major and let me go and
I will give you fifty million dollars . . . the same
for your two friends . . . just one bullet . . . I'll
pay every man outside . . . how many of them are
there . . . tell me . . .?' He was nodding like a
lunatic, 'tell them there has been a mistake . . .

tell them I am already dead . . . I will pay each of them five million dollars and you three will get fifty million each. Think about it!' he implored them.

If the Major was alarmed by this offer, he didn't show it. He just let Yaroslav Vasnetsov carry on making a fool of himself.

'You are going on a helicopter now Vasnetsov,' the Major told him, 'the journey won't be comfortable but it will seem like luxury compared to the cell we have waiting for you. Your billions of American dollars will buy you nothing there. It is very small and very cold and you will rot and die in it.'

The colour had gone from Vasnetsov's face. He already looked like death.

The Major then turned towards Mikhail, who had been cowering silently in a corner while a commando held a gun on him. He walked up to him and, astonishingly, shook Mikhail's hand. 'Mikhail Datsik, you are a hero of the motherland. My president salutes you. You will be rewarded for your services to the state.'

Mikhail just blinked at him but Vasnetsov immediately understood, 'Mikhail! You bastard! You fucking traitor! I'll rip out your guts!' and he launched himself forwards but one of the commandos grabbed him by the shoulder and punched him back down. Despite the blow, Vasnetsov carried on ranting, 'You fucking Judas, Mikhail. It doesn't matter where they put me, I'll kill you. I'll put one hundred million dollars on your worthless head. They'll kill you, they'll kill your wife, they'll kill your fucking children!'

'What do we do with him?' asked one of the men and he jerked his head towards me.

'This piece of shit?' answered the Major. 'He is a drug dealer. Take him into the woods and shoot him.' Then he eyed Mikhail keenly, 'Take the banker outside with you,' Mikhail went pale, 'to wait for the second helicopter.'

Two men held Vasnetsov while the Major opened a small case and advanced with a new weapon in his hand; a hypodermic needle. When Vasnetsov saw it, his eyes widened in terror and he tried one last desperate time to free himself from the grasp of the two soldiers, but they held him firm. I witnessed the needle go into his arm and watched Vasnetsov's terrified face until his eyes rolled back into his head and he slipped into unconsciousness. When he awoke again, he would be back in Russia.

I was forced from the room along with the banker. One of the soldiers pushed us out through the front door and made us walk across the court-yard. Mikhail was talking to himself manically, praying perhaps, or just muttering in a panic, despite what the Major had told him about being a hero of the motherland. There were many more soldiers standing guard, hefting machineguns or quickly and efficiently preparing to leave on the first helicopter which had landed a hundred or so yards away. Vasnetsov's bodyguards still lay on the ground where they had fallen. The location was so far from civilisation that Vasnetsov's attackers could have brought heavy artillery and the authorities would still never have heard a thing.

We left the building behind us and trudged across the snow just as a second helicopter landed in the courtyard. I turned to look behind me and there were three soldiers following us, all armed.

'Keep moving,' one told me. There was no sign of the Major.

Christ they were really going to do this. They were going to shoot us both and leave our bodies in the woods.

'Keep walking and shut up,' the soldier was addressing Mikhail but he was beyond reason now. His voice just went higher as his panicked rambling continued in earnest. He began to sob between the words. Me? I stayed silent, waiting for a miracle.

We walked on until we reached the edge of the wood and both turned to face our killers. The first soldier took a pistol from his holster and gestured with it for us to go on. Mikhail shook his head and the commando smacked him round it with the gun, drawing blood. The banker howled in protest and the other two soldiers hauled him into the trees. They gestured for me to walk and I followed dumbly. What choice did I have?

The cold air was biting and my breath was coming out in white plumes, my feet made the snow beneath my boots crunch with every step.

I'd done this before, marched on ahead while a killer held a gun to me and forced me to walk to my grave. That time I'd been saved by Palmer but he wouldn't be coming to my rescue now. Nobody would. I was twelve hundred miles from home, in a foreign land. There was no way back now and the men behind me couldn't be bought. Vasnetsov had already tried that.

We reached a clearing, an open space in the woods where the leaves of the overhanging trees parted above our heads, creating a space in the canopy that allowed us to look up and watch as the helicopter flew over our heads with its precious cargo; Russia's most wanted man. Everyone watched the helicopter disappear and, along with it, went my last chance of salvation. I turned towards the men who were about to kill us.

'We do it here,' said the soldier, with no trace of emotion.

Burly hands rested on my shoulders and I was pushed down on to my knees. Beside me the sobbing Mikhail was forced into the same position. I don't think he'd shut up once since we'd left the house but he finally fell silent now. I watched as the soldier went round behind Mikhail. In one swift and simple movement he raised the gun, aimed and fired. The bullet went straight into the back of Mikhail head and came out the other side, obliterating his face. His body pitched forward until it slumped lifelessly onto the ground. The snow around him was spattered with fresh blood.

'Jesus Christ,' I gasped.

The soldier frowned. 'You are a Christian?'

I tried to say something but I couldn't because I knew I was next and it would soon be my blood splashed all over the snow.

'You can stand up now,' the soldier told me and when he saw the confused look on my face, he actually laughed, 'you thought we were really going to do it?' And his men laughed too. 'That was just for him, and for Vasnetsov. You needed them to think we killed you too.' There was no disputing that but I couldn't believe they had taken the trouble to march me all the way out here just to fake an execution. I took a deep breath and my knees gave way. I stumbled to my feet and had to put a hand out in front of me to stop myself from pitching forwards face first into the snow.

'Do you think we don't keep a promise, English?' the soldier asked me, 'that we have no honour? You helped us take a man we have been trying to capture for ten years. You think we would kill you for that? No, you are our friend now, a hero of Russia,' he told me, 'but I think it is better for you if no one knows that.' I managed to nod. I was fighting back the bile in my stomach, trying not to puke at the sight of Mikhail's brains in the snow.

'Thank you,' I managed and slowly, very slowly, I climbed back to my feet.

'Obviously, English, we cannot give you a ride,' the soldier told me and there was more laughter from his men, 'and I don't think you want to go where Vasnetsov is going.'

'No,' I agreed.

'You should leave quickly . . .' He didn't finish the sentence, but didn't need to elaborate. When the Finns worked out that a smash and grab commando raid had been carried out by Russian special forces on their home soil, there was going to be one almighty row.

'And the money?' asked the soldier who'd done all the talking. 'The two million dollars at the house?' he gently enquired, and I did not hesitate, not even for a second.

'Keep it,' I told him and he looked a little affronted, as if I might be daring to imply he was corrupt. 'A gift to your president,' I added quickly, 'for his re-election campaign.'

He smiled and nodded, 'I am sure he will be most grateful.'

I didn't give a shit whether he kept some or all of the money, gifted it to his Major, his intelligence chief or the president himself, all I cared about was my life. I started to walk back towards the house, treading carefully to avoid the blood-drenched snow.

When we reached the house, the second helicopter was ready to leave. The dead bodyguards had all been piled up just inside the house and I watched as they were doused with petrol. The commandos moved briskly, as they removed all evidence of their presence. The Major spotted me and walked over. He handed me a set of car keys. 'Silver Mercedes' he told me. We both looked at a row of cars parked not far from the building and, sure enough, a silver Merc waited patiently among them. I turned back to the Major and he handed me a padded brown envelope.

'From the banker,' he told me, 'as you requested.'

'Thank you.' I said.

'Good luck Blake,' he told me, then he was gone without waiting for a reply.

I walked towards the car as the commandos melted away from the building and the sound of helicopter rotors whirring intensified. A charge went off inside the building. It didn't make a huge amount of noise but it must have been an incendiary device because a fire broke out and spread quickly. I watched as the helicopter took off and rose vertically above the trees, then tore off at an eye-watering speed until it was gone, disappearing into the darkness. I climbed into the Merc and started the car as the fire really took hold. I drove away from the house just as the first window exploded.

EPILOGUE

I drove back into Helsinki as quickly as I dared. I left the car in the underground car park of a large hotel. Then I went shopping. I bought new, casual clothes and a traveller's rucksack then walked for a while until I found the small, family-run hotel. I collected the package waiting for me under an assumed name and took it to my room. In it was the passport Palmer had acquired for me and some money. Once in the room, I changed my clothes and emerged wearing backpacker jeans, T-shirt, baseball cap and the blandest jacket I could find. I bagged up the suit in a black sack and ditched it in the large bin at the rear of the hotel. Before I left the place, I gave them the padded, brown envelope to mail out for me then I took a bus to the airport.

I sailed through Customs with the fake passport and boarded a flight to Stockholm, just to get me clear of the country. Then I took another flight from Stockholm to Berlin. I checked into a hotel, took a long hot shower and fell into bed.

I planned to stay in Berlin for one night only. I hadn't finished travelling yet, not by a long way.

You can buy English papers in Berlin and the next morning one of the broadsheets wrote. 'International condemnation is mounting against the Russian government following the alleged kidnapping and repatriation of a western-based oligarch who is resident in London. Yaroslav Vasnetsov, a long-time campaigner for human rights and a staunch opponent of the Russian President, was apparently snatched from a house near Helsinki by agents of the GRU or FSB, the Russian Military Intelligence and State Security Service, following a pitched battle with his bodyguards, which reportedly left several people dead. The President of Finland was said to be outraged by such an inflammatory act on Finnish soil.

The Russian government has denied the kidnapping, stating instead that Vasnetsov had returned to Moscow voluntarily, to answer numerous criminal charges levelled against him. A business associate of Vasnetsov has described this as laughable, adding that, 'A return to Russia is just about the only thing Yaroslav Vasnetsov was afraid of'.

Vasnetsov resurfaced in the Russian capital yesterday, standing in the dock of a Moscow court in handcuffs and regulation prison uniform, where he was charged with nine counts of tax evasion, embezzlement, money laundering, sponsoring terrorist organisations and treason. If convicted, he faces a life sentence in a Siberian prison. Human rights organisations have dismissed the spectacle as a show trial with the verdict already beyond doubt.

Mystery surrounds the fate of an unnamed British businessman who was also reported to have attended the high-level meeting near the Finnish capital. However, the Foreign Office stated that it was not aware of any British citizen being harmed.

Though there has been denial of any state involvement in the alleged kidnapping, a source close to the Russian Security Service said, 'Russia staunchly defends its sovereign right to defend its territorial borders against the threat of international terrorism. Terrorists and their sponsors do not have human rights. Yaroslav Vasnetsov was not taken on foreign soil but when the west does this, you put your suspects in orange suits and fly them to Guantanamo, locking them away for years without charge or even the opportunity of a trial. The Americans call this 'extraordinary rendition'. When the Russian government is accused of returning one of its own citizens to his homeland to stand trial, the American President and the British Prime Minister call this kidnapping. The hypocrisy of the western *so-called* democracies is staggering.'

'It was the US who launched a commando raid into another sovereign state, Pakistan, to carry out the assassination of Osama Bin Laden. The Russian government did not sanction a similar raid in Finland to seize the terrorist Vasnetsov but, from the precedent set by the United States of America, it seems we would certainly have been within our rights to do so.'

I was happy with the coverage. It made my subsequent disappearing act a lot easier. We ensured reports of a British national being caught up in the shoot-out at Vasnetsov's estate reached journalists and the DNA that was eventually recovered from the banker's body in Helsinki matched that of north-east businessman David Blake. The little package the Major gave me contained a sample of hair and blood and I had handed it on to the pretty receptionist at the hotel, so it could be mailed back to the UK. Sharp got it into the evidence room and filed it under my name. There was also a buccal swab, which I knew all about thanks to our recent experience with Henry Baxter. One of the commandos had kindly stuck the swab into what remained of the banker's mouth, catching his saliva and blood in the process. This also went into Sharp's evidence bag. It was labelled as DNA, apparently taken from me during a routine investigation into the death of a Glasgow gangster some years earlier. Sharp then went into action, making strident demands of his counterparts in Finland to release the DNA evidence taken from a corpse with an obliterated face they apparently discovered on land formerly owned by the oligarch Yaroslav

Vasnetsov. When the two DNA samples were compared, Sharp was able to categorically prove that the man murdered and left in the woods near Helsinki was none other than 'Tyneside gangster, David Blake'. I didn't mind that last bit. Sharp could have his moment in the sun. After all, you can't slander the dead. My stated occupation also tempered the outrage of the British Foreign Office, which was keen to avoid another row with Russia.

I paid DCI Sharp half a million pounds to go along with it and he was convincing. After all, he had a lot riding on it. Even my own lads believed it, by all accounts. They were a little upset to begin with but Vasnetsov was gone and there was no one else to take revenge against. Since they weren't daft enough to go to war with an entire country, they reorganised and settled down and, after a while, it was business as usual, just as I had predicted.

I looked after Palmer too. He was the only other member of my crew, apart from Danny, who knew the truth. As well as getting me the fake passports from one of his old contacts, it was Palmer who approached the FSB, to broker my deal. When Vasnetsov's people gave me the location of our meeting, Palmer passed it to them in a dead-letter drop. Helsinki was a dream come true for the Russians, since Finland is on their border.

An investigative journalist would later win awards for his report into the Vasnetsov case. He revealed the Russians were able to locate the oligarch's estate using one of their sixty orbiting, Cosmos-class, military satellites, to monitor the area around Helsinki and track the progress of the British businessman's hire car from Vantaa airport, which led them straight to Vasnetsov's estate.

The commando team flew in below radar from a base in Russia outside the city of Vyborg in the Isthmus of Karelia, just a hundred and thirty miles away. They set down a few miles from their target and yomped overland so nobody heard the helicopters till the firefight was over. Fortunately, Major Uri and his men were happy for me to be pretend-dead as opposed to the real thing. Maybe they thought I had no reason to own up to the deal I'd made with them and they were right. Vasnetsov might have been rotting in a Siberian prison but he still had a lot of money and a long reach. There was no way I could just resume my old life in Newcastle and I didn't want to. If Vasnetsov didn't get to me, sooner or later someone else would.

Sarah played her part to perfection, she really did. She was the grieving partner, the single mum left alone just a few short years after her dear old dad had disappeared. The local plod wanted to turn her into a poster-girl for the crime-doesn't-pay lobby. They came round the house for days afterwards making cups of tea, helping themselves to the biscuits, while they offered Sarah all manner of state-funded help because they didn't want to think of Emma missing out if times got really hard. All they wanted in return was a breakdown of everything Sarah knew about my business. Why waste a perfect opportunity to arrest everyone who ever knew or worked for me? That way they could really clean up the city.

Trouble was, Sarah turned out to be a complete airhead; a dumb blonde who knew nothing about my line of work. She admitted she knew I was a bit dodgy but, according to her, she didn't know where the money came from.

'And I never asked neither. I didn't want to know.'

The way she spun it, all she cared about was buying new clothes and having lunch with her mates. Now she had no idea what she was going to do. After a couple of weeks, the police stopped watching her, convinced she was a waste of effort. They had her tagged as a gangster's WAG whose biggest worry before now was wondering exactly when and where to get her nails done.

When a WPC went round the house a couple of months later, to ask some routine follow-up questions, she was surprised to learn that Sarah had gone. The furniture was still there and most of Sarah's possessions but she hadn't been seen in days and nor had her little girl.

Rumours abounded; Sarah had turned her back on the dirty money and gone down south to start a new life, earning an honest wage from a proper job. Some said she'd waited till the heat died down then left with suitcases full of cash she'd been squirrelling away for a day like this.

There was a more outlandish notion that it was all a put-up job and David Blake was very much alive, still controlling things in exile, pulling the strings from a country hundreds of miles away, but then they used to say that about Bobby Mahoney and no one ever saw him again.

There was another theory; Sarah Mahoney hadn't left with her daughter at all, she had been brutally murdered, along with her poor little girl. She knew too much about some very powerful villains on Tyneside and had to be silenced, before she ran out of money and went over to the dark side as a SOCA supergrass, spilling everything in return for immunity and a living wage. Their bodies were never found but that just lent the story a more chilling element.

The rumour of Sarah's death was the one that really took hold. Detective Chief Inspector Sharp made sure it was the strongest line of enquiry pursued by Northumbria Police. Sharp assured everybody that contradictory reports of Sarah leaving the north-east suddenly and of her own free will were just disinformation, put out by parties who wanted to ensure the authorities didn't delve too deeply into her disappearance.

My deal with Sharp was a sweet one for both of us. He agreed to do three more years as a DCI, before suddenly retiring early on health grounds; we agreed stress. Only then will he receive all of the money I've promised him, in return for sending the investigation down a series of blind alleys, while we made a different life for ourselves under new names at the other end of the world.

Auckland is a beautiful place; a laid-back haven, eleven thousand miles from home, where they still speak the same language we do. The weather in New Zealand is great, the people friendly and there's plenty to do. Emma loves it already and Sarah and I are just happy to have fallen off the grid. Last night we both slept without nightmares for the first time in a long while, despite the absence of bodyguards at our rented house. We kept our first names, so Emma doesn't get completely confused, but have a new surname on the passports Palmer provided for us all.

I'd been skimming off the top for a while now, stashing the cash, because I knew this day had to come, sooner or later. I didn't get to the magical four million, because I had to look after Sharp and Palmer, but I wasn't too far away in the end and I don't need to be flash out here. I just want to keep my head down and live a real life.

You see I always knew it would never be over for me until I was finally dead. Well, I'm a dead man now right enough, but that was the easy part. Want to know the tricky bit? Staying dead. That's the act I've got to pull off; for me, for Sarah, for our little girl.

I said we were like magicians in our firm, making people look the other way while we pull off our trick and that's just what Sarah and I have done. There's an art to that; distraction, misdirection, sleight of hand.

THE END